Miss Dimple
and the
Slightly Bewildered
Angel

Center Point
Large Print

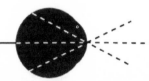

**This Large Print Book carries the
Seal of Approval of N.A.V.H.**

Miss Dimple
and the
Slightly Bewildered
Angel

Mignon F.
Ballard

CENTER POINT LARGE PRINT
THORNDIKE, MAINE

The text of this Large Print edition is unabridged.
In other aspects, this book may vary
from the original edition.
Printed in the United States of America
on permanent paper.
Set in 16-point Times New Roman type.

ISBN: 978-1-68324-314-4

Library of Congress Cataloging-in-Publication Data

Names: Ballard, Mignon Franklin, author.
Title: Miss Dimple and the slightly bewildered angel / Mignon F.
Ballard.
Description: Center Point Large Print edition. | Thorndike, Maine :
Center Point Large Print, 2017.
Identifiers: LCCN 2016056592 | ISBN 9781683243144
    (hardcover : alk. paper)
Subjects: LCSH: Women teachers—Fiction. | Elementary school
teachers—Fiction. | Murder—Investigation—Fiction. | Large type
books. | GSAFD: Mystery fiction.
Classification: LCC PS3552.A466 M565 2017 | DDC 813/.54—dc23
LC record available at https://lccn.loc.gov/2016056592

Make new friends, but keep the old.
One is silver and the other, gold.
—Girl Scout Song

For Tommye and Jim,
because you're gold

Acknowledgments

With thanks and appreciation to St. Martin's Hope Dellon and Silissa Kenney, for staying the path with Miss Dimple and Augusta, and to my agent, Laura Langlie, for her faith and friendship through the years.

Thanks also to my friend Lee Linn of The Ridge Books, for her valuable help and expertise.

Chapter One

"What are we going to do about supper?" Lily Moss asked, gazing longingly at the door that led to the kitchen.

"There's still plenty of that applesauce Odessa put up last month, and I suppose I could stir up some buckwheat cakes," Phoebe Chadwick suggested. As proprietor of the rooming house, she was responsible for providing appetizing as well as nutritious meals for her guests, but that was becoming more and more of a challenge with all the rationing and shortages during what seemed like a never-ending war, and now their reliable cook, Odessa Kirby, was leaving them to care for an aging aunt.

Dimple Kilpatrick had grown up eating buckwheat cakes. She hadn't liked them then and she didn't like them now. And besides, hadn't Phoebe served them only a few days before? Still, she kept her objections to herself. Phoebe was a dear friend and she was doing the best she could under the circumstances. All of the boarders had been pitching in to help as much as possible, but with teaching duties taking up most of their time, it was difficult to plan and prepare affordable meals that would appeal to everyone. Why, just the other day she had stirred up a batch of her fiber-filled Victory Muffins, which were intended to inspire one to become healthy and patriotic, as well as regular. It seemed odd to her that no one seemed especially hungry that morning, as most of the muffins were left on the serving platter. She even thought she saw part of one crumbled underneath the bird feeder in the front yard, but, of course, that was *surely* her imagination.

Annie Gardner tried not to think of Odessa's succulent baked chicken, her crispy fried fish and hush puppies, or her vegetable soup with golden-brown corn muffins. "How long does Odessa plan to be away?" she asked as she helped clear away the empty soup bowls from their midday meal. Because it was Saturday, they hadn't had to rush back to school and had taken their time over canned tomato soup and grilled cheese sandwiches.

The youngest of Phoebe's roomers, Annie was in her third year as a fourth-grade teacher at Elderberry Grammar School and had recently become engaged to Frazier Duncan, a young lieutenant currently serving somewhere in France—or at least that's where he was the last time she'd heard.

"I suppose we'll be without Odessa until her aunt Aurie is able to get about on her own," Phoebe said. "Odessa said she had a nasty fall and had to have surgery on her hip. She's no spring chicken, you know, and these things take time to heal."

Lucky Aunt Aurie! Annie thought. All she had to do was lie up in bed while Odessa served her all the good things they would be missing out on.

And then she felt ashamed of herself for being so selfish. The poor woman was probably in pain, and would be helpless without Odessa's kind nurturing. . . . Still, she *did* miss those heavenly desserts Odessa seemed to concoct out of practically nothing.

"We do have eggs," Phoebe reminded them, "and I could grate a little cheese for an omelette."

"Then I'll try my hand at biscuits again, if you'll let me." A novice at cooking, Annie had burned the last batch so badly, they'd had to throw them out. "And this time I promise to watch them." She shrugged. "I don't suppose there's any bacon?"

"We should have enough ration stamps if Shorty has any to sell," Phoebe said, speaking of Shorty Skinner, the local butcher. "Half a pound will have to do, if he has it. We don't have enough stamps for more."

"Virginia's holding a book for me at the library," Miss Dimple said. "I'll stop by the butcher's on my way." A great fan of mysteries, she was looking forward to reading John Dickson Carr's latest, *Till Death Do Us Part*, said to be a clever locked-room puzzle, and Miss Dimple enjoyed the challenge.

But lately, that was about the only thing she enjoyed. She was fond of her first-graders, as always, but had recently found herself lacking her usual enthusiasm for teaching and just about everything else. Dimple supposed it was because of the war, which seemed to define everything and everybody. Looking into the faces of her small charges, she often found herself thinking of others who had sat in those tiny green chairs years before: Peyton Hodges, who read so fast, the rest of the class had trouble keeping up. And she'd had to train herself to accommodate his natural inclination to write with his left hand. The young soldier had been killed the winter before in the Marshall Islands. And Chester Mote, with his big brown eyes and snaggle-toothed grin, had died when his plane ran out of gas during General Dolittle's bombing raid over Japan. Now, more recently, word had come that Dennis Chastain, who joined the marines early in the war, had been killed in September during the Battle of Peleliu in the Pacific. Tall and lanky, he had thrilled onlookers with his Tarzan-like antics in the trees on the playground, and was said to have been in great demand on the dance floor during high school years.

Miss Dimple tucked the required ration books into her worn purple handbag, patted her lavender hat into place, and stepped into the bright October afternoon, determined to find *something* encouraging in this day. At least the weather was cooperating, she thought, as the sky was so blue it almost hurt her eyes, and the large oaks on Katherine Street canopied the sidewalks in a patchwork of crimson and gold. Dimple Kilpatrick took a deep breath and straightened, walking quickly and with purpose, as was her custom. But today her purpose evaded her. *What was the matter with her? Why, this wouldn't do at all!*

This, too, shall pass, she reminded herself. You have a job to do, Dimple; now get on with it! Miss Dimple had never doubted the importance of her work. The children under her care deserved the best she could offer, but lately, she felt that hadn't been enough. If only she would hear from Henry. Her brother had been eight and she fourteen when their mother died, and Dimple had taken on the duties of rearing him in her stead. Henry Kilpatrick had become a fine man and a skilled engineer, as well as a loving and supportive brother, and she was proud of the job he was doing at the Bell Bomber Plant in nearby Marietta, Georgia. Although he seldom spoke of his work, she knew it was important to the war effort. Lately, however, Henry had become distant and uncommunicative, almost to the point of being rude, and it was most unlike him. She had received a brief note from her brother a few months before, but nothing since, and he had ignored her recent letters. Dimple missed their occasional visits, missed the warmth and understanding the two of them shared. Of course she had Phoebe and her fellow teachers at the boardinghouse, and she could always rely on her friend Virginia Balliew, the sole librarian at the town's quaint log cabin library. Perhaps, she thought, if things were quiet at the cabin today, the two might have a chance to talk. Dimple disliked unloading her troubles on anyone, but this time she couldn't ignore the need.

Collecting the half pound of bacon at Shorty Skinner's sawdust-smelling shop, Dimple stopped briefly to exchange pleasantries with Jo Carr, whose daughter Charlie taught the third grade in the room opposite from hers, and hurried across the street to the small park, where the library nestled in the shade of glossy magnolias and a sandy pathway circled the fountain, where lazy goldfish swam.

As a rule, the cabin with its wisteria-shaded porch had a calming effect on Dimple and the cares of the day fell away, at least for a while, when she stepped inside the door. For a few precious minutes, she could browse among the books, lose herself in another place, another time, and become immersed in an experience far removed from Elderberry, Georgia, and a war that seemed to go on forever.

The afternoon sunlight cast its enchanting

autumn spell across the cabin porch, pooling between rocking chairs and a couple of Boston ferns, and at first Dimple thought it was only a shadow she saw. And then it moved.

The woman stood with her back to the diamond-paned window, her hands clutching a large paper bag, and looked as if she wished she could become a part of the building itself. She wore a dark green skirt and tailored white blouse, with a gray sweater thrown about her shoulders. Her light brown hair curled beneath a knitted beret of dark red and gray.

Miss Dimple smiled. "Good afternoon," she said. "Lovely weather to be out-of-doors."

The woman nodded but didn't speak. Perhaps she had been to the library and was waiting for someone to come for her, but she didn't seem to have a book in her hand. Dimple had never seen her before.

"Is she still there?" Virginia whispered as soon as Dimple closed the door behind her.

"If you mean the woman with the paper bag, then *yes*. Why? Is there a problem?"

Virginia shook her head and frowned. "Well . . . no, but she's been out there all afternoon. I asked her if she'd like to come inside, but she said she only wanted to sit on the porch for a while."

Miss Dimple stepped over Cattus, the library cat, stretched out on a braided rug by the fireplace, although there was no fire this afternoon. "She seems to be waiting for someone, and . . . well . . . I have a feeling something might be wrong."

Virginia smiled. "Oh, you would! You and your mysteries. But she does seem a bit odd. Tell you what, let's give her a while, and if she's still there in half an hour, we'll try and get to the bottom of this." She frowned. "Is something wrong, Dimple? You look a little down in the dumps today."

And Dimple Kilpatrick returned a book to the shelf with a thump. Where should she begin?

"Have you spoken with Henry over the phone?" Virginia asked when Dimple told her of her concerns. "I realize long-distance is expensive, but in this case . . ."

"But I *have* called, several times, in fact, but Henry's never at home, and Hazel always answers. Of course she promises to relay the message, and I suppose she does, so why doesn't he reply?" Miss Dimple shook her head and frowned. "I'll have to admit, Virginia, this has me most distressed."

Virginia made a noise that sounded very much like a snort. "Oh, that Hazel! For heaven's sake, I wouldn't trust that one as far as I could throw"—she glanced about and pointed to a huge book on a stand—"that copy of *Webster's Dictionary* over there! You give her too much credit, Dimple."

"Well, she is Henry's wife, and I want to

16

keep peace in the family," Dimple said. Still, she never had understood her brother's choice of a wife. Hazel never went anywhere without her unpleasant sister, Imogene, who lived with the couple and had the personality of a slug.

She didn't mention the air of gloom that seemed to have settled upon her. Why burden her friend with a matter that couldn't be helped? After all, she was bound to snap out of it soon.

"I know!" Virginia suddenly clapped her hands. "Send him a telegram! That's certain to grab his attention."

"But, Virginia, that would be cruel." Everyone knew telegrams were the most frightening things one could receive. The small yellow piece of paper struck terror into the hearts of any recipient, as it might be a notification that a loved one was missing in action, or perhaps even wounded or dead.

Virginia only shrugged. "Do you want to get his attention or not?"

"I suppose you're right," Dimple agreed. "And if I still haven't heard from him by next week, I believe I will do just that."

Dimple collected the book her friend had been holding for her and selected two more. She was preparing to leave, when Virginia reminded her about the stranger on the porch. "I'll walk to the door with you," she offered. "I want to see if our visitor's still there."

"And what if she is? Are you thinking of collecting rent?"

Virginia laughed. "That might not be a bad idea if it looks like she's taking up residence."

But Miss Dimple waved that away with the back of her hand. "Oh, I expect she'll be long gone by now."

But she wasn't. The woman, who looked to be in her late thirties, had made herself comfortable in a rocking chair, with her eyes closed and her chin on her chest, and at first Dimple thought she was asleep, but she sat up abruptly, apparently startled at their approach.

"I hope we didn't alarm you," Miss Dimple said. "Wouldn't you like to come inside?"

The stranger looked quickly about, as if to assure herself she was where she should be. "No, thank you. I believe I'll just sit here, if that's all right."

"Of course, but it's already turning colder, and I'll be closing the library soon." Virginia introduced herself and Dimple. "Is everything all right? There's a telephone inside. Is there anyone I can call for you?"

"Oh, no. No. I'm fine, really." The woman hugged her paper bundle to her chest as if it were a baby. "It's just that . . . well, I wondered if I might stay here tonight."

Virginia's eyes widened. "Where? Do you mean here on the porch?" She glanced at Dimple, who shook her head. "I'm sorry, but I'm afraid that won't be possible. Besides, it's going to be cold out here, and where would you sleep?"

"Surely you have family who might help," Dimple offered in what she hoped was a gentle voice. Their guest seemed as easily spooked as a young colt. "You can phone them from here."

But the woman, who finally told them her name was Dora, only shook her head, and as Dimple stood there with Virginia, puzzling over what in the world to do, she noticed that Dora was trembling.

"Well, my goodness, you're getting cold out here. Let's get you somewhere warm. Have you had anything to eat?"

Reluctantly, Dora admitted she'd had only a banana and part of a pack of cheese crackers all day. "But I still have a few of them left," she added, patting the bag in her lap.

"Well, I know where we can remedy that," Miss Dimple said, urging her from the chair. "We'll work on the other problem once we get there."

And so while the strange newcomer sat in Phoebe Chadwick's kitchen, eating canned chicken noodle soup with bread and cheese and a cold baked apple left from the day before, Miss Dimple Kilpatrick attempted to explain the situation to her fellow boarders.

"She's been on the cabin porch all afternoon,

19

and I can't get a thing out of her except that her name is Dora," she told them. "The poor thing has nothing but a light sweater for a wrap, and it's supposed to turn colder tonight."

"She looks about my size," Velma Anderson said. "I've an old tweed coat I was getting ready to put in the Bundles for Britain, but it'll do just as much good here at home. I'll run get it before I forget. It's right there on my closet shelf." Organized to the hilt, Velma, who taught secretarial science at the high school, hurried upstairs to retrieve the coat. Dora had accepted it gratefully, she told them a few minutes later.

"But what can we do about a place for her to stay?" Phoebe asked. "There's no extra room here, and I'm sure she's harmless, but after all, we don't know anything about her."

Lily Moss gulped. "Oh, you're right, Phoebe! Why, she might be . . . well, running from the law, or even a murderer. We could all be killed in our beds—hacked to pieces or stabbed or something. Why, I read just the other day about—"

"Oh, for heaven's sake, Lily! You've been reading too many of those gory paperbacks," Velma said. "We'll make some phone calls. I'm sure we can find a place for the woman to stay, at least for the night."

"What about that tourist home just on the other side of town?" Annie offered. "They take in travelers for about a dollar a night, and I'm sure they don't require credentials. Couldn't we chip in and pay for a night or two?"

Miss Dimple smiled. "That's an excellent idea, Annie. I believe that's Warren and Opal Nelson's place. You remember Warren? Works with Bobby Tinsley at the police department. I'll call Opal right now and find out if they have a room available. She and I have served several times together for the Red Cross Blood Drive, and she seems to be an understanding person. I'll just explain to her about Dora."

After a few minutes' deliberation, Opal agreed to let Dora stay for the night. "And let's just see how that goes before we add on another," she told them.

"What about nightclothes?" Phoebe asked. "Do you think she has a gown or clean underwear in that bag she carries?"

Velma offered an extra pair of pajamas but said Dora was on her own for the underwear. She did add that she would be glad to drive the woman to the Nelsons' in her Ford V-8, which looked every bit as new as it had when she bought it in 1932.

"I'm sure she'll be relieved to know she has a place to stay," Miss Dimple said. "And tomorrow, maybe Dora will feel more inclined to tell us about herself. Now, I imagine she's tired and ready for a good night's rest. I'll go and tell her."

But when Miss Dimple returned to the group a

few minutes later, it was obvious that she was upset.

Annie jumped to her feet. "What is it, Miss Dimple? Is something wrong?"

Dimple Kilpatrick sank into the nearest chair and sighed. "She's not there," she told them. "When I went to the kitchen to tell her, she was gone."

"Did you look in the bathroom?" practical Velma asked, and Dimple nodded. "The bathroom door was open and I stood in the hall and called to her, but I never got an answer. I'm afraid it looks like Dora has decided to leave."

"Should we try to find her?" Annie frowned. "Where do you think she might go?"

But Dimple shook her head. "She knows we'll help her if we can. That's all we can do. Maybe she'll change her mind and come back."

"I don't think so," Velma said. "She seems afraid of something, or somebody. I don't believe she trusts us."

Phoebe nodded sadly. "I doubt if she trusts anyone."

Dimple Kilpatrick slept little that night, thinking of the woman wandering alone in the cold and dark. At least, she thought, before drifting off into a restless slumber, she has Velma's warm coat to help ward off the chill.

The next morning on her way downstairs for breakfast, she was relieved when the doorbell rang, and being the only one awake and stirring at the time, hurried to answer it. Surely Dora had decided to seek their help and make the best of her situation, which was exactly what Miss Dimple would have advised her to do—if she had been asked, which she hadn't.

But it wasn't Dora who waited on the porch, and Dimple Kilpatrick, who usually took everything in stride, found herself at a loss for words at the woman's appearance.

She stood there wrapped in a voluminous cape of deep emerald, with flyaway folds lined in shimmering plum. A tam that seemed to be woven of bronze silk sat crookedly on hair the color of which Dimple had never seen the like, except perhaps in paintings by some of the old masters, and a tapestry handbag about the size of a boxcar sat on the floor beside her.

"I do hope I'm in the right place," the woman said, clutching her cape about her. "I'm afraid I came away rather hurriedly. Last-minute notice, you know."

"No, I'm afraid I don't know." Miss Dimple struggled to regain her breath. "And what's all this about a last-minute notice?" She didn't want to be unkind, but two *very* strange people in less than a day was really just too much!

Her visitor smiled, and for some reason Miss Dimple felt her frustration begin to fade. She found herself smiling back. "I'm afraid it *is* rather sudden," the woman acknowledged. "I received my instructions only this morning. I've been assigned here, you see. There are problems, I believe?" And drawing her cape more snugly about her, she shivered in what could only be described as a lovely and delicate way. "My goodness, it's quite cold here, isn't it?"

And of course Miss Dimple stepped back and invited her inside. What else could she do? "You were assigned here for what reason?" she asked, closing the door behind them. *What was that she smelled? Strawberries in mid-October? Was this some new cologne?*

"Why, to help, of course. Augusta Goodnight at your service." With one quick motion, she swirled her cape to hang it neatly on the coat-rack, and set her bag sedately aside. "A place for everything and everything in its place," she said. "Now, where can I begin?"

Stunned, Miss Dimple heard a gasp behind her and turned to find Phoebe standing there. "Well, for heaven's sake, Dimple," her friend said, "tell her to start in the kitchen."

Chapter Two

"But where in the world did she come from?" Miss Dimple whispered to Phoebe. "The woman dropped in out of nowhere, and I don't believe she even knows why she's here."

From the kitchen she heard the sizzle of batter being poured into a hot waffle iron, and her mouth watered at the sound of it.

"Coming in on a wing and a prayer . . ." the newcomer sang as she whisked into the dining room with a large pitcher of orange juice before again disappearing into the kitchen.

"Off-key!" Dimple muttered, wondering how the curious woman had managed to squeeze that many oranges so quickly. "And we don't know a thing about her."

Phoebe smiled as she dealt out silverware for six places. "I suppose she read the notice I put up in Harris Cooper's store."

"Would you give me a hand with the napkins, please, Dimple? You'll find clean ones in that second buffet drawer."

Dimple Kilpatrick knew very well where the napkins were kept. After all, hadn't she lived in this house for almost thirty years? "What notice?" she asked, placing the napkins, thin from years of use and laundering, around the table.

Phoebe sighed. "With Odessa gone, it became obvious I needed help around here, so I put a little notice on the bulletin board—you know, the one by the stove in the back of the store."

This woman, Augusta Goodnight, if that was indeed her name, didn't seem the sort to fit in with the cigar-smoking, yarn-spinning bunch who kept the chairs warm around Harris Cooper's old woodstove, Dimple thought. "When did you put up the notice?" she asked.

"Strangest thing! It was only yesterday morning. I asked Annie to put it there for me when she went downtown to the post office." Phoebe smoothed the cloth and set a bowl of pansies on the table. "Must've been our lucky day."

"I suppose so," Dimple said. Well, time will tell, she thought, and those waffles *did* smell wonderful.

"Mmmm . . . It's almost like Odessa's back!" Annie took a deep breath as she helped herself to another waffle. "And this strawberry syrup is out of this world! Have I died and gone to heaven?"

Phoebe smiled at the newcomer. "I think Augusta's brought us a little heaven on earth," she said.

"Well, I hope you won't be in a hurry to leave." Velma sipped her second cup of coffee. "You must be new in town, Augusta. I don't believe I've seen you around."

"I think an angel must've brought you," Lily said, declining another waffle. "Have you found a place to stay?"

It appeared the thought hadn't occurred to the newcomer. "Do you suppose I might stay here?" Augusta looked about, and her smile seemed to light up the room.

The woman certainly had her nerve. Dimple shaded her eyes and blinked. It must be the morning sun in the window.

"Oh, dear! I'm afraid all our rooms are taken." Phoebe looked as if she might burst into tears. "But I'm sure we can find you a place somewhere."

Velma laid her silverware across her plate and spoke up. "There is that room at the foot of the stairs. No one's lived in it since Elwin Vickery.

"It seems like forever since he boarded here, but it was only a few years ago," she explained to Augusta. "It's used for storage now."

"Couldn't we move some of those things to the basement?" Lily asked. My goodness, they couldn't take a chance on losing someone who made waffles like those! "I'll be glad to help."

"So will I!" Annie echoed, glancing quickly at Phoebe. Had she spoken out of turn? After all, it wasn't *her* house.

"I expect I should get rid of some of that clutter," Phoebe said. "Meant to do that months ago. I'm afraid I've let it collect."

"I'm sure Charlie will help," Annie said, speaking of her friend and fellow teacher. "As far as I know, we don't have anything on our social calendar for the afternoon."

And with both of their young men serving overseas, she thought, that possibility wouldn't be likely until this war was over.

"I thought we might have heard from Dora by now," Annie said to Miss Dimple that afternoon as they bent over a large box, sorting items former boarders had left behind: a badly stained raincoat with buttons missing; one mud-caked boot dangling a buckle; three hats so flattened, it was impossible to tell if they had begun as bowlers, Panamas, or berets.

Charlie tossed aside a wool sock with a hole almost large enough to jump through. "Who's Dora?" she asked, and Miss Dimple told her of their strange encounter the day before.

"She just disappeared," Annie said. "I hope she found someplace warm to sleep. It was much too cold to be outside last night."

"She seemed to be running from something or someone," Dimple said. "I believe the woman was afraid."

Charlie frowned. "Afraid of what?"

"I don't know," Miss Dimple said, "but I suppose we'll find out sooner or later."

It turned out to be sooner.

"Why, Augusta, I can't believe what you've done to this place! It doesn't look the same." Phoebe stood in the doorway of the room they'd been using for storage and shook her head. "How in the world did you manage to do this so quickly?"

Annie spoke from behind her. "You must have

a magic wand. Do you mind if I borrow it?"

After eliminating the clutter and transferring the remaining items to the basement, they had left the room dusty and bare a few hours earlier. Annie and Charlie had then pitched in to help with cleaning, until Augusta thanked them and shooed them away, announcing she would finish on her own.

Now the patchwork quilt Phoebe had discovered tucked away in a trunk looked almost new on the bed that had belonged to her mother, and its mahogany headboard gleamed with polish, as did the floors they had cleaned earlier. The braided rag rug they'd found rolled up in the closet made the room look cheerful and bright, complementing the blue-and-yellow curtains in the windows.

"Those can't be the same curtains that were here before!" Phoebe fingered a corner of the fabric. "And you've washed the windows, as well."

Augusta smiled. "It only took a few minutes and a little soap and water."

"But how did you get them dry?" Annie asked. She knew she hadn't seen them hanging outside on the line.

"I imagine you ironed them, didn't you?" Phoebe said, looking about. "And you must have mixed sunshine in with the wash water. I've never seen this room looking as bright."

Augusta Goodnight only smiled in reply as she

29

settled in the old bentwood rocker they had brought down from the attic and began to stitch on a bit of shimmering fabric she'd taken from her large tapestry bag.

She wore a shirtwaist dress of turquoise and rose with a wide white collar and three-quarter-length sleeves. It was an ordinary dress from an ordinary pattern, but it looked anything but ordinary on Augusta. She kept her lustrous hair away from her face with a narrow scarf of emerald green knotted under one shell-like ear, and a long string of glimmering stones dangled from her neck, the colors changing from amber to gold, purple to crimson, and a host of colors in between.

Miss Dimple watched all this from a distance. There was no doubt the woman was extraordinary. In minutes that morning, Augusta had concocted waffles with strawberry syrup better than any she'd ever eaten, and in a matter of hours she'd converted a stuffy storage space into a room anyone would be happy to call home. So why did it prey on her mind?

That evening after a supper of cheese grits and eggs with a sprinkle of leftover bacon, they gathered in the living room for a game of bridge, with the exception of Lily, who didn't approve of playing cards on Sunday, and Augusta, who seemed preoccupied with her needlework and her thoughts.

Phoebe had turned on the radio earlier, as no

one wanted to miss Edgar Bergen and Charlie McCarthy, and of course they all wanted to hear the news that followed.

Augusta smiled in all the right places during *The Edgar Bergen–Charlie McCarthy Show*, laughing outright at times, but it seemed to Dimple their mysterious visitor was waiting for something to happen. But what? Where in the world had she come from, and what had brought her here to Elderberry?

Dimple Kilpatrick examined the cards she'd been dealt and decided to pass. But she wasn't passing on Phoebe's newest guest. One way or the other, she meant to find out why this person calling herself Augusta Goodnight had come to stay with them on Ivy Street.

Chapter Three

Bob Robert Kirby, Odessa's husband and part-time sexton at Elderberry First Presbyterian, frowned as he glanced up at the town clock in the courthouse tower. Was it almost six already? He'd sure better hurry and ring the bell for vespers. Mr. Evan Mitchell had always treated him fair and square, but the preacher was a stickler about ringing that bell on time, and he still had to climb all those steps and then the ladder to get to the platform to reach the rope. Bob Robert usually rang it for the morning service, but today their congregation had met at the Methodist church, where the combined choirs presented a long-rehearsed program of patriotic music for an early celebration of Navy Day, just as they had observed Army Day in April.

Several people spoke to him as they filed into the small stone church, some having stopped to catch their breath halfway up the steep steps that led to the door.

"Whew! This sure doesn't seem to be gettin' any easier," one of the older members said as he paused to wipe his face. "One of these days, Bob Robert, you'll understand what I mean!"

Bob Robert shook his head and smiled. He had a pretty good idea already.

The small closetlike room to the side of the narthex smelled close and musty. It always smelled close and musty, as it was used only as storage for church records dating way back before the turn of the century and stacks of ancient hymnals thick with dust, but that didn't bother Bob Robert. All he wanted to do was ring that bell and hurry home for supper. Odessa had promised chicken croquettes with mustard sauce tonight, as it was a favorite of her aunt Aurie's. Hooray for Aunt Aurie! Bob Robert smacked his lips as he pushed open the door to the narrow stairway that led to the steeple.

Or, he *tried* to push open the door, but some-

32

thing was in the way. He muttered under his breath. Were these young'uns playing a joke on him again? It seemed the higher they advanced in school, the more their spirits rose, especially the boys, probably because they knew their carefree days were limited, as the war loomed like the bogeyman ahead of them.

"You boys get away from this door," he said sternly. "Service gonna start any minute now and I've gotta ring that bell." He gave the door another push, but nothing happened.

"Mr. Evan sure isn't going to like it when he finds out you-all wouldn't let me get to that bell rope. Come on, now. You don't want to be late for church. You hear me?"

Bob Robert paused, but nobody answered. Not even the usual giggle, whisper, or scuffle. Sighing, he gave the door one final shove and succeeded in opening it just wide enough to see what was in the way.

At first, he thought it was a pillow wedged behind the door, but it was too heavy for a pillow, and what would a pillow be doing back there? And then he saw the shoe, a brown laced-up oxford like a lot of women wore, and in that shoe was a foot!

Bob Robert's first inclination was to slam that door and run, but what if this person was injured? What if she needed help? And he knew the person was a *she* because he could now see the hem of her skirt below the folds of her coat, a slender hand flung to one side.

"Ma'am?" Bob Robert stepped cautiously into the small enclosure at the foot of the steps and knelt beside her. She didn't move, nor did she respond. He didn't recognize her as a member of this church or as anyone else he knew, but he couldn't get a good look at her face. "Ma'am?" he said again, and touched her wrist. He didn't try to find a pulse, because her wrist was cold, and he knew it had been some time since there had been a pulse there. The woman lay on her side, her body stiff in death. The one eye he could see was open and glazed, and a dark trickle of what had probably been blood had dried on her mouth. It looked like she'd fallen from the steps or the ladder above them. But what had she been doing up there?

Bob Robert didn't stick around to find out, but backed quickly from the tiny enclosure, shutting the door firmly behind him, and hurried through the stuffy records room to the narthex, where a few stragglers were still making their way into the sanctuary.

He had to tell somebody—but who? That poor woman was way past needing help, but he couldn't just leave her there! *Oh Lord!* He felt like he didn't have any bones in his legs to hold him up, and Bob Robert gripped his hands to keep them from shaking. He had seen dead people

34

before, even helped lay some of them out, but this was different. He had never just come upon somebody like that. *Crazy woman had no business in that steeple anyway!*

Those chicken croquettes didn't sound so good anymore.

Doc Morrison! He needed Doc Morrison. Oh, why couldn't the doc be Presbyterian instead of Methodist?

"Bob Robert. Are you all right? You look like you've seen a ghost." Phil Lewellyn, the local druggist, paused in the doorway and took him by the arm. "I think you'd better sit down."

Mr. Phil! He would know what to do. Bob Robert wanted to hug the man. "The steeple— she's at the bottom of the steps in the steeple, and no use calling a doctor," he said. "Don't know how long she's been there, but she's way past helping now."

"Who in the world could be at the door at this hour?" Phoebe glanced at the clock as she put away the playing cards. "Why, it's ten-thirty already."

"Do you think it might be Dora?" Annie, who was folding up the card table, looked around for Miss Dimple, but she had gone to the kitchen for a cup of her ginger mint tea before bedtime. The others had all retired to their rooms.

"It might be an emergency." Dimple, steaming

cup in hand, appeared in the doorway. "I'll see what they want."

"We'll *all* see what they want," Phoebe said, flicking on the porch light, and one glance at the two men standing there warned them that something was terribly wrong.

Bobby Tinsley, Elderberry's young police chief, removed his hat as he stepped inside. "Sorry to bother you so late, but there's been an incident at the Presbyterian church, and I need to speak with Miss Velma right away."

"Velma?" All three gasped in surprise at the idea of the proper middle-aged teacher being involved in anything illegal, or—heaven forbid—illicit.

Doc Morrison's voice was soothing. "Now, why don't we all sit down. We didn't mean to upset you. Your friend hasn't done anything wrong, but the chief here just needs to ask her a few questions."

"Well, of course she hasn't done anything wrong! I'm surprised at you, Ben Morrison—and you, too, Bobby Tinsley, coming here in the middle of the night like this." Phoebe barely paused for breath. "There's such a thing as a telephone, you know."

The two men looked duly chastised. "I'm sorry," the doctor said. "We just wanted to get to the bottom of this as soon as possible."

"Get to the bottom of what? What in the world's

going on?" Velma Anderson stood in the hallway, hugging her blue flannel bathrobe closely about her.

Chief Tinsley twisted his hat in his hands and sighed. "Well, it seems a young woman fell from that ladder that leads to the steeple over at the Presbyterian church—"

"My goodness! Who was it?" Phoebe sank into the nearest chair. "Is she going to be all right?"

Chief Tinsley shook his head. "I'm afraid not. That's why we're here. She had no identification, but the coat she was wearing had your name in the label," he said, addressing Velma.

"Dora!" the four women exclaimed together.

"When did this happen?"

"What was she *doing* in the steeple?"

"Do you know how she fell?"

"Is she very badly hurt?"

A chorus of questions followed, but the chief waved them aside.

"I'm afraid Chief Tinsley is trying to tell us Dora is dead," Miss Dimple said quietly before he could continue.

He nodded. "We're hoping one of you might be able to give us a last name or some other information about her. She had no identification other than a stub from a bus ticket that was in the pocket of her skirt. It seems she bought the ticket a couple of days ago in some little place in south Georgia. . . ." He paused to consult a small notebook. "Fieldcroft. That's not too far from Savannah, I believe." He glanced at Velma. "Know anybody there?"

Velma Anderson looked as if she was ready to paw the floor and snort. She had not taught Bobby Tinsley in any of her secretarial science classes at Elderberry High, but she had supervised him in study hall and remembered how, on several occasions, he'd tied Franny Sue Boulware's dress sash to the desk behind her.

"Don't you get smart with me, Bobby Tinsley. The only thing I know about Dora, other than her first name, is that she was hungry and needed a warm coat."

"Perhaps I had better explain," Miss Dimple said, and told the men how she and Virginia had found the woman on the porch of the library the day before. "She had no place to stay and we were arranging for her to spend the night at Warren and Opal Nelson's place, but she left without saying a word. We had no idea where she might've gone."

"I wish you ladies would have a seat, because I'm going to," Doc Morrison said, and plopped into the wing-back chair by the fireplace. "I think I know where she went," he continued. "She walked a few blocks over to the Presbyterian church. They never lock their doors, and I expect she curled up to sleep in one of those pews until, for some reason or other, she took a notion to climb that ladder to the steeple."

"But that was last night," Annie said. "You mean she fell . . . she's been lying there all this time?"

Chief Tinsley nodded. "Sure looks that way. Bob Robert found her there when he went to ring the bell for the evening service. Poor fellow was so shaken up over it, Doc had to give him something to steady his nerves."

"Did you not find any kind of identification in that bag she had with her?" Velma asked.

The chief frowned. "What bag?"

"A brown paper bag, like the kind they use for groceries," Phoebe told them.

The two men exchanged glances. "I don't suppose you know what was in there?" Bobby said.

Miss Dimple shook her head. "We assumed she might have a change of clothing and perhaps a small change purse with whatever money she had—if she had any. She told us she'd only eaten a banana and a few cheese crackers all day, and she didn't carry a pocketbook."

Annie's eyes filled with tears. "Poor Dora! If only she'd stayed with the Nelsons last night, this wouldn't have happened. I wonder what made her leave here like she did."

"And why would she climb that ladder to the steeple in the middle of the night," Miss Dimple asked, "unless she was running from someone?"

Chapter Four

"Would you mind some company?"

Dimple paused in the doorway the next morning as she started on her usual walk, umbrella in hand, only to find Augusta—cape, tam, and all, beside her.

"Of course not," she said, although to be honest, she'd rather have had this time alone, especially today, as she had a lot on her mind. But she'd found it almost impossible to be discourteous to someone who made her smile in spite of herself —*and* was keeping them all extremely well fed, apparently with little effort. Earlier, she had peeked into the pot of oatmeal, smelling delightfully of apples and cinnamon, keeping warm on the back of the stove, and noticed the pan of biscuits ready to pop into the oven. Perhaps, just this once, she might cut her walk a little short and forgo the Victory Muffins.

"I hope our visitors didn't disturb you last night," Dimple said after they had walked a while in silence. Augusta's room was on the first floor, across from the kitchen, and she would have had to have been deaf or comatose to sleep through all that racket. "I'm afraid we received some rather distressing news."

The two paused beneath the tulip poplar on the

corner while Dimple told her of Dora's appearance and then disappearance on Saturday and the tragic accident the following day on the stairs that led to the steeple. Yellow leaves like tulip blossoms swirled about them and the autumn air was as crisp and sweet as a new apple. It was Dimple's favorite time of year and she had never outgrown the joy of the holidays that followed. For Dora, there would be no holidays. No joy.

Listening, Augusta fingered the strand of stones around her neck as the colors changed from amber to green to dark violet. "How sad," she said. "How very sad." And then: "Are they sure this was an accident?"

"I'm inclined to believe it wasn't." Miss Dimple speared a bit of litter with her umbrella as they crossed the street, then put it into the paper bag she carried for that purpose. "I think she went into the church looking for a sheltered place to sleep and someone frightened her into seeking safety in the bell tower."

"How long had she been there when they found her?" Augusta asked.

"Doctor Morrison thinks it must have happened sometime last night. She left our place at a little after five on Saturday, and I imagine she wandered around a bit before settling on the church as a safe place to spend the night."

"It appears she was running from someone," Augusta said. "I wonder who or why.

"Have the authorities been able to find out anything about her background?" she asked.

"Unfortunately, no. I remember her having a rather large paper bag when she came with us to Phoebe's, and I assumed it held the belongings she had with her, and possibly some identification, but Chief Tinsley said they had found no sign of it."

"Then someone must have taken it." Augusta frowned. "It sounds as if they were looking for something."

Dimple nodded. "I wonder if they found it."

Augusta shook her head and frowned. "I'm afraid this is not what I expected. I wish I knew . . ."

"What do you mean?" Dimple asked. "Knew what?"

But Augusta either didn't hear her question or chose to ignore it. "I suppose I'd better get back and put those biscuits in the oven," she said as they circled the small business district and turned left onto Myrtle Street. "Have you ever noticed," she said, looking about, "how these willow oaks hold on to their leaves long after others have fallen?"

Miss Dimple nodded. "True, but I believe these are water oaks."

Augusta's necklace jangled as she walked a little faster. "Really? Are you sure?"

Having been born and bred in the Georgia countryside, Dimple Kilpatrick was as sure as she knew the sun rose in the east and set in the west, but she didn't dispute the matter. "I believe there's a reference book on that subject in the bookcase by the stairs," she said. "We can look when we get back."

She might not be able to stir up waffles or decorate a room at the wink of an eye, but she knew a water oak when she saw one! And Dimple Kilpatrick picked up her pace. *Just who was this stranger who seemed to have landed on their doorstep?*

"Any more word about what happened to Dora?" Dimple asked, leaving her umbrella in the stand by the door.

Phoebe put a pitcher of orange juice on the sideboard and searched in the drawer for spoons. "Not yet," she said. "I do hope they'll be able to find out who she is and why she came here. Odessa phoned this morning, all upset about Bob Robert finding that woman like that."

Dimple nodded. "Not something he'll easily forget, I'm afraid.

"And how is Odessa's aunt?"

Phoebe smiled. "From what I hear, Aunt Aurie seems to be a bit of an autocrat. She's probably doing a whole lot better than Odessa."

"Well, you'll never guess what's happened now," Phoebe announced when everyone returned for the noon meal that day. "I ran into Lizzy Vaughn in the post office this morning. She's in charge of the nursery department at the Presbyterian church, you know, and she told me somebody telephoned Jesse Dean Greeson at Cooper's grocery store late Saturday and asked him to deliver a couple of boxes of vanilla wafers to the church kitchen."

"I suppose they wanted them to keep the children happy during the Sunday-morning service," Velma said, and then frowned. "But they didn't have a Sunday-morning service, did they?"

Phoebe dealt out silverware with a clatter. "And that's not all," she continued. "Lizzy says she didn't order them and neither did anybody else."

Lily shook her head. "I still don't understand. . . ."

"Neither did I," Phoebe admitted, "until several people reported seeing Jesse Dean using that side door to the church *at about the time Dora was killed,* and apparently somebody called and gave that information to the police."

Miss Dimple adjusted her bifocals, as if that might help her to understand. "Does Jesse Dean remember who called in that order?" she asked.

Phoebe explained the store was winding up their harvest sale and getting ready to close for the day. "He doesn't even remember if it was a man or a woman," she added, "but of course the police had to interview Jesse, since he was in the church during the time in question and could've easily had access to the steeple from the kitchen area."

Annie sighed. "Why in the world would Jesse Dean want to kill Dora what's her name when he didn't even know her?"

Miss Dimple's voice was calm. "I'm sure our Chief Tinsley is well aware of that, but it seems someone is trying very hard to make him look guilty."

"But who would want to do that?" Phoebe asked. "And why?"

It was not until that afternoon that they learned the paper bag containing Dora's few possessions had been found in a trash can at the depot. Inside were a pair of pajamas and a few other items of clothing, as Miss Dimple had surmised, as well as a small purse containing a little less than twenty dollars and a handwritten letter to Dora from an address in Tennessee.

"Whoever she was running from must not have been after money," Chief Tinsley told them when he dropped by later that day. "They didn't bother to take the purse, and I doubt if they saw the letter, as it was tucked into the folds of her underwear." He sighed. "At least now we know who she is—or was."

"Well then, who was she?" Velma demanded. She still hadn't forgiven him for getting on his high horse with her the day before.

It looked for a minute as if he might smile, but the chief managed a businesslike expression before continuing. "Name's Westbrook—Dora Westbrook, but the letter was addressed to a Mrs. Leonard Westbrook."

"Where? Surely not here," Phoebe said.

Bobby Tinsley shook his head. "Little place called Fieldcroft, just below Savannah. Letter was sent to a street address there—Lucia Lane, I think it was. I forget the number, but we checked it out. Seems this woman—this Dora—took off a couple of days ago. Mother-in-law answered the phone when I called. Said Dora's husband—Leonard, I presume—was frantic. Told me he'd been scouring the countryside, trying to find her."

"Did she have any idea why Dora left?" Dimple asked.

"Seemed to think she might've had a breakdown of some sort." The chief frowned. "I got the idea she thinks this Dora had mental issues.

"From what we could judge by its contents, we believe the letter came from the woman's sister in Tennessee, an Elaine Arnold. In it, she said she hoped Dora would be able to make it back home for Christmas this year, but she didn't mention the possibility of her leaving immediately. Return address was a little town in Tennessee—Lewisburg, I think it was. Dora might have been on her way there, but why did she get off in Elderberry?"

"Then, for heaven's sake, why didn't she *say* something?" Annie asked. "Why didn't she tell us she needed help?"

46

"It was easy to see the poor thing was afraid," Phoebe said, shaking her head. "She didn't know if she could trust us or not. I wish we had taken more time to get to know her better. Perhaps we could have helped."

"We *did* try, Phoebe," Velma reminded her, and frowned. "I wonder why she left here like she did—just took off without so much as a by-your-leave."

Miss Dimple spoke up quietly. "I think I know. We were talking about finding a room for her that night, remember? She must have been listening from the kitchen when I suggested we get in touch with the Nelsons, and I believe I might've mentioned that Warren worked with you, Chief Tinsley, at the police department."

"So . . . do you think she was running from the police, as well?" For about the third time, Chief Tinsley ran his fingers through hair that looked as if a hen had been scratching there. "We checked with the police down there, but, strangely enough, they were only recently informed she was missing."

"Well, that sounds peculiar." Lily hugged herself and shivered. "She was obviously in danger, and for all we know whoever was after that poor woman might decide to come for us next. Velma, I think we should lock the doors to our rooms tonight."

"Well, it sounds pretty fishy to me," Velma said,

ignoring her. "If her husband was all that frantic to find her, looks like he would've reported her missing."

Annie agreed. "And I wonder where this *Leonard* was the night she fell from that ladder in the bell tower—*if she fell.*"

Chief Tinsley turned to them with a smile that wasn't a smile. "Thank you. Thank you, all. I'll keep that in mind." And with a mock bow, he made his way to the door.

"Well," Annie said as the door closed behind him, "I didn't mean to step on his toes."

"Why, I don't believe you were standing close enough to step on the man's toes." Augusta spoke from the doorway, where she'd been observing the chief's visit.

Miss Dimple smiled as they filed into the dining room, where a tureen of something with a tantalizing aroma beckoned. "It's only an expression," she explained, wondering where this whimsical person had been hiding. "Annie meant she didn't intend to take charge of someone else's business."

"I understand," Augusta said, smiling, but it was obvious to Dimple that she didn't. The misunderstanding, however, was soon forgotten when they sat down to a succulent fish stew with yeast bread warm from the oven.

Phoebe started to ask where Augusta had found the fish, as she hadn't seen any lately at Shorty

Skinner's, but she decided she really didn't care, and helped herself to a second bowl.

Miss Dimple was quiet as she and Annie cleared the table after supper. Augusta had declined offers to help, saying it would take her only a minute, but Dimple pretended she didn't hear, and Annie followed suit. Both were curious to find out how the new boarder accomplished things in such a great hurry. Annie smiled as she stacked empty bowls on a tray, while from the kitchen she heard Augusta humming to music from the radio. Was that Bing Crosby's recent recording of "Swinging on a Star"? Over Augusta's attempts at singing, it was hard to tell for sure.

Miss Dimple seemed preoccupied as she gathered the soiled silverware and added it to the tray with a clatter. "Is everything all right?" Annie asked. Her respect for the older teacher had deepened into friendship during her past two years in Elderberry, and she had learned that when Dimple Kilpatrick was concerned about something, there was usually a good reason.

Miss Dimple dismissed her question with a wave of her hand. "Oh, it's nothing really. It's just that the mention of that town in Tennessee made me think of some friends I once knew near there."

"Lewisburg? Do you suppose they're still there?"

But Miss Dimple shook her head, and there

was an expression in her eyes that Annie had never seen before. "I'm afraid it's been far too long," she said. "Now, let's get these dishes into the kitchen and give Augusta a hand."

But she couldn't hide the flicker of sadness in her eyes.

The scene that greeted them in the kitchen, however, made the two break into laughter. To the music of the King Cole Trio's "Straighten Up and Fly Right," Augusta whirled about the room, twirling a dish towel in time to the music. Noticing she had company, Augusta reached for Annie's hand and drew her into the dance, while Dimple, finding it impossible to maintain her dignity, collapsed into a chair and laughed until the tears came.

"Oh my goodness," she said, wiping her eyes with her ever-present handkerchief. "I don't know when I've laughed so hard."

Before they knew it, Augusta had submerged the dishes in a sinkful of bubbles, and in a blink, it seemed, they were sparkling clean. "Laughter can be as cleansing as these suds," she said, flinging her apron aside. "I find it wise to air one's emotions from time to time rather than holding them inside.

"And, by the way," she said to Miss Dimple, "I looked in the reference book as you suggested, and you are right about the water oak. There are many things, I'm learning, that I need to review."

Review what? And where had Augusta been that she found this necessary?

Miss Dimple thanked her and smiled, knowing she'd been right about the trees all along. But she had a very strong feeling Augusta's comment about emotions had been directed to her, and her alone.

How could she possibly know?

Chapter Five

"Sure sounds like murder to me. Drat! Looks like I've been missing all the excitement!" Charlie Carr leaned against the back entrance of the faded brick building that housed grades one through four at Elderberry Grammar School and watched her small third-graders chase one another on the playground. As a child, Charlie had gone to school in these same classrooms, and two years before had returned to her hometown to teach, bringing along Annie, her college roommate, who now taught beside her.

"Fie, fie on you!" Annie told her, misquoting her favorite source, the bard. "The poor woman has 'shuffled off her mortal coil!' I do believe you're 'as cold as any stone.'"

Charlie looked silently at her friend for a moment and then brought her hands together. "Oh-h-h, *very* good, but I don't think they're

51

holding auditions for Shakespeare this week."

The day after Dora's tragic accident, the whole town of Elderberry had learned of her death, and of course Annie had filled Charlie in on the woman's disappearance from Phoebe's.

"The chief says her last name was Westbrook and she lived somewhere in south Georgia . . . but get this—he said she'd left home a couple of days before and nobody knew she was gone because her husband had spent the night on the farm with a sick calf and wasn't aware she'd left. Said her husband seemed—

"Donald Lee Thompson, you put down that stick right now!

"Now . . . where was I? Oh, yes . . . said her husband was worried to death and went out looking for her."

Charlie frowned as she pulled her sweater closer about her. "Did the chief say why she left home?"

Annie told her of Bobby Tinsley's conversation with Dora's mother-in-law, and how police had now found the bag Dora carried. "He said as far as he knew, everything was still inside, including some money."

"Where did they find it?" It was time for the bell to end morning recess, and Charlie clapped her hands to summon the children to form a line.

"In a trash can at the depot," Annie told her, doing the same.

"Then how can they believe her death was an

accident?" Charlie asked over the clanging of the bell.

The only reason Dora would climb that ladder would be to hide or get away from someone, she thought. Was her killer somebody who wanted whatever she carried—or what he *thought* she carried—in that paper bag?

"And now somebody has tried to drag Jesse Dean into it," Annie said as they herded the children inside, and she told Charlie about the cookie delivery to the church. "What if it's somebody we know—somebody right here in Elderberry?"

What would Miss Dimple have to say about it? Charlie wondered. Unlike her, the older teacher usually reserved her opinions until she had more of the facts. Still, it seemed odd that no one had mentioned the woman's mysterious death when the three had chatted that morning before the children arrived. In fact, Miss Dimple had little to say at all.

"Does Miss Dimple seem unusually quiet today to you?" she whispered to Annie as the children lined up at the water fountain inside.

Her friend nodded. "Seems to have something to do with a town in Tennessee. Chief Tinsley said Dora had a sister there, and I noticed she didn't have much to say after he mentioned that place, only that she used to know somebody there."

• • •

"Virginia," Dimple said to her friend when she dropped in at the library that afternoon, "do you think I hold my emotions inside?"

Virginia looked up from her position on the floor, where she was reshelving books, and brushed a stray lock of once-red hair from her face. "Why do you ask?" she said, struggling to her feet.

"It's just a remark someone made about it being wise to air one's emotions rather than hold them inside." Dimple stooped to stroke Cattus, who immediately jumped to the top of a shelf. "I feel certain it was directed at me."

Virginia frowned. "Who? Who said that to you?"

"She didn't exactly say it *to me,* but I sensed the implication."

"She? Who is *she?*" With one arm, Virginia scooped the cat from the shelf and set her on the floor.

"Augusta, our new boarder." Dimple explained how the newcomer had come in answer to a notice Phoebe had posted in Cooper's Store. "It was the strangest thing," she added. "She just appeared at the door wearing a huge green cape and carrying a handbag I believe I could climb inside." She sighed and shook her head. "Most unusual woman —seems a bit fey, as if her feet aren't firmly on the ground, but I'll have to admit, she makes the best waffles I've ever put in my mouth, and her fish stew? Virginia, it's absolutely *heavenly!*"

"And she's staying at Phoebe's? Where?"

"In that room across from the kitchen. It's been used mainly for storage since the last boarder left. And that's another thing," she added. "It took all of us most of an afternoon to clear that room of its contents, but by suppertime she had it looking like something out of *Good Housekeeping.*"

"Did she say where she's from?" Virginia asked.

"I assumed she was from some kind of agency, because she mentioned something about 'being assigned'—and apparently in a hurry—but Phoebe seems to think she came because of her notice."

"Dimple Kilpatrick." Virginia took her friend by the hand and led her to a chair. "Did it ever occur to you that this stranger might've had something to do with what happened to Dora?"

But Dimple smiled and shook her head. "Not at all," she said.

Taking a seat beside her, Virginia Balliew sighed and wondered for a second or two if her friend wasn't the one who was fey. "Do you mean it hasn't occurred to you at all, or that you don't consider that a possibility?"

"Both. Augusta had nothing to do with Dora's death," Dimple said.

"And how do you know this?"

"I know she would never do anything evil.

You'll understand when you meet her." The woman was curiously perplexing, and, yes, Dimple thought, a bit full of herself. Yet Augusta appeared to have a way of getting people to do as she wanted without their ever knowing it. And what's more, they seemed to enjoy doing it.

Virginia helped Dimple select a book on home decorating that Phoebe had requested, as she'd decided to spruce up her bedroom, and her friend was getting ready to leave when Virginia asked if she'd heard from her brother.

Dimple hesitated at the door. "Henry?"

"Yes, *Henry*. As far as I know, that's the only brother you have," Virginia said.

Having remembered what she'd promised, Dimple was eager to avoid the question. "Not yet, I'm afraid," she murmured.

"Then you know what you have to do," Virginia reminded her.

"But don't you think that's a bit harsh? Poor Henry! A telegram might frighten him to death."

"He deserves to be frightened. Besides, Henry's a big boy now, Dimple. He should be ashamed for worrying you so."

"All right, Virginia. I'll send the telegram tomorrow."

"Would you like me to go with you to the telegraph office?" Her friend's voice was soft.

Dimple smiled. "Thank you, Virginia, but I'm a big girl now, too, you know."

She had started across the street before it occurred to her that her friend hadn't answered the question she'd gone there to ask.

Dimple didn't know what made her look back, other than the fact that she always liked looking at this peaceful place set surely by God's hand among the glossy magnolias and winding walks. But today it didn't seem peaceful, and Dimple didn't know why. There seemed to be an aura about it, a cold, gray, shivery something, and Dimple drew her purple tweed jacket closer and clutched Phoebe's decorating book to her chest like a shield. Peering through bifocals, she looked closer. Was that someone standing under the magnolia by the porch? A slight breeze ruffled the tree's dark leaves and she thought she saw movement there. A limb shifting with the wind? The shadow of a person?

"You are letting your imagination run away with you, Dimple," her mother would have told her, as she had many times years before. "You're too old now to believe in fantasies."

But Dimple Kilpatrick had never grown too old for fantasies. And this, she decided, was no fantasy. Straightening her shoulders, Dimple marched right back across the street to the library and burst without ceremony into the book-lined room.

Virginia, who had been tossing a handful of

wilted chrysanthemums into the trash can, looked up, startled, empty vase in hand. "Good heavens, Dimple! You look like the hounds of hell are on your trail. What on earth is the matter?"

Dimple had to stop and calm herself before she could speak, and she was perturbed at the tremor in her voice. "I don't mean to alarm you, Virginia, but I believe there is someone just outside who might possibly be up to no good."

"How do you know? Did you see somebody?" Virginia set the vase aside and wiped her hands on her skirt.

With effort, Dimple resisted the impulse to offer her friend the use of her lace-edged handkerchief. "I just know, Virginia. You're going to have to believe me. Something is very wrong. I want you to telephone the police, and tell them to come quickly." And with those words, she stepped briskly to the door and slid the bolt into place.

Virginia Balliew had depended on her friend in too many times of trouble to ignore her now, and so she did as she was told.

Of course Officer Warren Nelson, who answered the phone, wanted to know the emergency.

"Will you just get over here, Warren? If Dimple Kilpatrick says there's cause for alarm, then there's cause for alarm. Now, hurry!"

And being familiar with Miss Dimple, the policeman didn't argue, but checked the revolver at his hip, grabbed his hat, and drove the three blocks to the library, going at least ten miles an hour over the speed limit.

Watching from the window behind the checkout desk, the two women saw the police car pull up out front and heard Warren shout "Halt!" as he stepped from the vehicle. "Halt!" he yelled again, and then disappeared from view.

"Where is he?" Virginia asked. "Can you see where he went?"

Dimple hurried to a window by the porch and leaned against the glass, but the light was already fading, pitching the area into deep shadow. Hardly daring to breathe, she listened until the crackling of branches and rustling footsteps faded into silence. Had something happened to Warren? Thank goodness she hadn't heard gunfire. Still, Dimple began to wish they hadn't called for help.

"Oh, good! Here comes Chief Tinsley," Virginia called from her vigil on the other side of the room. "Warren must have radioed for help." And for the first time since Dimple had demanded she phone the police, Virginia began to believe everything was going to be all right.

Both women jumped a few minutes later when someone pounded at the heavy oak door. "Miss Dimple? Virginia? Are you all right?" Bobby Tinsley shouted. "You can open the door now," he added.

Although the temperature had dipped into the

forties, the chief mopped perspiration from his face with a large handkerchief, while Warren fanned himself with his hat. "You were right to call," Officer Nelson told them. "There was somebody out there all right. Ran as soon as he saw my car."

"So it *was* a man," Dimple said. "I could only see enough to tell there was someone standing there."

"Couldn't see *that* well," Warren told her. "Might've been anybody, man or woman, but whoever it was must've been up to no good to have run off like that."

"I chased them all the way to the railroad track," Warren told them, "and soon as I leave here, I'll drive around over there, see if somebody turns up, but no harm was done—not yet anyway. Can't very well arrest somebody just for running."

"This person was waiting out there for a reason," Dimple reminded him. "I don't know what he had in mind, but I can assure you, it wasn't good, and if the two of you hadn't shown up when you did, I don't like to think what might have happened."

Bobby Tinsley looked at the levelheaded teacher who had shared her wisdom with several generations and helped guide the police through more frightening situations than he cared to count. Rarely did this woman reveal her emotions, but today Dimple Kilpatrick had let down her guard.

And she was afraid.

"I promise we'll keep an eye on this place in case this person shows up again," he told them. "Could be a tramp waiting around to try to hitch a ride when the freight train comes through, but if he comes back, we'll be ready.

"And now, just this once, why don't you ladies let us give you a ride home?"

This time, neither of them argued. And as soon as Dimple stepped inside the front door of the place she called home, the welcome aroma of a succulent chicken stew enveloped her. For a few brief seconds, she had the sweet sensation of her mother's arms around her, and Dimple Kilpatrick knew she would be safe here.

For now.

Chapter Six

"What is this dessert, Augusta?" Velma asked, and spooning up the last fluffy morsel, she licked her lips. "It tastes like lemony clouds."

Augusta smiled. "Then that's what it is— lemony clouds. It uses very little sugar, but you do have to whip it a lot."

Annie groaned. "I am *so* tired of all this worrying about sugar and rubber, and practically everything else. And what about leather? I've had these shoes resoled twice already and I don't know when I'll ever get another pair. *Use it up, wear it out, make it do, or do without!* I'm sick of hearing it."

She soon grew aware of the silence in the room, but the others were too polite to look at her. Worse than that, they acted as if she weren't there at all.

"Is anybody going to eat that last biscuit?" Lily asked finally, and Phoebe passed the platter, as requested.

"You know if you eat the last one, you'll be an old maid," Phoebe told her, and then gasped, realizing what she'd said.

But this time, Lily surprised her—surprised them all. "I guess it's a little late to worry about that," she said, and with a slight laugh, reached for the biscuit.

"I hear it's supposed to get colder tonight," Miss Dimple said, turning to Augusta. "Would anyone like another cup of tea?"

"All right! All right! I'm sorry!" Annie pushed aside her plate and closed her eyes, but only for a second. "I know I shouldn't complain. I know I should be grateful for everything we have, and glad to do without the things we don't have while so many are sacrificing their lives, and I *am.* Believe me, I am grateful. My own brother Joel is over there risking his life in a fighter plane, and Frazier . . . well, the last I heard from my fiancé, he was somewhere in France. . . ."

Annie rested her head on her arms and began to

cry. "I am so tired of this horrible war. I just *hate* this war! I hate it!"

"We all hate it, dear." Phoebe spoke gently as she placed a hand on Annie's shoulder.

"I'm sorry. I don't know what came over me." Annie sniffed as she accepted Miss Dimple's offer of a handkerchief.

"I think we all feel like crying sometimes," Miss Dimple told her, glancing briefly at Augusta. "I know I do, but what brought this on so suddenly?"

Annie dried her eyes before answering. "I don't know. I suppose it must've been the book."

"What book?" Velma asked, frowning.

"That decorating book. The one Miss Dimple brought home from the library today."

"My goodness!" Phoebe said, shaking her head. "I was hoping it would give me some new ideas for my bedroom. Everything looks so drab in there, but if that book upset you this much, I think I'd better rush it back to the library."

Annie saw that Phoebe was smiling, and so were the others at the table. In fact, she felt a smile coming on herself. "I found myself looking at the house plans in there," she admitted. "All those pretty cottages, and . . . well . . . I was thinking how wonderful it would be when Frazier comes home, if maybe one day *we* might have a house like that—just a small one with a yard, and we would fence it in so our children could play there. I even planned what kind of flowers I'd plant.

And then the horrible thought hit me: *What if he never comes back?*"

"We can't let ourselves think like that, Annie," Miss Dimple told her. "It won't help Frazier and it won't help you." She remembered the agonizing weeks the past summer when Annie's Frazier and another officer had become separated from their unit during the breakout at Normandy in Operation Cobra. For Annie, each day had begun with hope and ended in despair until she finally received word he was all right.

Phoebe nodded in agreement. She had recently learned that her own grandson, Harrison, was now helping to build an air base in the Dutch East Indies after being a part of the Battle of Morotai in September. There were some things, she realized, she would rather not know. That was one of them.

"Please let me help with the dishes," Annie insisted after supper, discouraging offers from others. She needed something to do with her hands—something useful.

Later, alone in the kitchen with Augusta, she slowly dried each yellow-striped bowl and stacked them one by one while outside a stiff wind sent the last of the brown leaves scurrying from the apple tree by the back door.

Standing at the sink, Augusta scrubbed the big stew pot, humming as she worked. Annie didn't recognize the tune, if there was a tune, but the funny little air seemed to float about like dandelion fluff in a breeze, reminding her of a summer day when she was five or six. Her family had gone on a picnic on her grandfather's farm, and while Joel and her cousins splashed in the creek, the grandfather they called "Papa Jake" taught her to make tiny houses from moss, sticks, and stones. As the other children played, the two of them created a small village with pebble-lined paths, giant daisy "trees," and "gardens" of buttercups.

Papa Jake had died when Annie was twelve, and she couldn't remember the last time she had thought of the fairy-size village in the woods and the happiness she'd felt there. But tonight, in this soap-scented kitchen with Augusta, she experienced it once again.

Annie Gardner took a deep breath, gave the dish towel a snap, and said, "Ahhh!"

Augusta turned with a smile. "I hope that means you're feeling better?"

"I am, yes. Thank you. For some reason, I remembered a special day with my grandfather when it seemed the most important thing in the world to do was nothing. Maybe it was that song you were humming, but suddenly I felt like . . . well . . . I can face whatever comes along."

Why am I telling this to someone I hardly know? Annie wondered, but what did it matter if her heart felt ten pounds lighter?

Augusta nodded. "When I want to go to a

peaceful place, I think blue," she said. "Tiny blue violets, calm blue waters, sky like a porcelain bowl. It calms me."

"I can't imagine you being any other way," Annie said. She watched Augusta stoop to store the large pot under the counter. She had never seen it so sparkling clean. "What did you use on that besides elbow grease?" she asked.

Augusta winked. "That and a sprinkle of angel dust."

Annie yawned as she climbed the stairs for bed. It had been a very long day and she was ready to snuggle under her comfy quilt and let the wind lull her to sleep.

The newcomer is an amazing cook, she thought, but sometimes she says the strangest things.

Miss Dimple had decided not to say anything to the others about what happened at the library that afternoon. Although the prowler acted suspiciously, he or she hadn't actually broken any law, and for all she knew, it might have been some poor creature frightened by the sudden frenzy. Still, she felt uneasy about the situation and was glad Bobby Tinsley had promised to keep an eye on the place.

Unable to sleep, she sat alone by the dying fire in the parlor with one of Agatha Christie's recent Miss Marple mysteries, *The Moving Finger.* Tomorrow was a school day and she needed her sleep. Perhaps reading would make her drowsy.

"Oh, I'm sorry. I didn't know anyone was in here," Augusta said from the doorway. "I was going to bank the fire for the night, but I hope you'll join me for a cup of tea?"

"Thank you. That would be delightful," Miss Dimple said, closing her book.

Augusta had left the kettle on a boil, so Dimple sat, warmed by the fire, as amber embers winked on the hearth, and she had almost nodded off when Augusta returned with two steaming mugs and a small plate of thin spice cookies she had made that afternoon.

Miss Dimple said she didn't usually eat sweets before bedtime, but found she'd consumed at least three of them before she even realized it.

"Miss Dimple, is anything wrong?" Augusta asked, sitting across from her in the small mahogany side chair, its flowered needlepoint seat now beginning to fade. "You seem as if something is bothering you."

Dimple sipped her tea. Not as good as her lemon-ginger brew, she thought, but hot and soothing just the same. She sighed. She really didn't know this newcomer well at all, and thought it a bit forward of her to ask such a personal question. Why should she unburden herself to a stranger?

But the words were out of her mouth before she even realized it. "I have to send a telegram," she said, and told Augusta of her concerns about Henry.

"Tell me about him," Augusta said, giving the fire a poke. And Dimple spoke with pride of her brother's work at the Bell Bomber Plant near Marietta. "I know he's doing something important for the war effort," she said, "but Henry doesn't talk about it."

Augusta nodded. "That's where they build the aeroplanes, isn't it?" She pronounced the word in a peculiar manner, as if she wasn't accustomed to using it, and Dimple hid a smile.

"That's right," she said. "My brother helps to design them. He's an engineer, a special kind of engineer." She remembered how proud she had been to contribute part of her small teacher's salary to help with young Henry's expenses at Georgia Tech, and it had been worth every dollar and then some.

Augusta just smiled and nodded, as if she knew all about flying. What a strange little bird, Dimple thought.

"I suppose you've tried to reach him by telephone," Augusta suggested, and was told he was never there when Dimple called, and Henry's wife apparently had forgotten to relay her messages.

"Hazel—that's my brother's wife—told me he's been out of town a good bit lately," Dimple confided. "She thinks he's working on a special kind of project, but of course she doesn't know what it is, except that it seems to be important."

Augusta shifted in her seat, giving her skirt a twitch. Its colors of turquoise, gold, and rose seemed to blend in the fire's glow. "He *must* be at home sometime," she said. "Do you know when he goes in to work?"

"Early. Very early. I've thought of calling then, but I don't want to wake the entire household."

"Why not?" Augusta said, and Dimple examined her companion's serene countenance and thought to herself, *Why not indeed?*

"Then I'll phone in the morning." Dimple stifled a yawn.

Augusta smiled. "Before your walk."

"Yes, before my walk," Dimple agreed.

And she did.

Grumpy Hazel answered, her voice sounding as if she were hollering up a chimney filled with soot. "Who is this? Dimple? Is that you? I suppose you know you've waked the whole household."

The words *I'm sorry* were on Dimple's lips, but she swallowed them just in time. She wasn't one bit sorry. "That's too bad. I'd like to speak with my brother, please."

Dimple heard a rumble of voices in the background and finally Henry himself took the receiver in hand. "Dimple? What's going on? Is anything wrong?"

Dimple was so relieved to hear his voice, she

almost cried, but this wasn't the time for crying. "Of course I'm all right, Henry, but I've been worried sick about you. Why haven't you returned my calls or answered my letters? It's been months since I've heard from you."

She found herself listening to dead air for a few seconds until her brother finally spoke. "I'm so sorry, Dimple. I wasn't aware you had phoned, and it's been . . . well . . . stressful at the plant lately. One of these days maybe I can explain, but I'm all right, and I will write soon—I promise. Take care of yourself, now. I don't have but one Dimple."

As soon as Henry said good-bye, Dimple Kilpatrick buttoned up her coat, jammed on her hat, and grabbed her umbrella, but she waited until she reached the porch to let the tears begin. Now was the time for crying.

Chapter Seven

"Well?" Virginia asked when Dimple saw her in town the next day. "Did you send the telegram?"

Dimple had stopped in at Cooper's Store to pick up soy flour and molasses for her Victory Muffins, as well as bananas and cheese for Augusta, and heard Virginia calling to her from the sidewalk in front of Brumlow's Dry Goods.

"I didn't have to," she said, shifting her burden.

"I reached Henry on the telephone this morning—caught him just before he left for the plant."

Her friend made a harrumphing noise. "And what did he have to say?"

"Sounds as if things have been more stressful than usual at Bell Bomber. I don't know what's going on, but I can tell my brother has a lot on his mind. It must have something to do with a special project—some kind of plane, I imagine. He can't talk about it, of course." Miss Dimple managed a smile, although she didn't feel like smiling at all. "And he promised to write soon. That's about all I can ask."

"Did you find out why he didn't return your calls?"

Dimple shrugged. "Seems he didn't get the messages."

"Ah-ha!" Virginia said.

Dimple ignored the inference. What good would it do to make an issue of something she couldn't change? However, thanks to Augusta's advice, she was glad she had ignored Hazel's rudeness and insisted on speaking with Henry. "I don't suppose you've seen any more suspicious visitors at the library?" she said.

Virginia shook her head. "Bobby or somebody else on the force has been patrolling faithfully, and I can't say I'm not grateful." She frowned. "Whoever was out there might've meant no harm at all, but it made me feel uneasy. You sensed it, too, Dimple—and he *did* run from the police. Anyway, he's probably long gone by now."

Dimple hoped it was true. She didn't want to alarm Virginia, but she would be grateful if the police would continue to keep an eye on the library for a while at least.

"Bobby tells me Dora's husband is on his way here to see to her arrangements," Virginia said. "Wonder what kind of person he is, and why she left the way she did."

Miss Dimple wondered, too. "I've been thinking about a limeade all afternoon," she said. "Do you have time to stop at Lewellyn's?"

"Do you know what time they expect Dora's husband to arrive?" Miss Dimple asked after the two were settled in a booth at the drugstore. She laid her recent purchases on the seat beside her and put in her order with Cal Stewart, one of her former students.

Virginia said she thought he was due sometime the next day and wondered if there was a way they might be able to meet him.

Dimple wondered the same thing and suggested it seemed only natural the two of them be introduced, since they had been the first to greet the unfortunate woman.

Except for a few customers waiting for prescriptions in the back of the store, Lewellyn's was relatively empty, as the after-school crowd had thinned, but the store still smelled of hot dogs with mustard and onions. Dimple took a deep breath and inhaled the mouthwatering aroma. She knew such fare was unhealthy, but now and then it was impossible to resist. In a hundred years, she wondered, would the pressed tin ceiling and black-and-white tile floor of the building still smell of that drugstore perfume?

"I believe they're releasing her body to Harvey Thompson," Virginia said, referring to a local funeral director. "It would be rude, don't you think, if we didn't stop by and pay our respects?"

Miss Dimple stirred her drink with a straw and smiled when she saw tired Cal had remembered to add the usual maraschino cherry. "Indeed it would," she agreed.

Virginia poured a Coca-Cola over crushed ice, watching foam fizz to the top. "What kind of person is this husband of Dora's that she was afraid to identify herself even to the police?" she said.

"I suppose she assumed her husband had reported her missing and the police would certainly notify authorities there, and her husband as well," Dimple said. "But according to the date on the stub from her bus ticket, she left home a whole day before she showed up in Elderberry, so where do you suppose she was during that time? It shouldn't take that long to travel here, even with the bus stopping at every crossroad."

"I suppose she stayed with a friend," Virginia said. "She must've had help from someone along the way."

Noticing a smear of mayonnaise on the table, Miss Dimple slowly tore her napkin in two and blotted it away, wiping her fingers with the part that was left. "It seems our Dora was a mystery unto herself," she said, shaking her head.

Virginia smiled. "Which means you'll have your work cut out for you."

Dimple didn't argue.

"I suppose it will be all right if you and Mrs. Balliew speak with this fellow," Chief Tinsley said when Miss Dimple telephoned him later that afternoon. "After all, I imagine he'd want to know of his wife's last few hours.

"Of course," he continued, "I have a feeling you're going to see him with or without my permission, and frankly, I'd like your opinion. The man's background checks out okay, but I believe there's more involved here than a marital tiff."

Later, over a supper of a delightfully fluffy dish called cheese strata and some of Odessa's home-canned peaches, Dimple told the others of Leonard Westbrook's upcoming visit.

"Oh, Dimple, do be careful," Lily warned. "The poor woman must've had a reason for running away from that man, and you don't know one thing about him."

Dimple only nodded and smiled. That was exactly what she intended to find out.

For dessert, Augusta had made cookie bars of oatmeal, nuts, and honey with a touch of apple butter. Annie stared longingly at the last one on the plate until Augusta laughed and slid it in front of her.

"I sure did want that last one, but I'd die before I'd ask for it," Annie joked before taking a bite.

"I wish I could get a good look at this husband of Dora's," she said as they cleared away the dishes. "He's probably spooky and grim, with a long beard and bad breath."

Augusta laughed. "That in itself might frighten anyone away. Maybe Miss Dimple can give us a report after she meets him."

"But don't expect me to get close enough to judge his breath!" Miss Dimple protested. "I wish there were some way we could talk with Dora's friends in Fieldcroft—possibly a neighbor or two," she added. "You can't expect an objective opinion from the very person she was attempting to escape."

Augusta paused to tuck a stray strand under the scarf that kept her sunbeam hair in place. "But isn't there a sister? I believe the policeman who was here the other night mentioned a letter from somewhere in—where is it . . . Tennesaw, I think?"

A lifted eyebrow from Miss Dimple stifled

Annie's outburst of giggles. "You're right. A little place near Lewisburg. I believe her name was Elaine . . . something."

Augusta backed through the swinging door to the kitchen, a stack of dishes shifting precariously in the curve of her arm. "Yes! Arnold. Elaine Arnold," she said to Dimple and Annie, who followed to help. And with a motion as quick as a blink, she set the dishes next to the sink and began to scrape the few remnants of leftover food into a pail. "I should think she might be able to shed some light on the subject."

Miss Dimple nodded. "I'm sure Chief Tinsley plans to speak with her, if he hasn't already." Quickly, she snatched a dish towel and began to dry the dishes, finding it hard to keep up as Augusta dealt them, sparkling clean, into the dish rack.

Steam rose as Augusta scalded the silverware with boiling water from the kettle, and for a few seconds Dimple imagined a faint halo of mist around her hair. Of course, it was warm and humid in the kitchen and it had been a tiring day.

"There must be some way we can locate a neighbor of Dora's in that town where she lived," Annie suggested as she gave the kitchen floor a quick once-over with the broom. "Do you think Bobby Tinsley might give us her address?"

"Certainly he would understand if we wanted to write a letter of condolence to the bereaved widower," Dimple replied. And she managed to keep a straight face when she said it.

Harvey Thompson said he expected Dora's husband to meet him at the funeral home sometime in the early afternoon the next day, so Dimple prevailed upon a reliable room mother to help with her first graders so she and Virginia might get there in time to speak with him.

"I feel uneasy about this, Dimple," Virginia said as she locked the door to the library behind her and paused to look about. "Do you think Leonard Westbrook might've been the person we saw hanging around here the other day? And how do we know *he* wasn't the one who ordered those vanilla wafers from Harris Cooper?"

"But, Virginia, how could he possibly know Harris Cooper, or Jesse Dean, either, for that matter?"

Virginia chose to ignore that. "And has anyone checked to see where he was the night Dora died?"

"Chief Tinsley assured me the police in Fieldcroft can vouch that he didn't leave the county during that time. Seems the tires need replacing on his car, and with rationing the way it is, he hasn't been able to find others. You can't go far on bald tires."

"Then how is he going to get here today?"

"I imagine he'll either take the bus or ask

someone to drive him," Dimple said as she climbed into the passenger side of Virginia's faithful Plymouth and immediately rolled down the window. Even in late October, the small car became uncomfortably warm when parked in the sun. "At any rate, what reason would he have to stand out there under that magnolia and watch the library?"

Virginia didn't have an answer for that. "But if he can find a way to get here today, how do we know he didn't do the same when his wife met her end at the foot of that ladder?" she asked.

Dimple shook her head and smiled. "Why, Virginia Balliew . . . and you accuse *me* of reading too many mysteries!"

She was pleased to see Bobby Tinsley's police car parked in front of the funeral home when they arrived a few minutes later, and had to admit to herself she was a little uneasy about intruding on what should be a solemn and private occasion. Perhaps the two of them might be able to offer a few words of comfort to Dora's husband, but frankly, Dimple couldn't imagine what they might be.

Dora had looked to be in her late thirties or early forties, so Dimple expected her husband to be close to the same age or older, but the man who sat in the vestibule seemed much younger. Leonard Westbrook stood and took her hand and then Virginia's as Chief Tinsley introduced them, and Dimple found it difficult to speak when she thought of the shocking way his wife had died.

Of medium height, Leonard Westbrook was clean-shaven and tanned, as if he spent a good bit of time in the sun. They had learned earlier that the family owned a small farm outside of town, where they raised beef cattle. His brown hair was tinged with gray at the temples, and he wore a dark suit and white dress shirt, but no tie. He listened gravely as they spoke their condolences, and nodded and thanked them quietly, as, Dimple thought, any grieving family member might. Leonard didn't ask and they didn't tell him of Dora's visit to the library or the brief time she spent at Phoebe's, and neither Dimple nor Virginia saw the need to bring it up. They did, however, think to get the man's address from Harvey Thompson before they left.

"Well, what did you think?" Virginia asked as they drove away.

Dimple didn't answer right away. "I don't know," she said finally. "I was dying to ask him if he had any idea where his wife went when she left there, but I'll have to admit he wasn't at all what I expected."

"He seemed all right to me. Makes you wonder why she left him," Virginia said.

Dimple Kilpatrick took a deep breath and sat a little straighter. "And that's exactly why we need to get in touch with their neighbors," she said.

Chapter Eight

Jo Carr sat at her sister Lou's kitchen table and helped herself to the ginger cookies. "I shouldn't," she said, and took two.

"And why not?" Louise Willingham rolled her eyes. Her sister, at fifty-five, was still as skinny as a stick, while she seemed to put on weight if she walked past a bakery. Jo's daughter Charlie taught with Annie and Miss Dimple at the grammar school, and the two women were usually kept abreast of the goings-on at Phoebe Chadwick's rooming house. Recently, however, they sensed they were missing out on something, and that didn't suit at all.

Three days a week, the sisters, along with others from the community, boarded a bus to nearby Milledgeville, where they worked in the ordnance plant, providing much-needed munitions for the war effort. Tired at the end of the workweek, Jo usually walked the few blocks home, but today the two had decided there were puzzling issues they needed to discuss.

A few hours after Dora Westbrook's body was discovered at the foot of the steeple ladder, most of the people of Elderberry had learned of the tragedy. Later, Annie told her friend Charlie of the strange woman's brief visit at Phoebe's, and, of course, Charlie told her mother. But the rest of the story appeared to be shrouded in mystery—at least to Lou and Jo—and a bit of detective work seemed in order.

"Have you seen the new boarder who's helping out in Odessa's place?" Lou asked. "I ran into Velma Anderson in Lewellyn's the other day and she said she was a wonderful cook—seems to come up with mouthwatering dishes from practically nothing."

"Surely not better than Odessa's?" Jo's eyes widened. She could hardly cook at all and was in awe of Odessa's culinary accomplishments.

"No, no, of course not," Lou protested, not wanting to be disloyal. "It just seems she showed up there . . . well . . . all of a sudden. Velma said Phoebe had posted a notice at Cooper's just as Harris was getting ready to close the day before." She clicked her fingers. "And poof! There she was."

"Charlie tells me everyone seems to like her," Jo confided. "She's almost too good to be true. It appears odd to me, though, that she turned up the *very day* that poor woman's body was found, and now they say *somebody* tried to throw suspicion on poor Jesse Dean. At least Bobby Tinsley had better sense than to take it seriously; still, I don't like the idea that somebody *right here in Elderberry* would do such a thing. Why would he try to blame it on Jesse Dean unless he's the one who killed her?"

"Or *she.*" Lou rummaged in the refrigerator for leftovers to warm for supper. Her husband, Ed, was usually tired and hungry after standing on his feet at his dental office most of the day and would be ready to eat when he got home. She turned to Jo with a bowl of cold butter beans in her hand. "Surely you don't think there's a connection between this new boarder and that horrible thing that happened in the steeple?"

Her sister bit into another cookie and shrugged. "I suppose not, but still . . ."

"Still what?" Lou sliced leftover meat loaf into a pan and doctored it with catsup, waiting for Jo to continue.

"I know you can't believe half of what the child says," she began, "and of course you have to take his wild imagination into consideration. . . ."

Lou slammed the meat loaf into the oven. "*What* child, Josephine? What on earth are you talking about?"

Jo paused. "Well, I wasn't going to mention it, but you know that funny Willie Elrod—lives next door to Phoebe?"

"Of course I know Willie. Seems to spend half his time reading the comic books in the dime store and the other half at Lewellyn's soda fountain. What about him?"

"Charlie taught him in her class a couple of years ago, so I suppose he's in the fifth grade now, so you'd think he would've outgrown this craziness, but the boy told Charlie the wildest tale! I can't imagine how he makes them all up."

Jo eyed her sister silently and waited.

"He said," Jo began, "he saw that new boarder —what's her name? Augusta? Anyway, he saw her hanging out laundry one morning early. Seems Willie had gone out to feed his dog, and he told Charlie she hung clothes on the line, and then— *whiff!* As soon as she finished hanging them out, she turned right around and took them down, and Willie swears they were *dry!*"

Lou smiled. "And you believe him?"

"I'm only repeating what Charlie told me."

"The woman probably noticed it was going to rain and took the laundry in." Lou shook her head. "That child watches too many movies, and I'm sure he listens to all those wild radio programs like *Captain Midnight* and *The Green Hornet.*"

"Probably. But it's odd, don't you think, that we haven't heard anything more about this woman who was killed and what she was doing here in Elderberry?"

"I doubt if the authorities have learned any more details." Lou dropped a handful of silverware on the table and Jo took the hint and set two places for her sister and her husband.

"Charlie told me Miss Dimple and Virginia Balliew were going to try to speak to the woman's husband while he's here to make arrangements with Harvey," Jo said. "Wonder what they'll find out."

"Whatever it is, they won't tell us."

"Maybe they will, and maybe they won't." Jo smiled. "What's the name of that town where this woman lived? Somewhere in south Georgia, I think."

Lou nodded. "Fieldcroft," she said. *Now, what did her sister have up her sleeve?*

"If anyone has mending or something that needs hemming, pass it along to me," Augusta announced that evening. It was Friday, the school week over, and everyone relaxed in the parlor after enjoying a savory vegetable omelette with homemade bread and a piquant salad of apples, nuts, and bananas. And after halfhearted protests, Phoebe Chadwick and her boarders filled Augusta's mending basket to overflowing.

"Are you sure you don't mind?" Lily asked, tossing in a blouse with a torn buttonhole; others soon added a skirt with a jagged tear, another that needed hemming, and an assortment of holey socks. Phoebe was reluctant to contribute her old tweed jacket with a rip in the sleeve. "I don't even know if this can be fixed, Augusta, and I hesitate to ask you to take the time," she said.

Augusta shook her head and smiled. "Idle hands are the devil's workshop, they say, and I surely

84

don't want any dealings with that fellow, so let's at least give it a try."

The house was quiet the next morning, with Augusta tucked away in her room with her sewing basket, and others busy with various tasks. Dimple, with a stack of workbooks to grade, took advantage of the spacious dining room table and had settled down to work, when someone knocked at the front door. Being the closest to answer, she was surprised to find Jo Carr and her sister on the porch, and of course she invited them in, as it was a chilly October morning.

Jo came directly to the point. "You're just the person we wanted to see," she began. "Miss Dimple, I have an offer for you—"

At that point, her sister gave her a jab with her elbow and Jo stopped abruptly and then continued. "Excuse me . . . *we* have an offer for you."

What in the world are these two up to? Dimple wondered. They were too old to be selling Girl Scout cookies, and the Scouts had even discontinued that and switched to calendars because of war shortages.

The two women hesitated in the entranceway and looked about. "We were hoping to meet your new guest," Jo said. "We've heard such lovely things about her."

Miss Dimple nodded, smiling. "And I'm sure there'll be other opportunities, but Augusta has retired to her room to catch up on some mending.

It's been a rather hectic week, and I imagine she needs the rest." Augusta hadn't asked not to be disturbed, but Dimple had a feeling she needed this time alone.

Shoving the workbooks aside, she cleared a space on the table and pulled out a couple of chairs. "I hope you'll allow me to offer you a cup of ginger mint tea and some of my Victory Muffins," she said.

"Muffins?" Lou looked hopeful, but her sister knew better. "Oh, no thank you, Miss Dimple. We both had a late breakfast, and I honestly don't believe I could hold another crumb."

Lou frowned at her sister. "But, I—"

"And we really have to rush if we're going to get to the telegraph office before it closes," Jo hastened to say.

"Telegraph office? Oh dear!" Dimple clasped her hands under the table. "Not bad news, I hope."

"No, no. Nothing like that. But that's why we're here, you see." Placing both palms on the table, Jo took a deep breath. "My late husband, Charles, had a cousin who lived in south Georgia. Still lives there, as far as I know. I've looked at the map, and you won't believe this, but it's very near that little place that poor woman was from—the one who died over there in the church."

Dimple waited silently. Surely this woman would eventually come to the point.

"Claudia has been begging me to come for a visit," Jo continued, "and now, if you'll agree, I'd like to take her up on it."

Dimple frowned. "I don't understand . . ." she began.

Jo pulled her chair closer to the table and leaned forward. "Lou and I have come up with a plan. . . . Well, really, it's more of an idea. I'm sure you're as concerned as we are about that woman falling from the steeple ladder—*if, in fact, she did fall.* From everything we've heard, it sounds like the poor thing was afraid for her life. She seemed to be running from somebody, and we're supposed to believe she *fell?* How do we know the person who killed her isn't still around? Why, it might even be someone we know."

"Frankly, this has created quite a stir at our church," confided Lou, who had abandoned the Methodists for the Presbyterians when she married Ed. "Poor Evan—you know Evan Mitchell, our minister, and a finer man never graced a pulpit—well, it's near about worried him to death with such an awful thing happening not twenty feet from where Mildred Hufstetler was just getting ready to play the prelude.

"The congregation's up in the air about it, that's for sure, and I'm afraid things won't settle down until we find out who's responsible."

Jo jumped in when her sister paused for breath. "Lou and I believe we need to learn more about this Dora's background. And that's where you come in, Miss Dimple."

Dimple was beginning to wish she hadn't answered the door. "And how is that?" she asked, although she doubted if she wanted to hear the answer.

"You're so much more experienced at this kind of thing than we are," Jo continued, "and, after all, three heads are better than two. We should be able to stay with Cousin Claudia, and we hope you'll come with us. It's a fairly long drive, but Lou and I can go in together on the gas ration stamps, and we'll take my car, of course."

"I don't believe it will take more than a day or so to find out what we want to know," Lou added.

"And why do you think I might be able to help?" Dimple concentrated on polishing her bifocals.

Lou sighed. "Well, let's face it. People trust you, Miss Dimple. They open up to you, and we need to find out what kind of person this Dora was. What was going on in her life that caused her to run away? Maybe you could talk with some of her neighbors and others who knew her. *Somebody* must have helped her between the time she left home and then ended up here in Elderberry. . . ." Lou caught her breath. "*Ended up* . . . oh dear, I didn't mean to make it sound so final. But then it was final, wasn't it?"

"And when did you plan on leaving?" Dimple asked.

"Why, as soon as possible," Jo said. "Tomorrow, if we can get in touch with Claudia this afternoon. I don't think she has a telephone, so we decided to send a telegram."

"But there's no way we could get back here by Monday," Dimple explained, "and I couldn't possibly take time away from school." Why, the very idea, she thought. Except in cases of illness or extreme emergency, Dimple Kilpatrick would never miss a day of school of her own volition.

Jo shook her head sadly. "In that case," she said, "perhaps you could give us suggestions on what to say, and some questions we might ask." She wasn't ready to admit it, but Jo Carr had another reason for the impromptu trip to Fieldcroft. After serving for years as society editor of the *Elderberry Eagle*, Jo was ready to move on to more serious reporting with an assignment that didn't involve an excessive use of adverbs and adjectives. Not only would the experience allow her an opportunity to learn more about Dora Westbrook's mysterious past but, if she played her cards right, her story might even rate a front page byline.

"I can do better than that," Miss Dimple said after several moments of reflection. "I can give you Dora's address, but first you must promise to be careful. Be very careful."

She hoped she hadn't made a mistake.

Chapter Nine

"You did *what?*" Virginia said when Dimple dropped by the library that afternoon. "Why, Dimple Kilpatrick, you know how flighty those two are. There's no telling what kind of mischief they'll get into down there."

Virginia had built a fire in the old stone fireplace to take off the late-autumn chill, and the two women pulled their chairs close to take advantage of the warmth, while Cattus slept on the rug at their feet.

Dimple watched a flurry of red sparks disappear up the chimney. "Oh, well," she said. "I suppose I know them well enough to believe they'll go with or without my support." She found it difficult to be distressed while staring into the lazy, flickering blaze. "Besides," she added, "Augusta has a friend there who has promised to keep an eye on them."

Virginia sat up straighter. "Augusta? That new boarder at Phoebe's? She knows someone in Fieldcroft?"

Miss Dimple nodded. "In her line of work, I suppose she's lived in various places."

Virginia frowned. "Her line of work?"

"Cooking. Housekeeping. Filling in where she's

needed. She tells me she's a temporary," Dimple explained.

"And don't you find that a bit too convenient? What do you know about this woman, anyway?"

Dimple smiled. "I know she can cook, and she mended Phoebe's jacket so you couldn't even tell it had been torn."

Her friend answered with a sigh—one that was louder and longer than usual. *What in the world was the matter with Dimple Kilpatrick? She had never seen her as unconcerned and nonchalant.*

"Has this woman cast a spell on you? I do believe she's hypnotized the lot of you." She shook her head and whispered, "Emma Elrod says her Willie believes she's a *witch*."

Dimple turned to Virginia and laughed. "And since when did you become concerned about the things Willie says?"

"If I remember correctly, a few short years ago, you would've been in an unfortunate situation indeed, Dimple Kilpatrick, if it hadn't been for Willie Elrod's wild tales!"

And Dimple had to agree she was right. She and young Willie shared a bond of friendship she would treasure the rest of her life; still, she sometimes found it necessary to make allowances for his overly active imagination.

A log fell apart in the fireplace, causing the cat to dash under Dimple's chair in alarm, and she reached down to calm it, but Cattus slipped past her and jumped onto the windowsill. "I'm afraid we have to be practical, Virginia," she began. "Neither of us can take off several days right now to travel to south Georgia, and although I'm sure Bobby Tinsley's doing all he can, he's handicapped by the distance, as well. Fieldcroft, it seems, is smaller than Elderberry, and I was told its police department is even smaller."

Virginia added another log to the fire and stood to watch it take hold. "So . . ." she said finally, "we're sending Jo and Lou into battle without armor. Do they have any idea what they're getting into?"

"My goodness, Virginia, I don't believe I'd put it *that* way!" Dimple smiled. "Besides, Celeste will be there. Remember?"

"And just who is this Celeste when she's at home?" Virginia grumbled.

Miss Dimple spoke calmly. "Augusta's acquaintance in Fieldcroft . . . I believe she said her name was Celeste."

"And do the sisters know to look her up when they get there? How are they supposed to find her?" Virginia gave the fire a poke, although it didn't need it.

"From what Augusta said, I expect she'll find *them*."

"Dimple Kilpatrick! Are you deliberately trying to be exasperating?" Virginia let the poker fall to the hearth. "What have you done with my friend —the one who sets out her clothes before she goes to bed each night and plans her days accordingly? The one who gets as jumpy as a beady-eyed grass-hopper when things don't work out the way they should? I want her back."

"I'll have you know that never in my life have I been as jumpy as a . . . what was it you said? 'Beady-eyed grasshopper.'" Dimple Kilpatrick struggled to keep from laughing. "Is that a new expression, Virginia? I don't believe I've ever heard it before."

Virginia shrugged. "That's because I made it up—and it's true, I've never seen you jumpy, but you do get all quiet and kind of beady-eyed when something's on your mind." Folding her arms, she looked at her old friend. "And, well, I hate to say it, but you're acting like your mind's somewhere else, like you don't even *care* what's going on."

Dimple was about to tell her friend that she did indeed care and had made a detailed list of questions for Jo and her sister to ask, as well as those they should avoid. She was about to assure Virginia she intended to do her best to find out why Dora Westbrook died the way she did, but the two were interrupted by someone who wanted to return books.

"Wonderful! You've built a fire." Rose McGinnis, her arm in a sling, slid a couple of books onto Virginia's desk and hurried across the room to warm herself by the blaze. "Good reading weather, don't you think?"

Both women agreed that it was. "How's your shoulder, Rose?" Virginia asked, rising. "You were lucky to have escaped from that accident as well as you did, but I guess you know that already."

"You're so right! The doctor put my shoulder back in place, but I still ache from all the bruises. Thank goodness I'll be okay. Some of the others on that bus weren't—"

Rose shook her head and went to the piano, where she raised the lid over the keyboard and began to pick out "Wait 'Till the Sun Shines, Nellie" with one finger. It was the only song she ever played, and it seemed she felt obligated to play it.

Virginia wanted to go to her, but she knew it would only make the young woman cry. Rose had been returning from a visit with her young soldier sweetheart at Camp Gordon, in Augusta, when the bus met with a terrible accident. Someone driving in the wrong lane forced the bus off the road, where it overturned in a deep ditch. At least one person was killed and many were injured.

Finishing her solo, Rose browsed about the room, finally selecting a couple of Patricia Wentworth's Miss Silver mysteries.

"Oh, I just finished one of her latest, *Miss Silver*

Deals with Death," Miss Dimple said, observing the titles. "Have you read any of her others?"

Rose frowned. "I don't believe I have. Before all this happened," she said, calling attention to her arm, "Aunt Trudy and I had been terribly busy, and she hasn't been feeling well lately."

"I'm sorry to hear that," Dimple said. "Her arthritis again?"

Rose nodded. "Makes it difficult to sew. I'll just be glad when I'm able to help."

Virginia stamped the date on the books. "I'll be glad, too, and I'm sure your aunt would agree. Did Trudy enjoy the book you checked out for her the other day? Such a good story! *Mama's Bank Account,*" she said, turning to Dimple. "Published last year."

"Yes, I believe she liked it a lot," Rose said, and, thanking her, gathered her new selections to her chest.

"And what do you hear from that soldier of yours?" Miss Dimple asked, smiling. "I believe he's with the Twenty-sixth Infantry, isn't he? I suppose you watch and wait for the mailman as most of us do, it seems."

Rose frowned as she hugged the books closer. "You never know when it might be the last time—"

"Let's pray this war will soon be over," Miss Dimple said gently. "This time next year, perhaps they'll all be home again."

"Gertrude Hutchinson must be relieved to have her niece come here to live with her," Dimple said after the young woman left. A talented seamstress, Gertrude took in sewing and alterations in the old family home a few blocks from town. Apparently, Rose had lost her job in a defense plant near Atlanta and moved to Elderberry to live with her aunt soon after her fiancé enlisted the year before. In addition to helping with sewing orders, she had also opened a secondhand shop in a spare room off the back porch.

"I'm sure she's happy to have her," Virginia said, returning the books to their proper places. "Rose is her great-niece, I believe, a grand-daughter of her late husband's brother, Tate. Since Gertrude's almost crippled with arthritis, I honestly don't know what she would do without her. Gertrude says Rose can do more with one arm than most people do with two, and she seems to enjoy keeping her aunt well supplied with books."

Dimple had barely known Tate Hutchinson. He'd owned a cotton gin outside of town until it burned several years before, and he'd died of a heart attack not long afterward.

"Makes you feel good, doesn't it?" Dimple asked, turning to Virginia. "In spite of war and death and all the worry that goes with it, you can still offer this magical escape through reading?"

• • •

Later, it occurred to Dimple she hadn't reassured Virginia that she *did* care about what was going on and wanted as much as anyone to learn who was responsible for Dora Westbrook's death and why. The fact that her friend was in doubt nagged at her conscience like a persistent reprimand. Already halfway home, she paused, intending to go back to the library, but instead decided to drop by the police department and speak with Bobby Tinsley. Clutching her large purple handbag with the library book inside, Dimple Kilpatrick turned back toward town, hoping the chief would be available.

She was in luck.

"Why, Miss Dimple, what can I do for you?" Bobby jumped to his feet and immediately offered a chair.

She thanked him and told him of her concerns about her friends' making the trip to Fieldcroft.

"Oh dear!" the chief said, or at least that's what Dimple thought he said. "Do you know when they plan to leave?"

"Tomorrow, if they hear from Mrs. Carr's cousin down there. I believe they plan to stay with her." Miss Dimple had never been one to fidget, but she contemplated fidgeting now. *What on earth made her think the two would be safe on their own? What if she'd made a mistake?*

Bobby Tinsley ruffled papers on his desk, then

leaned back in his chair and shook his head. "Then I'd better give them a call. If they're determined to do this, I want them to get in touch with a fellow at the police station there—name of Reece Cagle. I don't think the town has more than two policemen, and he's the one I've spoken with. At any rate, I think they should be prepared."

"I've given them a list of questions they might ask, and they have the Westbrooks' address, so they can speak with some of the neighbors," Dimple told him. "They shouldn't be totally unprepared."

The chief surprised her by laughing. "I wasn't talking about our two ladies, Miss Dimple. I was referring to the Fieldcroft police.

"But if they *do* end up going," he added, leaning forward, "I'll try to give them a few guidelines. None of us here can get away to go all the way down there, so we might as well make the best of it."

Dimple Kilpatrick walked the few blocks home, feeling as if she were carrying a basket of rocks on her head. She was responsible for possibly putting those two women in danger, and she didn't know what to do about it.

But maybe this Cousin Claudia hasn't received the telegram, she thought. Maybe she has moved away—someplace far away, like California or North Dakota. Or perhaps she's come down with an illness and won't be up for company. Nothing too serious, Dimple thought with a smattering of guilt. A terrible cold would do.

Of course it didn't take long for her friend Phoebe to notice her troubled demeanor. "What on earth's the matter, Dimple?" she asked over supper that night. "You look like you've lost your last friend."

And Dimple reluctantly confessed what was on her mind, thinking it would make her feel better. It didn't.

After supper, Dimple sat in the parlor with her library book, hoping it would bring relief, however brief, from her concerns. She had read only a few pages when Augusta quietly joined her with a book of her own.

Augusta waited a few minutes to speak. "I don't think you should be so hard on yourself," she said, marking her place with a finger. "From what I heard during the conversation at supper, these two sisters seem to be loving, intelligent women who care very much about their families, their community, and their country. Jo raised a son, who's currently serving overseas, and it sounds as if her daughter is a devoted teacher. Lou is a wonderful wife, a loyal friend to many, and takes an active role in her church. From what I've heard, she's also one of the best cooks in town."

"I know that, Augusta," Dimple began.

"And that's not all," Augusta continued. "They both give their time three days a week in an effort to help win this war. Just because they enjoy a bit of adventure now and then and try to find happiness where they can doesn't mean they aren't capable. Don't you think you should give them more credit than that?"

Dimple nodded and sighed. She could feel the rocks lifting one by one. "So . . . you believe I'm doing them an injustice?"

"And yourself, as well," Augusta said, and she opened her book once more.

Curious, Dimple glanced at the title. "*Where Angels Fear to Tread.* Sounds interesting. That's one I've never read. Are you enjoying it?"

"It's just something I found in the bookcase," Augusta said with a smile. "Not exactly what I expected, but I find it amusing."

Chapter Ten

"Charlie tells me her mother and her aunt Lou are on their way to that little town in south Georgia— the one where Dora lived," Annie told the others after church the next day. "They're staying with a cousin, and Chief Tinsley's already spoken with the police there to let them know to expect them."

Remembering what Bobby Tinsley had said, Miss Dimple hid a smile. She felt strangely lighthearted, but a little resentful, too, wishing she might have gone along as well.

"Has he mentioned anything about talking with Dora's sister?" Velma asked, removing her small black felt hat with the blue feathered flower. "It seems that should be the next step."

Lily agreed. "Lives somewhere in Tennessee, doesn't she? Lewisburg, I believe."

Phoebe shed her newly mended jacket. "That's what the letter said." She turned to Dimple. "Now, there's one for you and your young detective friends," she said, meaning Annie and Charlie.

"Oh, but it's much too far. We couldn't possibly get away," Dimple protested. "Besides, I'm sure Chief Tinsley and his staff are perfectly capable of taking care of that."

"But, Miss Dimple, have you forgotten? We have two whole days at the end of the week, not including the weekend." Annie's eyes sparkled and she clasped her hands and looked so hopeful, Dimple hated to discourage her.

But she did. *She couldn't. Not after all this time. Over the years, the wound had healed. Still, she knew the pain slept deep inside. It waited for her there.*

"Annie's right," Velma reminded her. "Remember? The school scheduled two extra days for the children to help pick cotton to make up for all that rain we had earlier in the month." With most of the men away in the service, it had fallen upon those at home to harvest the crop so essential to the manufacture of uniforms and other necessary items, and although the younger children thought of it as a picnic, those in the upper grades considered it a competition to see who could pick the most pounds, and farmers paid them accordingly.

"I'm sorry," Dimple said, avoiding Annie's eyes. "But perhaps the two of you might go." And she quickly left the room and went upstairs to change.

Augusta, standing in the hallway, finally knew why she had come.

"Jo, pull into that filling station up there," Lou directed. "I've got to use the rest room."

"Again? We'll be at Claudia's in less than an hour. Can't you wait?"

"If I could wait, would I ask you to stop? And do go easy on the brakes. I have a full bladder," Lou demanded, grabbing for the door handle.

"I told you not to drink all that coffee when we stopped for lunch. This is the second time . . ." But Jo found she was talking to herself as her sister, pocketbook on her arm, was already making her way to her destination.

"Are you sure you know where we're going?" Lou asked when she returned a few minutes later. "Seems we should've gotten there by now."

"You're the one who's supposed to be reading the map. Besides, Claudia gave very clear directions."

"I just don't want to be on the road after dark."

"The speed limit's thirty-five, Louise. Do you want us to get stopped by the police? Quit worrying!"

And although Louise Willingham would never admit it, she *was* worried. She worried that without Miss Dimple's keen observations, she and her sister might not be able to carry out their mission as expected. She worried that the synthetic rubber tires on the old Chevrolet might blow out before they got there and back. And she worried that Claudia, whom she'd never met, might not have indoor plumbing. Lou remembered the days of going to the outhouse in the middle of the night, but she didn't remember them fondly.

Fortunately, it was not quite dark when they turned into Claudia's graveled driveway on the outskirts of the little town, and Lou was relieved in more ways than one when she learned that although their hostess didn't have a telephone, she did have an indoor bathroom.

Claudia's husband had died several years before and their grown daughter, Esther, lived with her mother and clerked at a dry goods store in town.

"I suppose working where you do, you must get to know just about everyone in town," Jo began over supper of a wonderful pumpkin soup, fried apples, and tiny sausages wrapped in pastry.

Esther laughed. "It didn't take long." She passed

along the platter of sausages. "Mama tells me you're here to get some information on poor Dora Westbrook. Terrible thing that happened to her," she said, shaking her head. "Always seemed unhappy to me. Makes you wonder what kind of life she had."

"Now, Esther," her mother admonished. "You shouldn't speak ill of the dead."

And Jo, tired after the rigors of the long drive, brightened considerably and hoped Esther would continue to speak ill, and then some.

"I'm not speaking ill of her, Mama, and besides, what difference does it make? The woman's dead. She doesn't know anything."

"I heard her husband took it kind of hard," said Lou, who had heard no such thing. "He must be grief-stricken."

"We really don't know the family," Claudia said with a warning look at her daughter, "but I'm sure he must be heartbroken over all this. Now, I hope you'll save room for apple brown Betty," she added after a pause. "I used honey for the sweetening. Our apple trees outdid themselves this year and we're doing our best to use them up. I hope you'll take some with you when you leave."

"Or she's likely to block the road. Our friends lock their doors when they see us coming," Esther said. "Mama used apples in the pumpkin soup, too."

"Well, whatever she used, it was delicious," Lou said, and meant it. "I'd love to have the recipe."

And while Lou exchanged recipes after supper in the kitchen with Claudia, Jo spent her time prying information from Esther.

She didn't have to pry very hard.

"I have Dora's address right here," she said, smoothing the folded paper she'd taken from her handbag. "Do you happen to know anybody on Lucia Lane?"

Esther's eyes narrowed. "Like who?"

Jo lowered her voice. "Well, anybody, I suppose. We might start with the Westbrooks' neighbors."

And so they did.

"When you say your prayers," Jo reminded her sister when they turned in that night, "remember to give thanks that we decided to bring those jars of Odessa's chowchow as hostess gifts instead of apple butter."

Slipping a warm flannel gown over her head, she turned out the light. "I think we'll have more than enough people on our list to take up most of our morning," she said. "That just leaves that fellow in the police department for afternoon."

Lou only yawned and stretched out on crisp sun-dried sheets and a pillow that smelled of lavender. Tomorrow would take care of itself.

"You're from *where?* Elderberry?" The middle-aged woman stood in the doorway with one hand

105

firmly on the knob. Frowning, she shoved a graying strand of hair from her forehead and took a step backward. "Isn't that where Dora Westbrook was killed?"

Jo nodded, her expression sorrowful—or what she hoped was sorrowful. "And everyone is devastated! Why, for such a thing to happen in our little town was . . . well, I can't even begin to tell you how shocking that was."

"The poor woman died *right there in our church,* you see," Lou added, "and they're saying it wasn't an accident. Well, it has all of us upset, and we're determined to learn the truth."

"None of us will be able to rest easy in Elderberry," Jo said, "until we find out who did this horrible thing.

"Oh, here we are acting like we don't have any manners at all," she exclaimed, clasping a hand to her chest. "I'm Josephine Carr, and this is my sister, Louise Willingham. We were hoping to speak with some of poor Dora's neighbors in order to learn a little more about her."

"Well . . . I've just finished putting up green tomato pickles, so I'm afraid the whole house reeks of vinegar, but I guess you can come in. We can sit right here in the living room. I'm Priscilla Barnslow."

Priscilla Barnslow wore a stained white apron over her blue plaid housedress, and, obviously noticing the stains, pulled off the apron and tossed it aside as they followed her into the first room off the hall.

"We won't take up much of your time," Jo said, after they were seated—she and Lou on a chintz-covered sofa, and Priscilla on a small parlor chair upholstered in what looked like rose brocade. "We just want to get an idea about her family life, her friends, or at least someone who might tell us why she left so suddenly."

Priscilla looked down at her hands, chapped and rough, probably from housework, as most women's were. "I really didn't know Dora all that well, although we've lived next door for almost ten years now. It did surprise me, though, that she left the way she did."

"What about her husband, Leonard?" Jo asked. "Was everything all right there?"

Priscilla didn't answer right away. "As far as I know," she said, sighing. "He spends a lot of time out at his farm. Raises beef cattle, you know, and Dora volunteered some . . . as most of us do. Things have to get done, and it's up to us to do it, isn't it?"

The sisters agreed that it was, and Lou smiled, thinking the smell of cloves and allspice coming from the kitchen wasn't unpleasant at all. "So I don't suppose she mentioned anything about leaving?" she asked.

"I usually saw her when we were hanging out clothes together, or we sometimes volunteered at the Red Cross—you know, rolling bandages, things like that. She never said anything about that to me, but of course she wouldn't. If Dora told anybody, it was probably one of her friends from church."

Glenese Pitts, Priscilla told them. They might check with her. She and Dora had chaired a circle together at the Methodist church, and she'd seen Glenese visiting next door from time to time.

Jo hesitated as they rose to leave. "About Leonard Westbrook," she began. "From what you've observed, do you think he might've had anything to do with what happened to his wife?"

Priscilla Barnslow drew in her breath. "Oh my. I really can't answer that."

"I'm sorry," Jo said. "I shouldn't have—"

"He did seem upset about her leaving—almost desperate to find her and bring her home," Priscilla added, following them to the door. "But it wasn't the sad kind of worry, the heavy kind that drags you down, shuts out all the light. . . ." She lowered her voice. "I didn't see that at all."

Chapter Eleven

Virginia Balliew was not one of those people who dreaded Mondays. Virginia loved just about everything to do with her job in what everybody called "the cabin," and she always looked forward to beginning a new week. She loved the warm, mellow smell of the place; the scent of new books, as well as the favorite old ones, read and loved over the years until the bindings were broken and ragged. And she especially loved the people she served there, knew what they liked to read and found pleasure in introducing them to something new and exciting.

Next Saturday, she would be assisting the Woman's Club with a Halloween costume party and story hour for Elderberry's children, and her mind was on the decorations when she parked her car that morning in her usual spot behind the cabin. A large jack-o-lantern for the mantel, she thought, and of course black and orange streamers crisscrossing from the rafters. As president of the Woman's Club, bossy Emmaline Brumlow would want to run things her way, but Virginia had learned that as long as she allowed Emmaline to *think* she was in charge, she could pretty much do whatever she pleased.

A heavy frost had covered the ground when she collected her milk from the doorstep that morning, and there was still a nip in the air. Although the cabin had another source of heat, a wood fire would be welcome this morning, Virginia thought, and was glad she'd remembered to have firewood delivered. Digging in her purse for the key, she shivered as she hurried to unlock the front door.

Now who had broken those branches from the nandina bush under that small side window?

Virginia stopped and inspected the crushed twigs and foliage, the bright berries scattered on the ground. What a thoughtless thing to do! She was planning to use those berries over the fireplace with fresh greenery during the Christmas season.

And then Virginia saw something that made her turn around and hurry back to her car. The glass in the window was broken!

"Now, Miss V., I want you to promise you'll stay in the car until I see if there's anybody inside," Sergeant Nelson instructed her after following Virginia back to the cabin. "You did the smart thing by not going in, and coming for me, and I'm almost sure whoever broke in is long gone by now, but we don't want to take any chances."

"But, Warren, I have to see what they've done! And Cattus is in there! What if they've done something to our cat?" Virginia disliked women who cried at the drop of a hat, but it was taking every bit of her willpower to hold back the tears. She could feel the sneaky little things stinging her nose, just waiting for a chance to explode. She sniffed. "I thought you all were keeping an eye on this place after what's been going on here," she said, but he was already making his way to the front door.

It took even more willpower to remain behind while Warren entered the building, and Virginia hurried to meet him as soon as he emerged.

"Did you see Cattus? Is he all right?" she asked.

"Well, it's a mess in there, but I didn't see any sign of a cat. Now, don't worry. He's probably hiding somewhere." With a hand on each of her shoulders, Warren blocked her way. "I don't think there's any big damage done, but they've . . . well . . . whoever did this has just thrown books everywhere."

Warren was a large man and strong, and it was a good thing. With one arm, he encircled this bewildered and irate woman, this guardian of the town's precious books, and guided her onto the porch and into a rocking chair.

"Now, I telephoned Chief Tinsley and he's on his way, so let's just sit tight until he gets here, ma'am. Is there anybody you'd like me to call?"

Virginia glared up at him. At least she meant to glare, but with little experience in that area, who was to know? She wanted Dimple, but Dimple was at school, and it would take an act of God to force her to leave. "I guess we could call Phoebe," she said at last. Phoebe had a level head and a kind heart, and Virginia needed both.

Virginia held back the tears until he went inside to phone, and Bobby Tinsley found her there on the porch, scrambling in her purse for a handkerchief, when he arrived a few minutes later. Fortunately, his wife had provided him with one freshly laundered and folded into a neat square, which he passed along to Virginia.

She accepted it gratefully but not silently. "There's no telling what's happened to poor Cattus! You were supposed to be watching out for us here," she reminded him. "What happened?"

Pausing beside her, he sighed, shaking his head. "Well, I suppose you could say being a little short on manpower happened, Miss V. We just couldn't keep an eye on the place all the time, and I reckon whoever broke in here last night was aware of that." And frankly, he'd thought the threat had been a bit exaggerated, but he sure as hell wasn't going to admit that.

When she was finally allowed inside, Virginia began to call the cat, and after searching every room, finally found him under her desk.

"Here, Cattus!" she called, "Come on, kitty. It's all right now." But even pleading on her hands and knees couldn't budge the cat from his hiding place.

Sighing, Virginia got to her feet. "Poor kitty! He's scared to death." She could only stand and look about. Although nothing was broken that she could see, it looked as if a wild animal had been on the rampage, with books tossed in every direction. While Warren dusted for fingerprints, Chief Tinsley checked the back door and windows in the two small adjoining rooms, and Virginia began to walk slowly about to take account of the damage.

She wiped her eyes, blew her nose, and tucked

the handkerchief away to launder. She was through with crying. But she wasn't through asking questions. "Why?" she asked. "Why would anyone do this?"

"It appears they were searching for something," the chief said. "Do you have any idea what it was?"

Virginia tried to turn her back on the disaster around her, but that proved impossible, so she stood and stared into the empty fireplace, the only thing that hadn't been disturbed. "I think it must have something to do with what happened to Dora Westbrook," she said finally.

Bobby Tinsley stood by the piano and looked about the room. It was littered with books: books open facedown; trails of books like stepping-stones; books piled in haphazard stacks. It was difficult to walk without trampling on them. He wanted to turn away, but there was nowhere else to look. "The day Dora Westbrook showed up here," he said, "you say she spent a good bit of time on the porch. Did she ever come inside?"

"We tried to get her to come in—Dimple and I— but she insisted on staying out there on the porch . . . until—wait a minute! Just before we left to take her to Phoebe's, she asked to use the bathroom."

"Was she gone very long?"

Virginia reached down and picked up one of the books at her feet, a copy of Walt Whitman's

Leaves of Grass. She stroked it, held it for a few seconds, then laid it carefully on top of an empty bookcase nearby. "I don't think so," she said. "Honestly, I can't remember."

"Try to remember this," he insisted. "Did you follow her inside at that time?"

Virginia shook her head. "No. I'm sure I didn't. Dimple and I waited on the porch until she returned, and then I went back inside to get my purse. I locked the door behind us and we drove to Phoebe's in my car."

"Well, it looks like she might have hidden *something* in here, and somebody wants it—wants it badly enough to kill for."

Virginia felt slightly nauseated and suddenly weak in the knees, but she didn't have time to sit. There was too much to be done. "Let's hope they found it," she said, and began gathering books in her arms.

"Now, listen to me, Miss V." Bobby gently took the books from her and set them aside. "There will be plenty of time to take care of all this. What you need right now is rest. If you don't feel up to driving, Warren or I will be glad to take you home."

"That's all right, Chief; I can do that." Phoebe Chadwick stood in the doorway, and it was obvious she was making an effort to appear calm. "It looks to me like you could use a good strong cup of tea," she told Virginia, enclosing her friend in a hug.

"Could you make that something even stronger?" Virginia said, and Phoebe saw she was smiling. "I'm all right, really, except for feeling like I've just been dangled by my feet from the Oconee Bridge." And again she stooped and began collecting books from the floor. "I need to have something to do, and this should keep me busy for a good while, don't you think?"

Phoebe looked at Bobby Tinsley and shook her head. Both knew it would be no use to argue further. "Well," she said, "I'm here to help, and I didn't come alone. And Augusta left a big pot of soup for the teachers' lunch, so we don't have to hurry home."

For the first time, Virginia noticed the woman standing by the door. The rich color of her voluminous cape made her think of the moss along the banks of the sun-dappled creek where she'd played as a child. A penny-colored tam covered her ears but not her hair, and Virginia found herself staring. She had seen maple leaves that color in the fall, but she had never seen hair like that. It shone with the radiance of firelight, and when the woman smiled, Virginia knew that somehow she would manage to get through this day.

"You must be Augusta," she said, crossing the room to greet her. "I'm glad to finally meet you, but wish it could be in better circumstances.

"I can't get my cat to come out from under the desk," she said. "He must be terrified, and I don't know what to do." *Now, what in the world made her say that to this woman she'd never even met before?*

Augusta didn't hesitate, but knelt and extended a hand under the desk. "It's all right now. You can come out," she said, speaking softly. "That's a good kitty, such a good kitty." And Virginia watched in awe as Cattus not only crept out from under the desk but allowed Augusta to scoop him up into her waiting arms, and she was so relieved to see he was unharmed, she even forgot to be jealous.

Setting Cattus on his feet, Augusta shivered and drew her cape closer about her. "Well, this is a mess, isn't it? But we'll soon take care of that. The first thing, I think, is to get some warmth in here." And while the others looked on in amazement, she soon had a bright blaze glowing in the fireplace, which had been dark only minutes before. "There! That's better!" Augusta rubbed her hands together. "Now we can get to work."

Well, hadn't Dimple said she was bossy? "How did you do that?" Virginia asked, moving closer to see if the fire was indeed real.

"Do what?" Augusta tossed her cape and tam on a chair and looked about. "Is there a cart we might use? Or a basket will do."

"How did you start that fire so quickly?" Virginia held her hands to the blaze. It was hot all right.

Augusta seemed perplexed. "The fire was laid, and I found matches on the mantel."

But the grate had been dark and empty . . . hadn't it? And she never kept matches out, for fear of mice. Virginia took a deep breath. Of course shock affects people strangely, and the room did feel warmer already, so what did it matter? Still . . .

"We'll be leaving now, but we'll be in touch," Chief Tinsley said. "Be sure you keep the doors locked, and we'll send someone to board up that window until you can get the glass replaced."

Virginia thanked them and locked the door behind them. Had the two men exchanged glances at Augusta's apparent expertise at fire building, or was she imagining things?

"This should help. I found it in the back," Phoebe said, pushing a small cart in front of her. "We can stack the books on this and it will make it a lot easier to put them back on the shelves."

"Exactly." Augusta crossed with an armful of books. "We'll have this place boat-shape in no time."

Phoebe, in the midst of picking up books from the floor, looked at her and laughed. "Oh, Augusta, only you could keep your sense of humor in a situation like this. *Boat-shape!* I suppose that's appropriate in this case. This cabin's not big enough to be a *ship*."

Augusta smiled but didn't reply and continued

to pile books onto the small cart until the stacks teetered unsteadily.

"Just a minute, please." Virginia stationed herself between the loaded cart and the shelves behind it. "All the fiction must be arranged in alphabetical order. Children's books belong in those two back rooms, and the nonfiction—well, there's a system for that."

"You mean Mr. Dewey's system?" Augusta examined the spine of a book.

Virginia brightened. "Why, yes. Are you familiar with that?"

"It's been a while," Augusta said, "but I believe I can remember. Why don't I put a few of those back and you can see if I'm doing it right."

Phoebe volunteered to begin sorting books in the children's sections, and in a little while, satisfied that Augusta knew what she was doing, Virginia went to check on her other helper. She was pleased to find Phoebe had worked her way through most of the *D*'s, and pulling up another stool, sat down to lend a hand.

"Phoebe," she said, keeping her voice low, "were you in the room when Augusta built that fire?"

Phoebe frowned. "No, I don't suppose I was. Must've been back here looking for the cart, but I sure am glad she did. Why?"

"It was so quick, almost instantaneous, and I honestly don't remember seeing the fire laid there before."

"Well, it must've been. Maybe Bobby or Warren built it there before they left."

"I think I would've noticed that." Virginia added a few more books to the shelf and shrugged. "Or maybe not. Don't they say your memory is the first to go?"

"Then we're all in the same boat," Phoebe told her, laughing.

Virginia shook her head and joined her. She had a nice warm fire and two good helpers. With luck, they should get at least a running start by noon.

It was almost one o'clock when Virginia glanced at her watch an hour or so later. She stood and stretched. "I'm ready for something to eat," she called. "How about hot dogs and malteds from Lewellyn's? My treat."

Phoebe groaned as she stood and said that sounded fine to her, and from the other room, Augusta replied she thought it a good idea, as well.

"I can't tell you how much I appreciate your pitching in to help me like this," Virginia said as the three took time about washing their hands. "It's backbreaking work, as you'll find out when you get out of bed tomorrow, and I know you both have other things to do this afternoon, so please don't worry about staying longer. With such a good start, I should be able to put things straight before you know it."

Phoebe protested, as Virginia knew she would,

but Augusta was strangely quiet, and Virginia didn't blame her. Why, my goodness, the woman still had to plan and cook supper for everyone at Phoebe's.

But when she stepped into the large front room, Virginia knew why Augusta had no need to volunteer further. Every book had been put back exactly in its proper place.

Chapter Twelve

"I thought it wasn't supposed to get cold in south Georgia," Jo said, pulling a warm knitted hat over her ears. "So, where should we go next?"

"I guess we should get in touch with Dora's circle friend, Glenese Pitts." Lou searched her purse for a small scrap of paper torn from the end of an envelope. "Priscilla wrote down her address," she said, finding it. "It's only a couple of blocks from here. Priscilla said she was one of the lucky ones, as her husband's a field artillery instructor stationed at Camp Gordon and not likely to be shipped overseas." She shaded her eyes against the sun. "We need to turn right on Sanders Street, just up ahead."

"Maybe we should have telephoned first," Jo said, turning up the collar of her coat. It seemed colder in the car than out and the sun had suddenly disappeared.

"What if she doesn't want to see us? I think we should take our chances. Dora didn't seem to be close to her neighbor. I'm hoping we'll have better luck with Glenese."

Glenese Pitts lived in a small white cottage shaded by a huge live oak in the front yard. Yellow and bronze chrysanthemums surrounded a small birdbath and more bloomed in a large pot by the front door.

The woman who answered the door was blond, thirtyish, and pregnant. A wailing toddler pulled at her skirt and a little boy about four appeared behind her, clutching part of a sandwich that at one time might have been peanut butter and jelly.

"I'm afraid we've come at a bad time," Jo said, introducing the two of them. Speaking above the toddler's cries, she explained as briefly as possible why they were there. "Priscilla Barnslow suggested we speak with you. We were told you were a friend of Dora Westbrook's, and we're trying to find out more about her background. . . ."

Frowning, Glenese scooped up her toddler and stepped back. "I'm sorry, but as you can see, it's past nap time here already."

Lou gave her a smile that had eased many a nervous patient when she'd helped her husband in his early practice of dentistry. "We understand. Perhaps we can talk at a more convenient time. You see, this terrible thing happened in our own town, and it's been a shock to all of us. Dora was running from someone. She was afraid for her life. We want to know why. Won't you help us, please?"

"Donald, why don't you be a good brother and take your little sister out to the kitchen. You can give her one of your animal crackers," Glenese said as she set the little girl on her feet.

Donald grabbed his sister's chubby hand, and yelled, growling, "Lion! Tiger! Come on, Betty!" And Betty squealed and followed him happily.

Glenese Pitts shoved a stray lock of hair from her face and sighed. "My mother will be here in a little while to stay with the children while I go to the grocery store. Why don't you meet me at Lulu's in about an hour? I'll be ready to take a break by then."

The sisters nodded agreeably. "Lulu's?" both asked at once.

Glenese smiled. "It's a little place downtown. You can't miss it. You can get a cup of coffee there, or a Coca-Cola or something, and they have good apple pie."

"What if she doesn't show up?" Jo asked when they were seated in an empty booth at Lulu's exactly an hour later. The only other customer was a small older woman wearing a hat decorated with bright red and blue flowers of no known origin. She smiled at them from a corner table.

It was almost one o'clock and both were hungry,

so they ordered apple pie à la mode and coffee, and at the risk of being rude, didn't wait to begin eating. Glenese was right, they found it delicious.

It was almost a half hour later when Glenese breezed in, slid into the booth next to Jo, and deposited a sack of groceries on the seat beside her. "I don't have a lot of time," she began, "and I'm not sure I can be of much help, but I was fond of Dora, and I'll try to answer any questions I can."

Lou leaned forward. "Do you have any idea why she was so afraid?"

Glenese started to answer but was interrupted by the waitress. "Just bring me a Coca-Cola, Myra," she said. Then: "Oh, what the heck! That pie looks too good to pass up. And give me scoop of ice cream, too.

"Well . . . I know Dora was unhappy," Glenese began when the waitress left. "I don't think she and Leonard had a . . ." She paused, as if searching for the right word. "I suppose you'd say a *comfortable* relationship. She told me once she'd like to leave, but what would she live on? She didn't have the money to do it."

"Do you think she was afraid of her husband?" Jo asked.

Glenese shook her head. "No. I hate to say it, but I think the marriage had just run its course. He spent most of his time on the farm. Why, he didn't even realize she was missing until she been gone at least twenty-four hours. And then Len's mother lived with them, you know. Sometimes that can be an advantage, but not in this case, I'm afraid.

"They tell me Dora's body was found in a church in Elderberry," Glenese said after the waitress brought her order. "And from what I've heard, the authorities seem to think it wasn't an accident. It just doesn't make any sense!"

The two told Glenese how Dora had turned up at the library in Elderberry and disappeared later that same day from Phoebe's. "Our friends had found a place for her to stay for the night," Jo said. "If only she had let them help her, she might still be alive."

"They had arranged for her to stay in a tourist home run by a local couple, but Dora must've overheard them say the place was owned by a policeman and his wife," Lou said. She shook her head. "For some reason, it seems she was afraid of the police. Do you know why?"

Glenese frowned. "The only thing I can think of is that she didn't want to be found. Didn't want to come back here."

"I don't understand why Leonard's mother didn't notice she was gone," Lou said. "Doesn't that seem odd to you?"

But Glenese shook her head. "Not really. They kept to their own schedules, and I think Dora stayed out of her way as much as possible." She smiled. "Lucille belongs to some kind of knitting society. I think they've knit enough socks to take care of the army, the navy, and the marines!"

"Do you know if she had any enemies?" Jo asked. "From what I've heard, she didn't seem the type."

Glenese finished her pie before answering. "You're right. I can't imagine Dora having a serious conflict with anybody."

"You said she didn't have the money to leave," Lou reminded her. "So, how do you think she managed to get as far as she did?"

"She must've had help from somewhere," Glenese said. She sipped the last of her drink and stood to gather her groceries. "Her parents both died fairly young, I understand, and she and her sister were raised by their grandmother. From what Dora said, it seemed the two were close, and then the grandmother died a few years ago.

"She always seemed lonely to me. I think she must've been headed to her sister's in Tennessee."

"But her sister wasn't expecting her until around Christmas, and she'd bought a bus ticket to Elderberry," Lou said. "I guess it was as far as she could get on the money she had."

"Or," Glenese suggested, "she was counting on somebody in Elderberry to help her." She sighed. "And that's when things went wrong."

Glenese Pitts tugged her coat around her bulging stomach and picked up her check to pay, but Lou intercepted her. "No. This is on us, Glenese.

125

And thank you for taking the time to talk with us."

Glenese nodded. "You will let me know if you find out what happened, won't you?"

Jo stood to say good-bye. "We'll let you know *when* we find out what happened."

"Well, if you aren't the confident one, Dick Tracy," Lou said, referring to the detective comic strip character, as the two walked to their car. "What makes you so sure we *will* find out what happened?"

"And how do you know we won't?" The car had warmed in the sun, and Jo tossed her hat in the backseat and climbed in. "Lou, do you think Dora was expecting help from someone in Elderberry?"

Her sister frowned. "What do you mean?"

"Remember? Glenese said she might've planned on getting help from someone in Elderberry but that things apparently went wrong."

"Well, that's a comforting thought." Lou turned up the collar of her coat. "I wonder who it might've been."

Jo shrugged. "Unless you have other suggestions," she said, "our next step, I guess, is to talk with the local police."

"Reece Cagle," Lou said. "Bobby Tinsley was to let him know to expect us, and if he can't tell us much, maybe we can find some people around here who don't mind a bit of gossip. I noticed a little bandstand on the corner back there where some of the older fellows seem to congregate."

"But first," Jo reminded her, "you'd better have remembered to bring along your gas ration book, or we'll never get back home!"

The Fieldcroft police station was a tiny red brick building just down the street from Edna's Groceries: *If It's Not Rationed, We've Got It!* At the reception desk, a woman with dandelion hair and wearing a tight pink sweater pointed them to the boxlike office behind her, and once inside, Lou was sorry she'd eaten the pie. There was barely room for the two of them plus Reece, and he couldn't have weighed more than 130 pounds.

An ashtray of cigarette butts filled to overflowing sat on his desk, along with a half-empty bottle of Orange Crush soda and a MoonPie, still in its wrapper. Reece, who looked to be a little shy of fifty, stood and offered them both a chair and a soft drink, to which they accepted the former and declined the latter. He had a receding hairline, a warm smile, and a soft pinkish complexion and looked nothing like what Lou expected. She wondered how in the world a man as agreeable-looking as Reece Cagle could manage hardened criminals. But then she doubted if there was an abundance of criminals in Fieldcroft, and realized she hadn't noticed a jail.

"I can't tell you a whole lot about the circumstances surrounding Dora Westbrook," the policeman began after introductions were made. "Her husband doesn't seem to have any idea why she took off the way she did, or why she ended up in your town." He took a cigarette from a pack of Lucky Strikes in his pocket and then thought better of it and put it back. Both sisters breathed a sigh of relief. "Had everybody out looking for her as soon as he realized she was gone. Seemed real anxious to find her."

"I suppose you have proof Leonard Westbrook wasn't in Elderberry at the time of his wife's death," Jo said.

"If he was, ma'am, you can bet your boots we'd be holding him for questioning." Reece spoke with a smile in his voice but not in his eyes. "Len Westbrook can account for his whereabouts every minute since his wife went missing."

Jo thought that seemed awfully convenient, but she refrained from saying so.

"We don't know what goes on in people's lives," Reece continued, rearing back in his chair. "As far as I know, the two seemed to get along okay, but something must've happened to set her off like that. Her husband thinks she was headed to her sister's in Tennessee. Now, why she ended up in Elderberry is anybody's guess."

"I suppose she ran out of money," Jo suggested.

He laced his hands together and considered that. "Well . . . she had money in her purse when they found it—not a lot, mind you, but probably enough to get to her sister's. Looks to me like Dora had a reason for stopping in your town."

"Do you have any idea why?" Lou asked. She didn't like the sound of that. "Have you been able to find any record of letters or phone calls—anything like that—to somebody in Elderberry?"

Reece shook his head. "Nothing's turned up yet."

"You will let us know if it does, won't you?" Lou asked, rising to leave. "Or anything else that might help. This is affecting innocent people through no fault of their own, and we want to get to the bottom of it." She wished Dora Westbrook had had the sense to stay on the dad-blasted bus all the way to the state line and then some.

"Of course I'll stay in touch, and I'd like it if you'd do the same," Reece said, standing to see them out.

Jo stopped and turned at the door. "We noticed a group of men sitting on a bandstand down the street. Do you think they might be able to tell us something?"

"That bunch of buggers? Why, I wouldn't believe a word they told me. Heck! If they don't have an answer, they'll make one up." He grinned. "Naw! If you're looking for somebody to speak out of school, you'll do well to go next door."

Lou frowned. "Next door?"

He nodded. "Yeah. Edna Watson of Edna's Groceries. Our Edna's got a lot more going on in there besides selling something to eat."

Chapter Thirteen

"Dimple, I tell you, you'd have to have seen it to believe it," Phoebe said to her friend that afternoon as the two set the dining room table for supper. "She had every last book back where it belonged, and even the cat was sitting in the window looking smug and licking its paws like nothing had happened at all!"

From behind the kitchen door they could hear Augusta humming something that might or might not have been "When the Saints Go Marching In," and Dimple couldn't suppress a laugh.

"Laugh if you want to," Phoebe whispered. "You know as well as I do that some of the things Augusta does aren't . . . well . . . *natural.*"

The hearty aroma of ham and bean soup coming from the kitchen smelled natural enough to Dimple, but she understood Phoebe's concerns. Augusta *was* different, but different in a good way, if one could overlook the bossiness.

"I suppose she's had some experience as a librarian, and she does seem exceptionally organized," Dimple said.

Phoebe nodded. "She did say she was familiar with that decimal system Virginia uses." She sighed. "Poor Virginia! I've never seen her so unsettled. And I'll have to admit, I didn't know if my two legs would hold me up when I walked in and saw our cabin like that."

Dimple frowned. "Did you hear any more from the police?"

"Not since we left there. Other than the broken window, which, I assume, is the way they got in, they didn't do any physical damage to the building," Phoebe said, "but it certainly wasn't good for the books, pitching them around like that."

Dimple patted the last folded napkin in place. "Well, whoever it was certainly seemed to be looking for something and didn't care how they went about it." She paused. "I wonder . . . is it possible it might still be there?

"Did you notice anything—anything at all—that might have been missing when you were putting things right?" Dimple asked as Augusta filled a blue crockery tureen from the pot on the stove.

Cheeks flushed from the steam, Augusta stopped to fan herself with a dish towel. "If we just knew what to look for, but I only saw books —books everywhere—and I can't imagine why any of them would be the object of such a frantic search—unless there was something tucked within the pages."

"That might be why they were treated so roughly," Phoebe said. "If somebody was looking for something they would've probably flipped through the pages and then tossed the book aside."

"Or something might've been hidden behind the books themselves," Dimple added. She smiled. "I remember how our mama would hide peppermints behind the cookbooks on her kitchen shelf from my young brother, Henry." She smiled. "He would've eaten them, every one! And chocolate drops—oh, how he did love chocolate drops!"

"And how is Henry?" Phoebe asked. "Have you heard from him recently?"

"Not since we spoke, but he has promised to call more often, or at least drop a note now and again," Dimple said. "Henry's all wrapped up in this project at the Bell Bomber Plant and it doesn't leave much room for anything else right now."

Augusta spoke softly. "I imagine your brother's work is especially stressful now with the responsibilities he must be shouldering."

Dimple nodded. "He can't discuss it, of course, and I don't believe I'd want to hear about it even if he could."

"Maybe Charlie has heard something from her mother down in . . ." Phoebe frowned. "What's that place?"

"Fieldcroft," Dimple told her, "but I doubt if they've had time to learn much yet."

Charlie hadn't heard a word, Annie told them at supper, but then, she hadn't expected a call. Neither her mother nor her aunt would telephone long-distance unless it was an emergency, as the cost was what Jo Carr referred to as "outlandish."

"Well, I hope they'll be careful down there," Lily said. "Whatever happened at the library last night must've had something to do with that Dora woman."

"I suppose she was in there long enough to have hidden something," Dimple said as she spread margarine on a muffin. She made an effort not to look at the product with distaste as she knew they should all be grateful to have it, but, oh, how she missed the real thing! The margarine was purchased in a round white glob with a red button of coloring in the middle that had to be massaged into the contents to color it yellow. She'd heard her first graders discuss how they competed with siblings for that honor, but Dimple Kilpatrick would be a happy woman when butter came in the color God made it.

"Augusta, this soup is delicious," Velma said. "I wonder if I might have half a bowl more?"

Augusta smiled and dished up a ladleful from the tureen. "Why, have all you want. There's plenty.

"I wonder," she continued, "if the next step— after Jo and her sister return, of course—is to talk with Dora's sister in Tennessee."

Velma put down her spoon. "I think that's an excellent idea, Augusta. I've been thinking, we have a long weekend coming up, and I've heard that's a lovely area. I've been frugal with my gasoline coupons, so I should have enough to get us there and back. This thing with Dora has worried me more than I'd like to admit. I mean, the woman was *here*—right here in this house—and I don't know about the rest of you, but I'd like to get to the bottom of it."

Annie brightened. "You can count me in," she said, passing her empty bowl to Augusta.

"It sounds exciting," Phoebe said, "but I suppose I'd better stay here. Somebody has to hold down the fort."

Augusta frowned. "The fort? Oh my! Are we under attack?"

Silence descended on those around the table until someone finally laughed. "Well, after all that's been going on here, it would seem so," Miss Dimple said.

"I suppose I'd better stay, too," Lily said. "Report cards are due soon and I've grades to tally."

"We've still room for one more," Velma said, looking pointedly at Dimple.

"Oh, I think you'll be just fine without me." Dimple rose hastily and began removing plates from the table. "You can tell me all about it when you get back."

"But you always know just the right thing to *say!*" Annie protested. "Please come, Miss Dimple. We need you." But Dimple Kilpatrick had already disappeared into the kitchen, leaving the door swinging shut silently behind her. Annie started to follow but was delayed when Phoebe put a gentle hand on her arm, and they watched as Augusta rose and slipped quietly into the kitchen.

"Memories can be fearsome things to face," Augusta said. She put the empty muffin basket on the table and filled a dishpan with hot water. Dimple stood at the window overlooking the dark backyard, where a bare branch of the apple tree brushed the side of the house. She didn't speak.

"I believe it was Emerson who advised, 'Always do what you are afraid to do.' And then our own President Roosevelt is noted for saying, 'the only thing we have to fear is—' "

" 'Fear itself.' *I know very well* what he said!" Dimple turned and began to rearrange fruit in a bowl on the kitchen table, shifting apples and bananas from one side to the other. "I don't see any justification in opening old wounds," she said.

"Unless perhaps they haven't properly healed." Augusta spoke softly.

Dimple crowned her arrangement with a final banana and pulled a chair up to the table. This was all in the past and she did not—absolutely *did not*—want to dredge it to the surface. Augusta stood by the sink and silently met her gaze.

"Why are you here, Augusta?" Dimple asked.

"Why, to help, of course."

"Help where? In the kitchen?" Dimple nodded in the direction of the vacant chair across from her and Augusta slipped into the seat and smiled. "Of course. Wherever I'm needed."

"And I hear you've experience with the Dewey decimal system, as well."

"It's been a while, but it comes back," Augusta said.

"Who sent you? Some kind of agency?"

"I suppose you might call it that."

"You are right. I am not interested in a visit to the Lewisburg area, although I believe you'll find it a lovely and hospitable place, and I hope you'll be able to locate Dora Westbrook's kin and find some answers there."

Augusta smiled but didn't speak.

"I don't know why everyone thinks it's so important for me to go along," Dimple continued, reaching for a small basket of pecans. *Crack!* With a nutcracker, she began to shell them and pick out the meats, dropping them into a cup with a ping.

"Once I found great happiness there," Dimple said, apparently addressing the basket in front of her, "but that's gone now. Only the scar remains."

"Surely memories remain," Augusta reminded her. "Good memories. Happy memories."

Against her will, Dimple Kilpatrick smiled. "Yes," she said.

"And nothing can ever take those away," Augusta said.

Dimple brushed pecan shells into the palm of her hand and tossed them into the trash. "I don't know why you're really here, Augusta, or how you came to know about these things in my past, but I don't believe it matters, does it?"

Augusta only smiled.

"Well?" Phoebe asked Dimple later as they sat alone in the small front parlor. "Did Augusta convince you to go to Tennessee with the others?" And Dimple answered with a nod and a sigh. "I think I just met up with Brer Fox and the Tar Baby," she admitted.

Chapter Fourteen

Edna's Groceries looked to be about a third the size of Harris Cooper's store in Elderberry and was crowded with only a handful of shoppers, none of whom, obviously, had made a list. One woman selected pecans one by one from a bin, tossing back the nuts that didn't suit, and another browsed over the glass counter in the rear of the store, where the butcher waited patiently for her decision.

"Is that little ole hen the best ya got, Al?" she asked, tapping on the glass.

Al wiped his hands on his spattered apron and grinned. "Now, Mrs. Hendricks, if you add a few onions and a stalk of celery to that bird, she'll stew up just fine."

"Well, I reckon it'll have to do." Mrs. Hendricks sighed and put a container in a brown paper bag on the counter. "This here's the grease I've been saving. Lid's not tight, so watch it don't spill."

Lou and Jo saved their cooking grease as well, as did many in Elderberry and elsewhere as it was used in the manufacture of ammunition for the war effort.

The little lady in the flowered hat they had seen in Lulu's earlier examined sweet potatoes, choosing a few before moving on to the turnips. The store smelled of earthy root vegetables and brine from a barrel of pickles, and while Jo browsed about, Lou selected apples from a basket on the counter. They were green and speckled with a yellowish tint and smelled so sweet, she couldn't wait to bite into one.

"Those are Disharoons brought in from north Georgia." The woman behind the counter, whom Lou guessed to be Edna of "talking out of school" fame, put them in a paper bag and rang up the sale. "Won't get these just anywhere," she said.

"They smell wonderful," Lou said. "Don't believe I've ever heard of this kind before."

Edna smiled. "Didn't think I'd seen you around. Where you from?"

"My sister and I are from Elderberry," Lou said. "We're only here for a day or so."

Eyes narrowed, Edna leaned over the counter. "Elderberry? Isn't that the town where poor Dora Westbrook met her maker at the bottom of a steeple?"

"Well . . . I guess you could put it that way."

"So," Edna said, making change for the pecan-buying customer, "do they know who did it yet?"

Lou shook her head and leaned closer. "Did you know her well? Dora, I mean."

Edna looked about. The pecan customer had left, as had Mrs. Hendricks and her fair-to-middlin' chicken. Miss Flowered Hat had moved on to examine the canned goods on the other side of the store.

"Known her since she came here, I reckon," Edna said. "But *well?* I doubt if anybody knew Dora Westbrook well."

Jo, joining her sister, selected a couple of packages of cheese crackers from a glass jar on the counter. "We were hoping to talk with somebody who might have an idea why Dora left the way she did," she said, speaking barely above a whisper.

Edna shrugged. "Looks like it took old Leonard by surprise, and most everybody else, as far as I know. Dora . . . well, she just wasn't the type to go bolting off out of the blue like she did."

"So, what do *you* think made her do it?" Jo put a dime on the crackers. "Was she running from something or someone?"

Edna flipped the dime into the cash drawer and frowned. "Seems more likely she was heading *to* somebody."

"What makes you think that?" Lou asked.

"It was just a feeling, but Dora acted like she might be expecting something to happen—something good." Edna lowered her voice. "Can't put my finger on it, but right before she left, seemed her whole attitude changed. She was like a different person. Maybe she thought she was coming into some money somehow. That Leonard's tight as Dick's hatband, you know, so it couldn't be coming from him."

Edna looked pointedly at Flowered Hat, who, at the moment, seemed to be considering a box of Post Toasties cereal. "Ready for me to ring that up?" she said, and the woman obediently brought her groceries to the counter, paid for them, and left.

Edna watched the departing figure with a quizzical look. "Did you notice that?" she asked.

"Notice what?" Jo asked, as she obviously hadn't.

Edna took a deep breath and sighed. "She smelled like peppermint."

"Hmm . . . maybe she was eating them." Jo had to agree the air in the little store had become peppery fresh. Was there such a thing as peppermint perfume?

"You were saying you thought Dora was on her way to someone," Lou reminded Edna. "Why?"

For a minute, she didn't think Edna would answer, as the woman seemed to be biting her lips to keep from speaking. "I shouldn't be repeating this," she said finally, "but it came from a reliable source, so I suppose there's some truth in it. I understand Dora had received communication from someone in South Carolina."

"What kind of communication?" Jo asked.

"How do you know that?" Lou's words tumbled out.

Edna pushed up her glasses and frowned. "Naturally, he didn't think anything about it until after Dora's death, but then, of course, he remembered the letters."

"Who? What letters?" The sisters spoke in unison.

"Why, Eli, our postman. He has one of those— what do you call it? Photogenic memories, and he remembered Dora receiving a couple of letters from there."

"Where in South Carolina?" Jo persisted.

"I believe it was Columbia." Edna thought for a minute and smiled. "Yes! Columbia."

"Would he remember who sent them or the return address?" Lou asked.

"Of course not! He only noticed the postmark. Why, that would be an outrageous invasion of privacy!"

"Seems to me," Lou said as they returned to the car, "if this Eli had a 'photogenic' memory, he could've at least remembered the return address on those envelopes."

Jo giggled. "Shame on you! Don't you know

that would've been an outrageous invasion of privacy?"

"So, what now? It's getting late and the stores will be closing soon."

"For one thing, we need to let Reece Cagle at the police department know about Dora's letters from South Carolina," Jo said. "Then he can telephone that information to Bobby Tinsley."

Lou nodded. "Jo, I don't know about you, but I feel that little piece of gossip has made this whole trip worthwhile. It looks, though, like we've just about run out of people to question."

"Not quite. There's still Dora's mother-in-law—right next door to Priscilla, remember?"

Lou frowned. "What makes you think she'll talk to us? From all we've heard, she doesn't come across as the warm, cuddly type to me. Besides, we don't even know her name."

"Mrs. Westbrook, I guess, unless she married again, but that shouldn't matter." Jo frowned. "We're not far away, but I'd like to speak with her before Dora's husband gets home. We can stop and see Reece after that."

"Jo, I'm afraid we'll just be wasting our time. That woman isn't going to give us the time of day."

Lou smiled as she pulled out of the parking space. "How could she turn us away when we've gone there to return a personal item Dora left behind?"

"What personal item? I don't remember her leaving anything."

"This personal item." Lou tossed a small paper bag on the seat between them and watched as her sister opened it to draw out a head scarf with a geometric design in patriotic colors.

"Then you'd better remove the price tag," Jo said, examining it closer. "According to this, it came from Murphy's Five and Dime."

"Well, *she* doesn't know that! Here, take off the tag and wad it up a little so it'll look like it's been worn."

Jo laughed. If her sister had gone to all that trouble, she supposed it would be worth a try.

"You came all this way just to return *this?*" Leonard Westbrook's mother stood in the doorway, holding the scarf at arm's length, as if it might contaminate. She wore her dyed black hair in a bun and had a mustache almost long enough to curl. She did not invite them in.

Lou forced a smile. "First of all, we want to tell you personally, Mrs. Westbrook, how very sorry we are about what happened to your daughter-in-law. This tragedy has upset many of us in Elderberry, and . . . well, we're doing our best to try to find out why it happened."

"I'm sure the police have taken a statement from you, but the authorities in Elderberry are still trying to act on every lead, and so, with their permission, we're following up on this," Jo added. "We're hoping you might be able to shed some light on why Dora left so abruptly."

"And why should I answer you? You don't look like Nancy Drew to me."

Was the woman actually smiling?

"I've already answered all the questions I intend to." With one hand on the door, Dora's mother-in-law narrowed the gap between them. "My son's wife was selfish, conniving, and what's more, she was a thief to boot!"

Whoa! "A *thief?* What did she steal?" Jo asked the door as it slammed in her face.

Lou shrugged. "Somehow I get the idea Leonard's mother wasn't exactly fond of Dora."

Chapter Fifteen

Except for Lily, who lingered over a dessert of applesauce cake with whipped cream, everyone at Phoebe's had finished supper when Charlie Carr exploded into the living room with news from the police in Fieldcroft.

"Chief Tinsley just called, and—"

Annie, who had been grading classwork, jumped to her feet, scattering lined Blue Horse notepaper all over the floor. "Oh, my gosh! Has anything happened to your mother? What about Aunt Lou? They haven't had an accident, have they?"

"No, no, they're fine," Charlie said. "Plan to start back home after breakfast tomorrow, but they found out something we didn't know before." She paused to catch her breath while the others crowded closer.

"Seems Dora received a couple of letters from somebody in South Carolina."

"You mean *after she died?*" Lily wiped whipped cream from her lips.

"Of course not, or she wouldn't have been able to read them, being dead and all," Charlie said, and a giggle oozed out in spite of her efforts to control it.

"I'm sorry, Lily," she added after a disapproving look from Miss Dimple. "No, it seems she received the letters a few weeks before she arrived here. They were from somebody in Columbia."

"How did they find this out?" Dimple asked.

"It seems Mama and Aunt Lou learned about it from a woman who has a grocery store there, and *she* heard about it from the postman who delivered Dora's mail. After Dora was killed, he remembered seeing the Columbia postmark."

Charlie collapsed into a chair and glanced at Lily's unfinished dessert. "Don't reckon there's any more of that cake, is there?"

"Of course." Augusta started to rise, but Miss Dimple held up a hand to delay her. "I'll get it, Augusta," she said, but turned and paused on her way to the kitchen. "Perhaps she had relatives there, but from the postman's reaction, it sounds very much as if it was rare for Dora to receive mail."

"Why, they might have even followed her here. . . . Could be the same person who ransacked the library." Phoebe looked fierce.

"Sounds like your mother and your aunt Lou made their trip to Fieldcroft worthwhile," Velma said. "Wonder who else they spoke with there."

"Chief Tinsley didn't say, but he did want to let me know they had gotten in touch with the police there and seemed to feel they'd accomplished what they came for." She laughed. "The chief said he probably should've asked me not to say anything about it, but he had an idea Mama and Aunt Lou were going to tell everybody anyway."

"I wish it didn't cost so much to call long-distance," Annie said. "I can't wait to hear what else they found out down there. Wonder if they talked with Dora's husband or her mother-in-law."

"Well, I'm more concerned with who wrote those letters to Dora from Columbia," Phoebe said, frowning. "So what brought her here to Elderberry? It's beginning to sound like somebody lured that poor woman here in order to take something from her—something valuable."

"But why Elderberry?" Charlie asked. "Why not Fieldcroft or somewhere else?"

"Oh, dear," Lily said, shaking her head. "What do you think we should do?"

Augusta's voice was calm. "The first thing, I suppose, is to get all our chickens in a line."

Annie laughed. "You mean ducks in a—"

"Whatever the fowl, Augusta's right," Miss Dimple said. "We need to decide what to do first in order of importance. I believe we should try to learn where Dora went when she first arrived in Elderberry."

Annie frowned. "You mean before she turned up at the library?"

"I suppose we could ask Clyde Jefferies at the Feed and Seed," Phoebe suggested. "That's where the bus stops here. Maybe Dora asked for directions."

Dimple smiled. "I taught all three of Clyde's boys. I believe the youngest, Richard, is with the navy somewhere in the Pacific. Why don't I give him a call, and we'll go on from there?"

The others could barely hear one end of Miss Dimple's muted telephone conversation in the hallway, but she was smiling when she reentered the room. "Clyde believes Richard is somewhere in the Philippines, but it's been a while since they last heard. He said he has a good feeling about it, though, and expects word any day now."

"I hope and pray he's right," Phoebe said. Her grandson, Harrison, had been a part of the invasion in the Marshall Islands, and like Clyde Jefferies and other families of those fighting overseas, she lived from day to day in fear of the dreaded telegram from the War Department.

Annie nodded. "I count each day as a good one when it ends without bad news," she said, and Charlie agreed. Both wrote faithfully to fiancés facing danger on a daily basis.

Velma leaned forward. "So did Clyde remember seeing Dora?" she asked eagerly.

"He said the only reason he remembered her was because she was so shy," Dimple explained. "Clyde said he thought she might have gotten off at the wrong stop and didn't know what to do, so he asked if she needed help."

"And what did she say?" Charlie asked.

Dimple hesitated before answering in words barely above a whisper. "She asked directions to Cooper's Store," she told them.

The silence seemed to shriek until Augusta asked if Dora had mentioned the store by name. "That afternoon at the library, you said she had a package of cheese crackers," she reminded them. "She must've been hungry, and she had to buy them somewhere. Perhaps she only wanted to find a convenient place to get something to eat."

"Augusta's right," Phoebe said. "It doesn't necessarily have anything to do with Jesse Dean."

But Dimple shook her head. "Clyde was certain she asked for Cooper's by name. It's just down the street, you know, and he remembered seeing her sitting on that bench out front when he went home for dinner at noon."

Velma snorted. "Another passenger on the bus could've told her about Cooper's. Besides, a lot of people use that bench—use it myself, and the awning protects you from too much sun. She was probably waiting there for someone."

Augusta caressed the stones in her necklace as she sat beside Velma, and the colors seemed to wrap them all in serenity: a cooling deep-in-the-forest green, sunset amber, and the smoky amethyst of twilight.

Velma immersed herself in the calmness and settled down to think. "Has anybody thought to ask who waited on Dora at Cooper's that day?" she asked.

Nobody had.

"Then that should be our next step." From the corner of the room, Lily stood and spoke up, spindly arms on her hips, and announced in a take-charge voice that Jesse Dean Greeson didn't know the dead woman, and would never in this world do anything to hurt anyone. "Why, I've seen him go out of his way to avoid stepping on an ant on the sidewalk," she told them. And her look let them know that anyone who disagreed would have her to deal with. But nobody did.

"I'll telephone Harris Cooper," Phoebe volunteered. "Maybe he'll remember. I need to order eggs anyway, and we're getting low on milk."

But that happened to be the day many of the stores were offering harvest specials, Harris told

Phoebe, and there were more shoppers in town than usual. He might've waited on her, he said, but he couldn't be sure. He *could* be sure, he added, that Jesse Dean had had nothing to do with what happened to that woman, and it was beyond him how anybody could believe anything else.

"We know Clyde Jefferies saw Dora on the bench outside the grocery, and sometime later, she showed up at the library," Dimple said. "That's not much to go on."

"And she seemed to be afraid—remember?" Phoebe reminded them. "I suppose she thought whoever she was afraid of wouldn't think to look for her at the library."

Augusta sat silently, watching the embers in the coal grate flicker and crumble into ash. "I believe it happened the other way around," she said at last. "I don't know why Dora asked directions to Cooper's, unless someone suggested it to her, or perhaps she was told to wait there until it was time to meet at the library, but I think the library was meant to be her destination."

Dimple nodded. "That could explain why she didn't want to leave. Virginia and I had trouble persuading her to come with us here to Phoebe's."

"That must've been when she left something behind in the library," Velma said.

"Either she left it there or somebody believes she did," Phoebe added. "I suppose she planned to go back for it the next day."

Annie shook her head. "Poor Dora. It looks like she was killed soon after she went inside the church. Bobby Tinsley said she'd been dead almost twenty-four hours when Bob Robert found her."

"And I imagine she was already dead when Jesse Dean came by to leave those vanilla wafers in the kitchen," Charlie said. "It's obvious that whoever called the store and ordered those cookies was trying to throw suspicion on Jesse Dean. Why, I doubt if he's ever been as far south as Fieldcroft, Georgia."

As far as anyone knew, he probably hadn't, but Dimple Kilpatrick remembered that his father had come from that area. Just now, however, she didn't see the need to share that information.

Chapter Sixteen

"I hope you're satisfied," Lou said as her sister backed out of the Westbrooks' driveway on Lucia Lane. "I told you she wouldn't talk to us—Watch out, Jo! You almost backed over that quince bush."

"So what? Prickly thing! I'll bet that evil witch in there planted it."

On the other side of the street, several soldiers, probably headed back to Camp Gordon, hurried to the bus stop on the corner. On the way to

151

Fieldcroft, Jo had given a lift to a young corporal returning from leave, and to a sergeant who had hitchhiked all the way from his grandfather's funeral in North Carolina. Those in the armed services were seldom left waiting long for a ride.

"What do you suppose she meant by saying that Dora was a thief?" Lou wondered.

"She probably saved up the grocery money to buy her bus ticket," Jo said. "And speaking of tickets, something just occurred to me," she added, turning into the street. "The stub they found in her bag was dated on the day *before* she showed up in Elderberry, so she must have stopped somewhere Friday night and then bought another ticket."

"You're right, Jo. And here I was thinking *I* had all the brains in the family. I guess we'll have to find out where that bus stopped along the route. Dora had to have spent the night in one of those places. Wonder why she kept only the one stub?"

"Maybe she didn't want anyone to know where she'd stopped. I suppose we'd better drop by the police station and find out what Reece Cagle thinks about this, and we should tell him what we learned from Edna at the grocery store, too," Jo said.

Lou frowned. "You mean about the letters from Columbia? Don't you think he already knows?"

Jo shrugged. "We'll soon find out."

But he didn't. "Well, ladies, back again so soon?" Reece smiled and jumped to his feet, and maybe she was imagining things, but Lou thought it obvious the officer didn't expect them to have anything important to share.

"And Edna said the letters were postmarked from Columbia?" he said when they told him what they'd heard. Rearing back in his chair, Reece twiddled a pencil in his fingers, as if that might help to clear things up.

"That's what the postman—what's his name?— Eli told her," Jo explained.

The policeman tossed the pencil aside. "I wonder if Leonard Westbrook might still have those letters around," he said, picking up the phone. "On the other hand, it might be a better idea to find out in person." Abruptly, he returned the receiver to its cradle.

Lou nudged her sister and both stood expectantly. "I don't suppose we—"

"Not a good idea." Reece shook his head, but he smiled when he said it. "You've helped quite a bit and I thank you, but this is police business, and I think you'd best stay in the background."

"But you will let us know what you find out, won't you?" Jo asked. "After all . . ." She was going to say, "Turnabout is fair play," but that might be pushing it. "After all, we're leaving for Elderberry in the morning."

"We did give you our telephone number, didn't we?" Lou asked, and just in case, she scribbled it on a piece of paper.

He touched his hat in a farewell salute. "I'll call. I promise."

"Well . . . if that doesn't beat all!" Jo muttered as they drove away. "We do all the work and he gets all the glory."

"What glory? You've been watching way too many war movies, Jo."

"Maybe so, but do you think he'll call?"

"I guess we'll just have to wait and see." Lou yawned. "Wonder what kind of apple dish our cousin is serving tonight?"

"Oh, do have some more stewed apples," Cousin Claudia urged, "and how about another muffin?"

Lou helped herself to a second muffin—also apple—but politely declined the other. "The apples are delicious, but I've eaten way too much already, Claudia."

Claudia smiled. "I added a second stick of cinnamon this time and a little sliced lemon. Really perks it up, don't you think?"

Lou agreed that it did and nibbled at her muffin. If only Claudia had a telephone! They would have to wait until they drove all the way home to find out if Dora's husband knew about the letters from Columbia.

"So, did you learn anything interesting—about Dora, I mean?" Esther asked as she served a dessert of apple turnovers.

Jo told her about Dora's unaccounted-for stop

154

along the way and the rumored letters from Columbia. "But, of course, we don't know if there's any truth in that or not. We heard this second—no, thirdhand," and she explained about Edna and the postman.

But Esther waved that away with one hand. "Oh, Eli never forgets anything," she assured them.

"There is one person I neglected to mention," Esther added as they cleared away the dishes. "Dora was a big reader. I know that because I used to see her at the library—if you can call it that. There's a little place behind the fix-it shop where you can borrow a book. Woodrow Malone runs it but he's hardly ever there. You just write down your name and what you've borrowed. For the most part, the books are donated—kind of a swap, I guess, but it serves a purpose. There's not much else to do around here, and Dora spent a good bit of time there.

"Anyway, you might ask Woodrow if she said anything to him—if you can find him, that is."

"What do you mean?" Jo asked.

"Woodrow owns the little fix-it shop next door and I guess you could say he keeps his own hours," Esther explained. "He's there if he's working on something, but if he's not, he usually doesn't bother to go in."

Lou frowned. "So, what if somebody has an iron or a toaster or something that needs fixing? How would they get in touch?"

"Oh, they would just call him and he'd meet them there." Esther smiled. "And sometimes he hangs out at Lulu's, usually in that booth by the window."

"Then I guess we'll make a side trip before we leave in the morning," Jo said, and her sister nodded in agreement.

And so the next morning with a basket of Winesaps, three jars of applesauce and two of apple butter, they left the two women behind and turned back toward town.

"Hurry, Jo," Lou urged, looking over her shoulder, "before Claudia comes out with another basket."

"Looks like we're in luck," Jo said a few minutes later as they parked in front of the We Dare to Repair shop, whose motto, printed in smaller letters, was *Not Like New, But It'll Do!*

Lou laughed. "Well, I have to meet this man. Even if he can't help us, he must have a great sense of humor."

But the gnomelike man bent over a radio behind the back counter didn't glance up when they came in, and when he did, he greeted them only with a dour look and a raspy grunt. He had heavy-lidded, lizardlike eyes and chewed on a stub of a cigar.

"We understand you have a library here," Jo began, "and we thought you might—"

"Next door," the man muttered, nodding in the

direction of an adjoining door, then returned his attention to the inside of the small radio. "Just write your name and whatever you want to read in the logbook."

"Oh, we didn't come for that—although I'm sure you have some interesting books in there," Lou told him. "We understand Dora Westbrook was in there a lot and wondered if you ever had a chance to talk with her." That is, if you ever talk with anybody, she thought.

He glared at her over the counter. "Now, what would I talk with her about?"

"Oh, I don't know. The price of eggs in China?" Lou had had enough of the man's rudeness. "The woman was killed, you know. Murdered, and maybe you don't care, but we do, and we're trying to learn what we can about the weeks leading up to her death."

Woodrow Malone put down the radio and took the cigar from his mouth, then leaned on the counter and smiled. At least they thought he smiled. "Dora was a friend, and I don't have so many friends I can afford to lose one. I sure as hell didn't want to lose her.

"People come in here and talk about Dora, and if they don't know the truth, they just make something up—mostly malicious lies, and Dora's not here to defend herself."

Lou smiled. "But you are."

He sighed. "Darn tootin'!"

Jo explained who they were and why they were there. "Did Dora happen to mention why she planned to go to Elderberry?" she asked. But Woodrow shook his head. "I know she wanted to go back to Tennessee to be near her sister. She was born there, you know, and Dora was ready to get away. It was easy enough to figure out why."

The sisters waited for an explanation, but none seemed to be forthcoming. "I suppose it could be difficult having to live with your mother-in-law," Lou suggested, and that, of course, instigated the answer she expected.

Woodrow Malone drew himself up to his full height of close to five feet, give or take an inch or two. "With that one it would be," he declared. "A lot of families have had to make do under one roof with the war and all, and most get along just fine. They know they have to and make the best of it, but . . . well . . . if the devil had a sister, she'd be the spittin' image of Lucille Westbrook. She'd make a preacher lose his religion!"

"We thought she might've been headed to her sister's in Tennessee, but why would she stop in Elderberry?" Lou asked.

Woodrow's answer seemed long in coming. "Look, I believe she meant to meet somebody there. I assume she did."

"Who?" Jo demanded. "Who did she meet?"

"If I knew that, don't you think I'd tell you?"

"We were told she spent a good bit of time here in the library next door and were hoping she might've confided in you," Jo added.

"Dora wasn't one to talk about her problems, but most of us knew what she had to put up with at home. Leonard stayed out at the farm most of the time—probably to avoid his mother—so she couldn't count on him." Woodrow stuck the unlit stub of cigar back into his mouth and picked up the radio again. "I did what I could to help. It wasn't enough, and I reckon I'll have to live with that. One of these days, I hope to find out who did this to her, but right now I don't know any more than you do."

Jo wrote down her phone number and Lou's and passed it over the counter. "If you do hear anything—anything at all—please give us a call, won't you?"

And Woodrow, fiddling with the radio's insides, mumbled that he would.

"Well, that's that," Lou said as she returned to the car. "I don't know about you, but I think Woodrow knows more than he's telling." But her sister, she saw, was still standing on the sidewalk, peering in the library window behind her.

"Come on, Jo. Let's go! There's nothing in there to see."

Reluctantly, Jo turned away. "Well, somebody was there. I'm sure I saw our friend in the flowered hat leaving just as we arrived, and—"

"Well, why shouldn't she? It *is* a library, isn't it?"

Jo followed her to the car, but she didn't look happy. "But after she left, there was somebody in there watching us while we were talking to Woodrow. They were hidden behind the door, but it was open just enough for me to see somebody standing there."

Lou slid into the passenger seat and slammed the door, first glancing into the empty seat behind her. "Were you able to tell anything? Was it a man or a woman?"

"Couldn't see. It was just the barest motion, and the door moved about a fraction of an inch. I wanted to go over there and give it a big jerk, but it might've just been some little old lady curious about what we were doing in there. Didn't want to give her a heart attack or something." Jo shrugged. "Well, whoever it was is gone now, so I don't guess it matters."

"If it was a little old lady, she sure did get out fast." Jo backed out of their parking place and turned toward the small police station. "Let's go pay a visit to our friend Reece before we start for home."

Chapter Seventeen

She *must* talk with Harris Cooper. But when? It had to be when Jesse Dean wasn't around, and Dimple knew he usually made deliveries for the grocer during the morning hours, while she was teaching. Well, that wouldn't do, yet if anyone could give her the information she needed, it would be Harris.

The porcelain clock on the mantel said quarter to eight and Dimple knew the Coopers were early risers, which meant they would probably soon be turning in. Marking her place in the mystery she was reading, she hurried to the telephone and in a hushed voice asked Florence, the operator, to please ring the Coopers' number.

"Phoebe's asked me to see if we can put in an order for some of that good sausage he gets in, so she can pick it up in the morning. . . . No, I don't know who makes it—comes from somewhere in Alabama, I think—and, *hot?* Oh, my goodness, it'll burn the roof off your mouth, but we like it that way," Dimple lied. She was not aware of any special order for sausage, but everyone knew Florence McCrary listened in on private conversations, and she definitely did *not* want her to be privy to this one.

"Angela," she began when the grocer's wife

answered the phone, "I'm sorry to be calling so late, but could I please speak with Harris a minute? . . . No, no, we're all right, thank you. I just need to run something by him. Shouldn't take long." Dimple waited for the dead silence that meant Florence had put down the phone, and was relieved that the operator wasn't interested in obtaining the fictitious sausage from Alabama.

When Harris got on the line, she got right to the point. "Harris, I remember that you lived down the street from Jesse Dean's grandmother when his father disappeared sometime back in the late twenties. Seems like it was not long after his mother died." She paused. "Tell me, did you know the family well?"

If Harris Cooper thought that a strange question, he didn't mention it. "Well," he began, "Eugenia, Jesse Dean's mother, and I went to school together. She was a couple of years older than me but we were friends. She got dealt a rotten hand, Eugenia did. Sanford never was right after the war, and then she died soon after Jesse Dean was born. If she'd have lived, he wouldn't have had to live with his grandmother, crazy old Addie Montgomery. She just about ruined him for life."

"What about Sanford, Jesse Dean's father?" Dimple asked. "Do you know where he lived before he came here?"

For a minute, she thought he wasn't going to answer. "I think it was somewhere way down in south Georgia. Can't think of the name of the place right off hand."

Dimple hesitated. She didn't want to put words in his mouth. Instead, she suggested a few.

"It wasn't Moutrie, was it?"

"No. That doesn't sound right."

"What about Quitman?"

"Nope. That wasn't it."

"Brunswick, then?"

"I'm sure it wasn't Brunswick," Harris said.

"Could it have been Fieldcroft?"

"Fieldcroft . . . Fieldcroft . . ." Harris muttered. "I believe that sounds about right. I think Eugenia met him at a church camp meeting or something. Course that was before he went to war. Got a dose of that mustard gas over there, they say. Never was quite right after that."

"Harris, do you know if Sanford had any close friends, someone who might still remember him?"

"That'd be hard to say. I know he worked for Amos McIntyre at the old Hutchinson cotton gin—the one that burned out on Riverbend Road. Old man Tate Hutchinson owned it, but Amos ran it for him. Gosh, old Amos must be in his eighties now. I see him now and then at that Super Service Station his grandson runs at the north end of town. Guess it gives him something to do."

And now she had something to do, Dimple thought as she thanked Harris for his help. She would follow up with Amos tomorrow.

•••

Just as Harris had suggested, she found Amos McIntyre drinking Coca-Cola and eating boiled peanuts in the back of his grandson's service station. Miss Dimple treated herself to a Hershey bar, a favorite of hers, not always available since the war, and introduced herself to the older man.

"Of course I know who you are," he said, starting to rise from his chair. "I reckon you've taught every one of our grandchildren."

"Oh, please keep your seat," Dimple told him, and was relieved when he did. "I've come to pick your brain a little, if you'll let me."

He chuckled. "You're welcome to it if you can find it."

"Sanford Greeson worked for you at the gin a while, didn't he?"

"Sanford Greeson!" Amos grabbed another handful of peanuts and leaned forward in his chair. "You are going back a ways. Yeah, worked for us for several years, until he took a notion to light out. Never did know what happened to him, did they?"

Miss Dimple shook her head. "Not that I know of. I'm trying to find out about his background. I understand he came from a little town in south Georgia. Do you remember if he ever mentioned having family there?"

Amos tossed soggy peanut shells on the floor.

164

"Oh lordy! I have trouble keepin' up with my own folks, much less somebody else's."

Miss Dimple smiled. "I know, but this is important, so I hope you'll try to help me out. Did he have a brother back there, or maybe a sister?"

Amos McIntyre hitched up one overall strap and frowned. "You do realize that was an awful long time ago?"

"But I'll bet you remember who sat next to you in the first grade."

He laughed. "Fuller Hicks! Stayed in trouble as much as I did."

"And what was the best Christmas present you ever received?" she continued.

Amos didn't hesitate. "Why, my calf! Named her Tillie. You'll never find better milk than that cow gave, and gentle! Followed me everywhere."

Miss Dimple's voice was low. "Maybe Sanford had a calf, too. A best friend back home. A brother he cared about. Just think. *Please* think."

And Amos did. He even stood and walked to the front of the store and back again. "I'm sorry, Miss Dimple," he said at last, "but nothing comes to mind."

"Well then, sleep on it," she advised him, "and if you think of anything—and I mean *anything*—please give me a call. I'm at Phoebe Chadwick's —number's in the phone book."

Walking home, Miss Dimple noticed a figure standing on the corner at the end of the block, and on drawing nearer, saw that it was Augusta. "Are you waiting for someone?" she asked as she approached, and Augusta laughed and joined her.

"Yes, you," she said, tugging her hat over her ears. "I do believe it's gotten colder."

Dimple Kilpatrick seldom felt the need to share her concerns, especially with someone she'd known for such a short time, but the shocking death of Dora Westbrook had seemed almost like a personal tragedy after her strange appearance at the library. Although she didn't understand it, Dimple accepted the fact that Augusta sensed when she was troubled, and the two walked in silence for a while before Dimple finally spoke.

"I'm concerned about Jesse Dean," she admitted, "and frankly, I don't know what to do."

"Surely you don't believe he had anything to do with Dora's death," Augusta said. She had been told of the young man's background and of the friendship he shared with Dimple and the other boarders.

"Of course not, but it looks as if someone is attempting to make it look like he did, and I can't imagine why. Oh, I wish we could find out who ordered those cookies! I'm afraid there's a chance Jesse Dean might even be in danger himself."

"But he didn't know the person, did he? Was there some connection between the two? She came from another part of the state." Augusta pulled her cape closer about her and began to walk faster.

Dimple told her about her conversation with Harris Cooper. "Before he came here, I believe Sanford Greeson, Jesse Dean's father, lived in Fieldcroft or somewhere nearby. Of course, that was many years ago." And Dimple told her of her disappointment that Amos McIntyre wasn't able to remember more about the man's past.

"But that doesn't mean the young man had any reason to kill Dora. Surely the authorities wouldn't suspect him on that basis!" If Augusta had been a hen, she would've ruffled her feathers.

Dimple smiled. "I have no doubt of that, but if we can find the connection, it might help lead to the person who *did* kill Dora Westbrook."

Augusta nodded. "It would have to be someone who is familiar with Jesse Dean's background. They knew he made deliveries for Cooper's Store and ordered the vanilla wafers to be left at the church while Dora Westbrook lay at the bottom of that ladder, probably soon after she died, which leads me to believe whoever was responsible probably had knowledge of this town, as well."

Dimple had to agree, but the idea made her want to rush home, lock the door, and huddle in front of the fire. And it wasn't because of the cold.

She didn't expect Amos McIntyre to telephone that night and was frankly surprised when he called the next morning. "I don't remember the person's name," he explained, "but I do recall somebody sending Sanford soft-shell pecans a couple times around Christmas and him sharing them with the rest of us."

"Could they have come from his parents, or perhaps a brother or sister?" Dimple asked. But Amos didn't know.

"Seems funny, but I woke up this morning and that was the first thing that came to mind—those pecans! As to who sent them, I'm afraid I can't help you there."

She shared the news with Augusta over breakfast, but their small victory was short-lived, as Charlie phoned in much distress to report that her mother and aunt had not yet arrived from Fieldcroft, and except for Chief Tinsley's brief communication with Reece Cagle, no one had heard a word from them since they left for home.

Chapter Eighteen

"I guess you didn't expect to see us again," Lou said when she and Jo stopped by the local police station before leaving for home that morning. And Reece, occupied with a stack of papers on his desk, looked up in surprise.

"You're right. I thought you two would probably

be halfway to Elderberry by now." He started to rise. "What can I do for you?"

"We can't stay," Lou said with a dismissive wave of her hand, "but Jo and I thought we should share something Lucille Westbrook said. It might not mean a thing, but we think it's worth mentioning."

Reece nodded, gesturing for her to continue.

"She said Dora was a thief," Lou told him.

He frowned. "And did she explain why she thinks that?"

"She didn't explain anything," Jo said. "She was too busy slamming the door in our faces."

"I'd be interested to know exactly what she thinks the woman took."

"Well, good luck with that," Jo told him. "We'd like to find out, too. And I've thought of another thing," she added, "if Dora left home on Friday and didn't arrive in Elderberry until Saturday, where did she spend Friday night?"

"There should've been a ticket stub," Reece began, but Lou interrupted him. "The only stub they found just showed a date and point of origin, and part of that was torn off, but Bobby Tinsley—he's our chief of police, you know—anyway, Bobby said there was enough on there to tell the ticket had been bought here in Fieldcroft."

"She could've slept on the bus," he suggested. "Some of these routes stop at every little crossroads and it makes for close to a twenty-four-hour trip."

Lou hadn't thought of that. "Is there any way to check that out?"

Reece reached for his phone. "Sure thing. I'll just ring Edna." He smiled. "Oh, the grocery store serves as a bus station, too."

If Lou could've paced during Reece's long-winded conversation with Edna, she would have covered a lot of territory, but there was nowhere to pace, so she just fidgeted in place and looked around for somewhere to go to the bathroom before getting on the road.

"Well," Reece said at last, "Edna checked the schedule, and . . . Dora didn't buy a ticket to Elderberry at all that Friday. The fare she did buy was to Macon."

"Macon? Why Macon?" Jo asked.

Reece didn't try to hide his grin. "I reckon that's where she wanted to go," he said.

"Well, why didn't Edna tell us that in the first place?" Lou said. She had waited until Reece ended his long phone conversation to use the facilities, and now she was irritable and uncomfortable.

"Probably because Edna didn't sell Dora that ticket. Seems Dora purchased that the day *before* she left. That was Emmet Dixon's day to work. Thursday is Edna's day to volunteer at Camp Gordon with the Faithful Fieldcroft Friends." He grinned. "That's a group of women who serve coffee and cake—things like that—to the enlisted

170

men." He nodded toward the door to the tiny reception area up front, where a large woman with unnaturally yellow hair sat behind a desk. "Our Linda Pearl's a member, too. Wouldn't miss a Thursday."

"Sounds like Dora planned to buy her ticket while Edna was away," Jo said. "I wonder who she knew in Macon."

"And where she went when she got there." Lou frowned. "How are we going to find that out?"

"I'll check with Leonard, of course, but I think your best bet is with the sister in Tennessee," Reece told them, "and that inquiry will have to come from your Chief Tinsley, since it's his investigation."

"Good! Maybe by the time we get home, he might be able to let us know if he's learned anything," Jo said. "Oh, and by the way, did Leonard Westbrook know anything about the letters his wife was supposed to have received from Columbia?"

The policeman shook his head. "He says not. Even took some time to look for them, and I believe him. Of course his mother claimed she didn't know anything about them, either, but I wouldn't take a word that woman says to the bank."

"I wonder if they might've had something to do with whatever Lucille Westbrook thinks Dora took," Lou said. "If we could only find those letters, it might clear up the whole thing."

"I do think it's likely there's a connection." Reece followed them to the door. "Now, you ladies be careful on the road out there, and tell your Chief Tinsley if anything turns up here, I'll be in touch."

"Will you look at the time!" Jo glanced at her watch as they once again started for home. "It's already after ten, and at this rate, we won't get to Elderberry until midnight. We probably shouldn't even take the time to stop for lunch."

Lou groaned. "Who cares about lunch? All I want is a bathroom!"

"Well, for heaven's sake, Lou, why didn't you go back at the police station?"

"Because Ruby Linda, or whatever her name was, was permanently installed in there, that's why! I think she lives in there. Surely there's a filling station around here somewhere."

Jo pressed on the gas pedal. She knew she was over the speed limit, but if Reece stopped them, he could at least let Lou use the rest room at the police station. "I think I remember seeing one on the other side of town. Looked fairly clean, too. Just try not to think about it, Lou."

At this point, Lou decided she would not turn her nose up at an outhouse. A large tree might even serve the purpose, but all they could see were pines.

The blue-roofed Pure Oil Station a few miles

from town was a welcome sight, not only for Lou's relief but also because they needed to fill up the gas tank. They had traveled less than thirty minutes after leaving there when Lou noticed the car behind them. "Speed up, Jo, there's a car back there right on our tail."

Her sister frowned. It had begun to rain and she strained to see the road. "Well, if they're in such a hurry, let them pass." Jo slowed as gusts of wind pounded the car with sheets of water. They inched along, the only sound the *whack-whack* of the windshield wipers. "Are they still behind us?" she asked.

Lou twisted around to look. "Doesn't seem like they're going anywhere. They probably can't see any better than you can."

"Well, I wish they'd go on around. They're following too close," Jo said. "What kind of car is it? Can you tell?"

"Hard to see. Looks big, though. I think it's black."

"I don't like this, Lou. Maybe they'll drop back if we go a little faster." But the car behind them maintained the same speed, keeping a fixed distance between them. "Why would anybody do this?" she said. "Can you make out who they are?"

But in addition to the rain, the windows were so fogged up, Lou was unable to see. "Do you think it might be Leonard?" She shuddered. "Or maybe Lucille?"

"But what would they want from us?" Jo gripped the wheel and leaned forward, as if that would make the car go faster.

Lou clung to the overhead strap and bit her lip. "Maybe they think we know something. I sort of got the idea our friend Lucille didn't like us being here."

"Fine! I'm trying to leave as fast as I can. If there was only a place to turn off. How far are we from the nearest town, Louise? Do you still have that map?"

Lou scrambled about and found the dog-eared map on the floor under her feet. "We shouldn't be too far from Hazelhurst," she reported.

"About how far is that?"

"Looks like about ten miles, more or less. Maybe we could just pull over and let them pass."

"Pull over where?" Jo scoffed. "This road is a sea of mud already."

"That looks like a house up ahead," Lou said as the rain slacked. "Seems to be just off that side road up there. Maybe whoever's behind us will think we've gone visiting and leave us alone."

Jo took a deep breath and, singing the popular "Praise the Lord and Pass the Ammunition" as loudly as she could, swerved suddenly onto the narrow road on their right. The car behind them, apparently caught by surprise, continued down the road. "Lou, I think that's the woman with the yellow hair—Linda something—the one who works at the police station."

"I don't know what she wants with us, but it can't be good." Lou frowned as they turned into a rutted driveway. "I can't see a light inside. Doesn't look like anybody's home."

"Maybe they don't have electricity." Jo knew it wasn't unusual for people—especially in the country—to still rely on oil lamps and use woodstoves for heat. "But that doesn't matter, since I plan to turn around as soon as I'm sure that car behind us has gone."

A clump of evergreens screened them from the main road, but a patch of clearing allowed Jo to see if a car was in sight. She had turned off the engine to save gas, and with no heat, the car was beginning to cool. Jo shivered. Maybe the car behind them had only been using them as a kind of guide in the heavy rain. Her hand was on the ignition key, preparing to restart the engine, when Lou grabbed her arm.

"Wait, Jo! I think they're coming back." She leaned closer to see better. "They're slowing . . . looks like they're going to turn here. What are we going to do?"

Jo wished she knew. Miss Dimple would surely know. She closed her eyes and wished for one tiny spark of inspiration to tell them what to do. And then she waited.

The jarring crack of a falling tree made both

sisters jump and cling to each other. Lou held Jo at arm's length and examined her for injuries. "Are you bleeding anywhere? Am I? Oh Lord, I thought we'd been shot for sure!"

A fair-size tree had fallen over the side road, blocking the entrance from the main road. Jo laughed and turned on the car's ignition, and therefore the heater. "Good! Now whoever was following us won't be able to turn in here."

"And we won't be able to turn out, either," Lou reminded her.

"There must be another way. We can't just sit here." Jo put the gears in reverse in an effort to back down the drive, but the tires only mired in deeper. "Looks like we're stuck, Lou." She sighed. "What else can happen?"

"I'll put some limbs or something behind the tires," Lou said, and did. But it didn't help. "Okay, I'm going to try to push. We've got to get out of here. Our families will be worried sick wondering where we are."

But Lou's pushing only made the ruts even deeper as the tires rocked and spun in the mud. "It's beginning to look like we have no choice but to start walking," she said, wishing she'd brought galoshes.

"Walk where? You said the next town was about ten miles up the road." Jo could taste salty tears inching down her throat. *Why in the world had she turned onto this road?*

At first, she didn't notice her sister's insistent tapping on her shoulder. "Somebody's coming!" Lou whispered. "Somebody with a light."

She was hardly five feet tall, with a head full of smoky blue curls that tumbled loosely over her forehead. The hem of her flowered smock touched the top of work boots much like the ones farmers around Elderberry wore to town on Saturdays, and a cloak that seemed to be stitched from a forest of leaves swung from her shoulders.

"My goodness," the woman said, holding her lantern high. "Do come in out of this weather and get warm by the fire. There's bread baking, and the stew is almost done."

Jo shook off her sister's grasp, as she was losing feeling in her hand. "But our car . . . we have to get back home."

"Now, don't you worry. I'll have that taken care of, but first let's get the two of you warm and dry."

"A telephone," Lou gasped as they followed their peculiar hostess up a hill slick with pine needles and sodden leaves. "I have to call my husband." *Damn the expense! What else was she supposed to do?* But of course there was no telephone here. There was only lamplight and a welcoming wood fire on the hearth.

"We'll take care of that tomorrow." The tiny woman threw off her cloak and her curls bounced when she walked. "You'll find warm beds in the next room, and our supper will be ready soon. You should be on your way home soon after daybreak.

"My name is Celeste, by the way, and I was told to expect you."

"Who told—" Jo began.

"And that tree—" Lou chimed in. "What about our car?"

Celeste only smiled and waved her hand, as if shooing away a gnat. "Minor problems. Easily remedied."

"Why do I feel like Hansel and Gretel?" Lou whispered as they washed their hands and faces in basins of warm fragrant water.

Her sister only smiled. "Don't you recognize our hostess? She's the lady in the flowered hat. Haven't you noticed, the whole house smells like peppermint?"

Chapter Nineteen

"Suppose they've had a wreck?"

"Or they might be lost. Some of those roads aren't well marked, you know."

"It's those awful synthetic rubber tires! What if they had a blowout on some lonely country road?"

"And there're swamps down there, you know. . . ."

Phoebe Chadwick's breakfast table was in an uproar over the news that their emissaries, Lou and Jo, seemed to have disappeared, and although Dimple didn't join in, she felt largely responsible. Of course it wasn't her fault, but Augusta *had* assured her the two would be all right.

She turned to Augusta now and saw that she was calmly helping herself to a generous portion of grits. "Aren't you concerned at all?" she muttered, and was ashamed of herself for sounding so accusing. Almost ashamed.

Augusta smiled and added another biscuit to her plate. "Don't worry. They'll be fine. I'm sure Celeste—"

Dimple shoved back her chair. "Just who is this Celeste, and how could you possibly know that?"

Others at the table looked at the two in alarm. Why, it was almost unheard of for Dimple Kilpatrick to lose her temper. And my goodness, would you look at that? A hairpin hung precariously over one ear and her hands trembled as she picked up her plate.

Augusta buttered her biscuit and added a dollop of muscadine jelly.

Across the table, Phoebe tossed her napkin aside and jumped to her feet. This just wouldn't do. It broke her heart to see her dear friend in such a state. "Dimple," she began, and then the telephone rang again.

Annie, who happened to be closer to the phone and quicker on her feet as well, reached it in two steps. When she hung up, she was smiling. "Well, listen to this wild tale! That was Charlie," she explained. "Her mother just called from a little place called Hazelhurst, and said, like it or not, Chief Tinsley was going to have to pay for the call. A tree fell across the road yesterday, and then her car got stuck in the mud. They couldn't get away until early this morning."

"They must've been miserable, and terrified as well," Velma said. "Did they have to sleep in the car?"

"Believe it or not, some kind lady took them in. Charlie said her mother told her the food they were served was out of this world, and they both fell asleep as soon as their heads hit the pillow."

"Sounds too good to be true," Phoebe said. "How do I make reservations?"

"What luck she was there to help!" Lily said. "Who was she? Did they get her name?"

"I believe she said her name was Celeste," Annie told her.

"Would anyone else like another cup of coffee?" Augusta asked.

It wasn't until late in the afternoon that Bobby Tinsley called to ask if he might come by for a few minutes, and of course everyone eagerly agreed as they wanted to know if he'd learned what took place during their friends' stay in Fieldcroft.

"Mainly, I wanted to touch base with you about your upcoming trip to Tennessee," he began after everyone was seated in Phoebe's parlor. They had invited Augusta to join them, but she seemed to be in the middle of some endless tapestry she was working on and begged to be excused. "If it's something I need to know," she said, "you can tell me about it later."

And, as it turned out, it *was* something she needed to know, as it involved their intended trip. Dimple, feeling much like a remorseful child, had apologized for her overreaction at breakfast, but Augusta dismissed that by holding up one dainty pink palm like a stop sign.

"I should have explained," she said.

Miss Dimple sighed. Now they were back where they started. "Explained what?" she asked. "How did you come to know Celeste and how did you know she would be in the right place at the right time?"

Augusta concentrated on her glittering stitches. "We've worked together several times before," she said, not looking up. "And I was sure she would be there, because that's her job."

And Dimple knew she could pursue the subject, just as she could pursue the meaning of life and other perplexing puzzles, but was relieved when Annie called to let her know the police chief was waiting in the parlor.

"Two things," Bobby Tinsley said after everyone except for Augusta was seated. "First of all, we've learned, through Mrs. Carr's and her sister's efforts, that Dora Westbrook received several communications from South Carolina—Columbia, to be exact—before all this took place, but no one knows who sent them or where the letters are now.

"Also, Sergeant Cagle tells me they've confirmed that on the Friday she left there, Dora Westbrook boarded a bus to Macon. Apparently, she spent the night there and then bought a ticket to Elderberry the next day."

Annie frowned. "She bought two different tickets to get here, but you found only the one stub in the bag she had with her."

He nodded. "I suppose she threw the second one away upon arrival, but that's not important now. It would help if we could get in touch with whoever she stayed with in Macon. They might be able to tell us what she had in mind and why she came here to Elderberry."

"Wouldn't her husband know if she knew someone in Macon?" Miss Dimple asked.

"She did attend college there. Leonard Westbrook said he met Dora there during her sophomore year at Wesleyan, and they were married soon afterward. It wasn't a formal wedding. No attendants. Just a justice of the peace. He can't remember the names of any of Dora's friends at school there."

"Huh!" This from Velma. "Can't or won't?"

"How very sad," Lily said, looking a bit droopy herself.

"Then we need to find out from her husband what Dora's name was before she married," Annie suggested, "and look her up in the college annual. Maybe some of her classmates will be able to help."

"What about her parents?" Phoebe asked.

"From what we've learned, it seems Dora's grandmother raised her and her sister." Chief Tinsley inched his chair closer and clasped his hands in front of him. "And I believe there's an easier way to find that out. The sister's address is on the envelope we found in the bag Dora carried. Her name is Elaine Arnold, and I plan to telephone there today. If anyone can tell us about Dora's connections in Macon, it would be Elaine." Smiling, he looked about. "Don't you agree?"

Of course they all did, and although Miss Dimple had already thought of phoning Dora's sister, she was too polite to interrupt him.

Growing serious, he added, "Mrs. Carr and her sister—who, by the way, arrived safely a short time ago—admitted they had a bit of a scare on their way home last night. A car was following much too closely and they couldn't seem to shake it. That was when they turned into a side road and became stuck in the mud."

"Oh dear! Did the car go on by?" Lily asked, and the chief only nodded, because he didn't want to go into an explanation about a tree blocking the road and mysteriously disappearing the next morning, in spite of the sisters' conviction it had been hauled away.

Bobby Tinsley shifted in his seat. "If you're serious about making this trip to Tennessee, I want you to keep your eyes open. I'd feel better if we could send somebody along with you, but we can't. Keep in mind that we don't know anything about these people. I'm hoping they want as much, or even more than, we do to get to the bottom of what happened to this young woman." He shrugged. "We'll just have to see, *so be careful!*"

"We will. I promise." Annie's eyes gleamed. This was an adventure, and she was already packed and ready to go.

"It sounds to me, and to Reece Cagle down in Fieldcroft as well, that Dora was planning to meet somebody here in Elderberry, and I think it had something to do with the correspondence she received from Columbia.

"Now, I could ask her sister this when I call, but it would mean a lot more coming from you, face-to-face. Of course I plan to let her know some of you hope to speak with her. We'll try to keep it light, as I don't want to put her off or scare her. Just let her think you're in the area for the weekend and would like to drop by."

"We can certainly do that," Velma said, looking efficient and businesslike. "My car is gassed up and ready to go, and I'm sure we'll be able to find some decent motor courts along the way."

"We'll help with your expenses as much as we can," the chief said, standing, "and if you run into trouble, you know you can telephone from the local authorities there. *Just try not to get into trouble.*"

Dimple Kilpatrick watched the front door close behind him and sighed. "Do you really think it's necessary for me to go along? I could use this extra time to put my room in order and plan some art activities for Thanksgiving."

But Velma was having none of it. "Dimple Kilpatrick, your room is in order as much as it needs to be, and what else can you possibly add for Thanksgiving? As far as I know, the Pilgrims still came over on the *Mayflower*, landed on Plymouth Rock, and celebrated the harvest with the Indians. You can't tell me that after all the years you've been teaching, you don't have that subject fairly well covered!"

Miss Dimple looked around for help, but nobody offered. "I usually give Virginia a hand with the Halloween party at the library," she said. "It's this Saturday, you know, and there's always a lot to do."

This was met with silence until Phoebe finally spoke up. "Which suitcase would you like for me to get down for you? That embroidered bag that was left here, or the tan suitcase with stripes?"

Chapter Twenty

It was still dark when Jo awoke to the aroma of coffee and cinnamon. Or was it nutmeg? Beside her, her sister slept the sleep of the pure in heart, or the totally exhausted. Possibly the latter. Stepping onto a nubby rug—braided, if she remembered correctly—Jo felt for the clothing she'd left on a chair the night before and reluctantly slipped out of her warm flannel pajamas. *How were they ever going to get out of the mud and find their way back to the road?*

"Wake up, Lou," she whispered. "We've got to find some way to free the car and get home."

Lou didn't respond except to curl into a cat-like ball. *And why am I whispering?* Jo thought. Of the three of them here, her sister was the only one sleeping.

"LOUISE!" Jo gave the covers a jerk. "Get up! We have to find a way to let everyone at home know we're all right, and we're going to need help getting back on the road."

"Uh!" Lou sat up, hugged herself, and rubbed her eyes. "Oh dear!" she mumbled. "Ed . . . Good heavens, Jo! Ed will think we're both dead."

Jo thought of her daughters, Charlie and Delia, and the toddler grandson they called Pooh, who shared her home. They would all be frantic with worry, or at least her daughters would, and Pooh would miss her if she didn't come back, and wonder where she was. Now she was getting teary.

Stop it, Josephine Carr! She unrolled stockings over her legs and knelt to find her shoes. It was beginning to be light now. Maybe they would be able to see well enough to finally get her car out of the mud.

Their hostess, again in boots and flowered smock, and wearing a large white apron, stirred something in a big pot on the woodstove. "I hope you like oatmeal," she said.

Oatmeal would be just fine, they agreed, but it tasted like no oatmeal they'd ever eaten. Sprinkled with brown sugar and dotted with plump raisins and bits of apple, it reminded Lou of the kind they'd had at their grandmother's house as children, only better. Jo must have felt the same, as she ate two bowlfuls.

When Celeste brought a platter filled with thick slices of homemade bread toasted under the broiler and spread with butter and honey, both claimed they couldn't eat another bite. Instead, they found they could eat several. And did.

After breakfast, Celeste washed the bowls, cups, and spoons in a pan of hot soapy water while Lou rinsed them for her sister to dry. Each bowl was patterned with a different flower. Bright blue morning glories twined around the one Celeste had used; Jo's was a sunny cup of daisies; and pink-and-white hollyhocks marched around Lou's bowl. Lou wished she could find some like them, but something told her the set was one of a kind.

"Celeste," Jo began as she hung the dish towel to dry, "do you know anyone we can ask to help with my car? I'm afraid it's hopelessly stuck, and our families must be worried sick not knowing where we are."

Celeste tossed her apron over the back of a chair. "I'm sorry, I don't have a telephone, but your car has been taken care of." She smiled. "I think you'll find it ready to go."

"Really?" That sounded too good to be true. Would a fictional beast, who was really a prince, come stomping through the door and bellow that they would be required to remain here until they had accomplished some impossible task?

"How did they ever manage to get it out?" Lou asked. "Who can we thank for this?"

But Celeste kind of shrugged that away. "Friends. Good friends. It's a blessing, don't you think, to have friends we can count on? But no thanks will be necessary."

"I don't understand. When did this happen? I didn't hear a thing," Jo said.

"You fell asleep soon after supper," Celeste reminded her. "Both of you were so very weary. You must have had a tiring day."

They agreed that they had, and hurried to see

the car, all polished and shiny, parked in front of the house.

"Why, it looks like it's been washed and waxed," Jo said. Now and then, she and her daughters rinsed off the car with a hose, but she'd never had it waxed.

Celeste stood behind them. "And ready for the road," she added.

"My goodness!" Lou couldn't think of anything else to say, and then she remembered the tree. "Do you know of another way back to the road?" she asked.

"Oh, you can get out the way you came in," Celeste told her. "That tree's out of the way now. Roots must've been weakened in that heavy rain we had yesterday."

"My goodness!" Lou said again. "Who moved it? Your friends, I suppose. Please thank them for us."

"It was only a sapling," Celeste said as she helped them carry luggage to the car. "Didn't take long at all. Now, I'm sure you'll find a telephone in the town up the road, and I know your families will be relieved to hear from you."

After many thanks and minus two jars of apple butter and three of applesauce, the two finally got on the road back to Elderberry. "Lou?" Jo said after a few minutes of driving in silence. "Do you believe somebody really was following us yesterday, or was it our imaginations?"

Lou warmed her hands by the heater and turned up the collar of her coat. "I don't know, Jo, but I have a weird feeling if we were to try to find Celeste's place again, it probably wouldn't be there."

It was not until they got home that Jo discovered in her luggage a beautiful ceramic bowl covered inside and out with daisies, and Lou was delighted to find its twin in a colorful hollyhock design.

"Well, did everyone get away as planned?" Virginia asked Phoebe that Friday when she came to help decorate for the Halloween party.

"Whew! Finally. They left this morning, with Dimple dragging her feet the whole time. Planned to leave yesterday, but Velma discovered a crack in her fuel line and had a dickens of a time finding another." Phoebe sat down and began cutting orange crepe paper into streamers, a task Cattus found highly entertaining.

"Time for a little fresh air," Virginia said, depositing the cat on the porch and out of the way. "We'll never get anything done with that cat in here.

"But I'm a bit worried about Dimple," she added, searching in a box of cardboard cutouts. "She hasn't been herself at all lately. Why, you'd have to lock the Dimple I know in a closet to keep her from going somewhere new—especially if it concerns solving a murder."

"I think it has something to do with her fiancé. She doesn't like to talk about him, but she did tell me once he died of yellow fever during the Spanish American War," Phoebe said. "I believe she met him when she was teaching at a small school somewhere in rural Tennessee."

"Then I guess that explains it. It must've been near the area they're planning to visit, the one where Dora's sister lives." Virginia climbed onto a step stool to tape a trio of fiery-eyed bats over the door, and Phoebe stood to help her down.

"Poor Dimple! She must've been awfully young," Virginia said. "I don't think she was ever interested in anyone else."

Phoebe smiled as she began on another streamer. "You know our Dimple—loyal to the end and beyond, but I really don't think she ever cared about another man. Not that they weren't interested in her. She was still young when she came to live with us. My husband was alive then and active in the community. Young men were often in our home on some business or other, and I remember that some of them reached out to Dimple."

Virginia shook out a jointed scarecrow. "And what happened?" she asked.

Phoebe shrugged. "Dimple didn't reach back."

Just then, a blast of cold air ushered in Emmaline Brumlow, who was in search of the latest Dorothy L. Sayers mystery featuring her character Lord Peter Wimsey. "I've read most of them now," she said, adding a book to the stack by Virginia's desk, where she began to shuffle through the recent returns. "Has *Busman's Honeymoon* come back yet? Looks like whoever checked it out last is taking forever and a day. Why, it only took me three days to read *Nine Tailors*. Would've been two, but I had to host the church circle this week."

Noticing the festive preparations, she frowned at the shopworn scarecrow. "If you must put that up, why not hang it in the children's section?"

Virginia, who had an identical scarecrow for that area, said that was a fine idea and that Emmaline could find the book she wanted on the shelf under *S*.

"I don't know how I could ever manage this library without that woman's help," she said after Emmaline checked out her book and left.

Phoebe laughed. "So good of her to offer to help with the decorating."

Virginia stepped back to admire the scarecrow, now suspended from the rafters, which was where she'd planned to hang it in the first place. "I wonder what Dimple was doing in Tennessee," she said, continuing their interrupted conversation. "She must not have stayed very long."

"I imagine teaching jobs were few and far between then, and she was just out of what they called 'normal' school," Phoebe explained. "Her brother, Henry, would've been about twelve then, which meant she probably had to leave him at home with their father, and Henry, you know, was like her own child. I think she was offered a position closer to home a year or so later, and soon after Henry started at Georgia Tech, our Dimple came to Elderberry."

Later, during a break, Phoebe told Virginia about Dimple's conversation with Amos McIntyre. "She thinks there might be a connection to Jesse Dean's father, who left here years ago, and that town where Dora lived," she said. "Turns out Sanford Greeson probably did live there, or somewhere near there, before he came here."

"So what?" Virginia unwound herself from a clinging streamer. "The man's been gone for years. What difference could that possibly make?"

"None, except it connects Jesse Dean with Dora Westbrook."

"Oh, for heaven's sake! Jesse Dean Greeson has probably never been to Fieldcroft, Georgia, and I would bet a rib roast on that—if I had one, that is!" And Phoebe let the scissors slip to the floor, barely missing her foot.

Virginia laughed. "And so would I, but somebody—somebody who knows about Jesse Dean's background—obviously tried to use that to make it look like there's a connection between Dora Westbrook and Jesse Dean."

Phoebe frowned. "But who would do that? And why?"

"I assume it's the person who killed her, desperate, no doubt, to find somebody to blame in case suspicion was cast on him. He knew Jesse Dean delivers for Cooper's Store and that his father once lived in Fieldcroft."

"I've lived here for longer than I care to remember, and I had no idea Sanford Greeson lived in Fieldcroft," Phoebe said.

"But *somebody* did." Virginia set a fat orange pumpkin in the center of the table. "Somebody whose knowledge of goings-on in Elderberry goes way, way back."

"Well, that's just plain scary, Virginia." Phoebe shivered. "Maybe we don't even have to decorate for Halloween. It's spooky enough already.

"We did hear some good news, though," she said, eager to change the subject. "Lou and Jo got home safely late yesterday and they said Dora didn't come here directly from Fieldcroft. Seems she spent the night in Macon."

"Macon? I wonder why she went to Macon."

"Went to school there, Bobby Tinsley says. Wesleyan. He phoned her sister to find out who Dora might've been visiting there, but she wasn't much help. Said she'd look through some old letters and see if she can find the names of some of her sister's college friends."

"So I guess she knows the Elderberry Detective

Agency is on the way." The floor was littered with bits of black and orange construction paper, ancient cardboard cutouts, and strands of crepe paper, and Virginia, being unable to see her feet, looked around for the broom.

"That poor sister!" Phoebe said, grabbing a trash can. "She has no idea what she's in for."

And that was when Rose McGinnis breezed in and plopped Cattus in the middle of the debris. "Poor kitty was lonesome out there. Why did you shut him on the porch?" And she shuffled through the litter to browse among the books and perform her one-finger solo at the piano.

Having accomplished what they set out to do in the way of decorating, Virginia made a point to sweep under Rose's feet, hoping she would take the hint and go home, while Phoebe gathered the colorful litter into a bag to take to the trash. "I'll just get rid of this, Virginia, and we'll be ready to leave," she said in a voice barely below a holler, and stepped out the front door, almost colliding with her neighbor Willie Elrod.

"Oh, Miz Chadwick! I'm sorry! Hope I didn't step on your toes," Willie said, hurrying past her to speak with Virginia. "I was afraid you might already be closed and thought I'd check just one more time to see if anybody brought back *Huckleberry Finn*. I been wanting to read that book for ages, and we've got three whole days before we have to go back to school."

Virginia smiled as she stamped the desired book. "You just happen to be in luck, Willie, but aren't you picking cotton this weekend?"

He grinned. "Shoot! Picked I don't know how many pounds today—earned a whole dollar— but Mama's taking me to Atlanta tomorrow. We're going to Rich's. You know, that big store with the escalators! I've just about outgrown all my clothes."

"My goodness, Willie!" Phoebe looked closer at the boy's face and attempted to lift his chin. "What in the world happened to your eye?"

He dodged her hand and stepped away. "Oh, nothing much."

Frowning, Virginia looked closer. "Looks like you have a black eye to me. Must've been some fight."

Phoebe shook her head. "What were you fighting about?"

Willie Elrod tucked the book under his arm and grunted. "That R. W. Hawkins tried to take my cotton sack. We were standing in line to get it weighed and mine had way more in it than his did. He was trying to get me to trade." He grinned. "Guess I showed him! Nose bled like a river—you shoulda seen it! Hope he didn't bleed on the cotton."

Both women were familiar with R. W. Hawkins, who had repeated the seventh grade twice and held the school record for visits to the principal's office. Neither condoned fighting, but in this case, assumed R. W. probably got what was coming to him.

"Well, just try to stay away from him, Willie, and hurry home now before it gets dark," Phoebe warned. "We'll expect a fashion show when you get back from Atlanta."

Chapter Twenty-one

They had driven through the small town of Covington and were nearing the outskirts of Atlanta when Augusta began to laugh. She and Annie shared the backseat, while Miss Dimple sat up front with Velma.

Dimple had removed her lavender felt hat with a hint of a veil and now held it in her lap. "What's so funny?" she asked, turning to glance behind her.

Augusta leaned forward for a closer look out the window, and her laughter sparkled like soap bubbles, making everyone smile. "It's the signs," she said, pressing her forehead against the glass. "Look, there are more coming!"

Annie read them aloud as they passed:

At ease, she said
Maneuvers begin
When you get those whiskers
Off your chin
Burma-Shave

A few miles up the road, they all laughed at another series of signs advertising the popular shaving cream:

Many a wolf
Is never let in
Because of the hair
On his chinny-chin-chin

"My goodness," Augusta said, once again taking needlework from her bag, "I'd almost forgotten those funny little verses."

"How come?" Annie asked bluntly. "Where've you been?"

Augusta smiled. "Oh, here and there, but it's not always easy to stay in touch."

How could she possibly not stay in touch when the war has dominated practically every waking minute for three long years? Annie wondered, but just then Velma called their attention to the beautiful homes and spacious lawns spread along Atlanta's rolling hills, and the four of them discussed which they would like to choose for their own. Of course it was fun to pretend, Annie admitted, but she still had her heart set on that cottage with flowers in the yard.

They passed several hitchhiking servicemen along the way, but all were going in the opposite direction, until they drew near Marietta, where Dimple's brother worked at the Bell Bomber

Plant, and Velma slowed as she saw the young sailor up ahead. "Do you think we can squeeze him in the back?" she asked.

Augusta and Annie agreed to make room, and the young man grinned as he hurried to the car and slung his duffel bag at his feet. He was heading for Kennesaw, he said, the tiny village at the foot of Kennesaw Mountain, the site of the Civil War battle that preceded the well-known Battle of Atlanta. His name was Andy, he told them, and he was nineteen years old, and hoped to go to the university after the war and earn a degree in agriculture—to bring the family farm into the modern age, he confided.

His father, grandfather, and uncles, he claimed, were dead set against any kind of change, so it looked like it was going to be up to him to convince them.

Of course they all wished him good luck with that, and Annie asked if he had a special girl-friend.

He admitted that he did and fumbled in his bag for a small box that held a silver ring of intricate design studded with tiny turquoise stones. "It's not an engagement ring," he said, "but I hope it will do until I can afford the real thing.

"Her name is Anne," he confided. "She has the most beautiful hair, about the color of a new penny, and she's the prettiest girl I've ever seen. I know we have years ahead of us with college and all, but I'm hoping she'll love me enough to wait.

"I'm seeing her tonight," Andy told them when they reached his destination and dropped him off in front of the local drugstore. "Cross your fingers for me, won't you?"

And naturally everyone did. Everyone but Dimple Kilpatrick.

"Is anything wrong, Miss Dimple? You're awfully quiet," Annie observed. Since they had stopped at the drugstore, Augusta suggested they treat themselves to ice cream, and everyone seemed to be in favor.

"I was just thinking of that young man, Andy. I believe he said he would soon be shipping out."

"That's right," Velma explained. "That's why he's here on leave. I do hope his girl accepts that ring. It will give him something to dream about until he comes home."

But what if he doesn't come home? Dimple stopped herself from saying it aloud. After all, here was Annie, like so many others, bravely waiting out the war for the soldier she loved to return.

Like she herself would have done. And hadn't she just recently assured Annie it does no good to worry?

"I believe I'll have chocolate," she said as Velma blew the horn for service, and Augusta, admitting to feeling adventurous, said she hoped they had tutti-frutti.

Soon a young girl came out to take their orders, and a few minutes later brought them on a tray she attached to the window on the driver's side of the car.

"Has anybody noticed if Andy has come out of the drugstore yet?" With eyes on the door of the building, Annie finished the last of her strawberry cone and folded the paper napkin to use later. "I wonder who came to meet him."

Augusta smiled. "You mean you wonder if his flaming-haired sweetheart is with him there inside."

And as if on cue, the couple stepped outside, arm in arm, followed by a man and woman of middle age, whom they assumed to be Andy's parents. And the four in the car, including Dimple Kilpatrick, waved at him to wish him luck, but he only had eyes for the girl by his side.

"He was right," Velma said, and hoped no one could hear her sigh. "She really is lovely."

Over an hour later, they reached the tree-shaded streets of Calhoun, a tiny teacup of a town nestled in the foothills of northwest Georgia, and pulled into a service station to make way for the khaki convoy of soldier-filled army trucks heading south down Highway 41, probably for Fort Benning.

"Where do suppose we should stop for the night?" Miss Dimple asked later as they drove north through the towns of Dalton and Ringgold before crossing into Tennessee. It had already begun to get dark and she knew Velma didn't feel comfortable being on the road at night.

Velma frowned. "As soon as we see a likely place. Keep an eye out for a decent-looking motor court, and if we're lucky, there should be a place to eat nearby. That wouldn't be a problem if we were going as far as Chattanooga, but according to the map, we should be veering left before too long.

"See if you can tell what the next town will be," she said to Dimple, who held the map. "We should be getting close to it soon."

"Lynchburg." Dimple spoke so softly, Velma strained to hear.

"What did you say, Dimple?"

"Lynchburg," Dimple said again. She didn't need to look at a map. As much as she tried, she couldn't forget this part of Tennessee and the time she had spent here. If she closed her eyes, perhaps the memory would be less vivid, wouldn't cut into her heart.

A boulder was lodged in her stomach, and Dimple gasped for breath. After all these years, why did it still hurt so? "Stop. Please stop. I have to get out." Her hand was on the door handle when Velma pulled over on the shoulder of the road. "Dimple, what is it? Oh dear God, is it your heart?"

It *was* her heart, but not in the way Velma had in mind. Dimple tried to answer but couldn't speak.

"Breathe in this." Beside her, Augusta spoke in a gentle voice and held a paper bag to her mouth. The bag smelled like peanuts and she remembered Annie had brought some along to munch on. Now the peanuts were on the ground at her feet. "Slowly now . . . breathe deeply . . . in . . . out. . . ." Augusta touched her hand, and for a few seconds, the fragrance of strawberries surrounded her and then was gone. "Now, close your eyes and think blue. Summer skies, a field of violets, sunshine on a mountain lake . . . your grandmother's Sunday dress . . ." The words moved over her like a lullaby, and Dimple began to breathe normally.

"Oh my goodness!" Dimple looked down at the peanut litter at her feet, dismayed at what she had caused. "What a mess! I don't know what came over me, but thank you, Augusta. I must have been hyperventilating."

Why had she not thought of the paper bag remedy? Why, goodness, she had used it herself on occasion. And Dimple stooped to collect the scattered peanuts.

"Now, you sit right down." Annie led her back to the car. "I'll pick those up, Miss Dimple. Won't take a minute."

"Well, Dimple Kilpatrick, you gave us all a scare, and I'll thank you not to do that again!" It would've been impossible to ignore the tremor in her friend's voice, and Dimple gave Velma's hand a squeeze and promised to do better.

Darkness had fallen by the time they checked into the Victory Motor Court a few miles up the road, and they were relieved to find the cottages, although small, clean and comfortable. And Aunt Ella's Table, the restaurant on the premises, served vegetable soup and corn bread almost as good as Odessa's.

Velma, tired from the long drive, chose the first cottage, and Annie agreed to share it with her after Velma promised it wouldn't keep her awake if Annie sat up writing to Frazier all night long.

"Then I guess you're stuck with me," Augusta told Dimple as the two took time about brushing their teeth. "I hope you'll be able to get some sleep."

Dimple hoped so, too. She had made up her mind not to think of tomorrow. "Just one question," she asked as she pulled the quilt to her chin. "How did you know about my grand-mother's blue Sunday dress?"

"Oh, just a lucky guess!" And Augusta reached over and turned off the light.

Chapter Twenty-two

What could they have for supper? Marjorie Mote put aside her latest copy of *Good Housekeeping* and added a few chunks of coal to the fire. Maybe if she chopped thin slices of Spam, sautéed them with a little onion, and added some grated cheese, it might make a passable omelette. Her husband never complained, but it got tiresome eating the same old things when meat was so hard to come by.

John had dozed off earlier after listening to H. V. Kaltenborn's evening broadcast of the news. War news. Always war news, and she saw no need to wake him.

The demands of war were forever on her mind. The banners in the living room window were a constant and grave reminder of their two sons. The blue star represented Jack, who, as part of the Thirtieth Infantry Division, had recently played a crucial role in the capture of the German city of Aachen. The gold star was for Chester, who had been killed earlier in the war when his plane ran out of fuel and crashed during General Dolittle's bombing raid over Japan.

Marjorie lightly touched the banners, as if wishing her sons a good night, and had turned to go into the kitchen when she heard the crash.

At six o'clock, night had descended, but a pale yellow light from the streetlamp on the corner kept enough of the darkness at bay to reveal a small form curled on the sidewalk in front of the house.

"John!" Marjorie shouted, snatching an afghan from the back of the sofa as she rushed out the door. "Somebody's hurt out here—wake up!"

"Willie?" He opened his eyes when she called

his name. "Lie still now. . . . Don't try to get up before we see if anything's broken." Gently, she probed his arms and then his legs. "Where do you hurt? Do you know what happened?"

He tried to lift his head and moaned. "My head. Oh my head! It felt like somebody shoved me. Must've been hiding behind that tree, and he pushed me when I rode by."

"John, phone Emma Elrod, and hurry! Willie's been hurt," she called, seeing her husband approach.

"Now, keep still, honey, until you feel you can sit up." Marjorie draped the warm afghan over the boy and was glad she'd thought to bring it, as there was a noticeable chill in the air. She wanted to gather him into her arms as she had her own boys years ago, and would do the same now if only it were possible.

"Were you able to see who shoved you?" she asked. *Who would do such a cruel thing? And why?*

"No'me. I didn't see it coming, but I'm pretty sure I know who it was, and he's gonna wish he'd never been born." Willie grunted as he raised his head. "I reckon I can sit up now."

She put a supporting hand behind his head. "Just take it easy, Willie. Your mama's on her way."

"Oh, Miss Marjorie, my mama's gonna kill me! She told me to come straight home from the library, but, well . . . Junior Henderson and me, we been shooting hickory nuts at this old tin can. Junior's got him a great new slingshot. His brother made it for him. He's home on leave, you know. I sure wish I had a brother."

"Willie, what happened?" Breathless from her frantic dash across the street, Emma Elrod stooped beside him. "Tell me where it hurts."

"Mostly it's just my head, but my elbow's burning like crazy."

"Well, let's get you home. Do you think you can stand up? I've been worried sick about you, Willie! Virginia Balliew said you left the library over an hour ago. Where in the world have you been?" Emma Elrod picked up the afghan her son had thrown aside and folded it over her arm. She didn't appear sympathetic. Realizing that, Willie moaned. "Oh, it hurts to move my head. Hurts something awful!"

His mother touched his forehead. "I'm afraid you're going to have a knot there, and probably a bad bruise. An aspirin should help, and we'll put an ice pack on it when we get home." Softening, she kissed the top of his head while helping him to his feet. "How did this happen, Willie?"

Willie repeated what he'd said earlier. "That R. W. Hawkins is crazy if he thinks he's gonna get away with this! Just wait till I get my hands on him."

Emma Elrod exchanged knowing glances with her neighbor and shook her head. "Well, you don't know that for sure, so don't be jumping the gun. At least your bike doesn't look too worse for the wear, and it's a good thing . . ."

She stopped herself before saying "Because you can't get another until after the war." After all, the Motes had suffered an irreplaceable loss.

John Mote insisted on taking the two home in his car, and upon arrival, drew on his training as a former Boy Scout leader to remind Willie's mother to wake him a few hours after he fell asleep to be sure he didn't have a concussion.

"I don't believe I'll go," Phoebe said. "It's just too far, and the ceremony's not until five o'clock. It'll be dark by the time we get home."

She had been invited to the wedding of her cousin Ada's daughter, Marceline, who was marrying in the Methodist church in the nearby town of Washington. Frankly, Phoebe had never cared for Ada. After all, who would name a child *Marceline?* Of course, the poor girl couldn't help being named for some long-forgotten silent-film actress, and Phoebe wished her a long and happy marriage, but why did *she* have to be there?

"But if you don't go, Mrs. Ashcroft will have to drive all that way by herself," Lily reminded her. "It'll be dark when she leaves for home, and what if she has a flat or takes a wrong turn? Why, there's no telling what might happen."

Kate Ashcroft, who gave piano lessons and

taught music in the Elderberry schools, had roomed with Ada's younger sister at Agnes Scott College, in Decatur, and was to be the accompanist during the ceremony. Learning of Phoebe's connection with the family, she had invited her to share the ride.

"I can't see that my being along will keep her from having a flat, Lily. And everybody knows I have no sense of direction."

With everyone else away, the two were enjoying a late breakfast, and Phoebe, reluctant to leave the table, lingered over a second cup of coffee, something she seldom had an opportunity to enjoy.

Her face a mask of disapproval, Lily picked up her plate and headed for the kitchen. "After all, she *is* your cousin," she reminded her.

"Ada is my late husband's cousin." And since Monroe has been gone these many years, he's not here to make me feel guilty, Phoebe thought. "Besides," she added, "I sent the bride a whole place setting in her silver."

Lily sighed. "Well, I hope some of the family will offer to put Mrs. Ashcroft up for the night," she said, and disappeared into the kitchen.

"Why, Lily, I do believe you're trying to get rid of me!" Phoebe said on her return. "You must be planning a secret rendezvous."

"Why—why, Phoebe Chadwick, the very idea!" Lily's cheeks turned almost as pink as the fabric rose pinned to the neck of her blouse. "You didn't go with the others to Tennessee, so I just thought you deserved some time away."

"I'm sorry, Lily. You're right, of course, and I suppose I should go to the wedding, but what about you? I hate to leave you here alone."

"I won't be the only woman alone tonight. Just think of all those young wives whose husbands are fighting overseas. If they can bear the loneliness day after day, I can surely manage for one night."

My goodness, Phoebe thought as she tidied up the kitchen, Lily Moss sounded almost noble. She couldn't remember her being so eager to be left alone. Naturally, she wondered why.

Was love blooming between the modest sixth-grade teacher and the new assistant principal? Or perhaps it was portly Craig Defore, who came there to teach history and math. But Phoebe shook her head. Neither seemed her type.

As it turned out, demure Lily *did* have a rendezvous of sorts in mind, but it wasn't the kind Phoebe had suggested. Earlier in the month, the scandalous new novel *Forever Amber* had been confiscated when one of the more daring seventh-grade girls was found relishing it behind a textbook in Ethel Willoughby's English class. The forbidden book was then placed in a locker in the faculty room, where it became available to any of that group who wanted to take advantage of the information.

There was little doubt that Lily Moss lacked in that area more than most. She intended to remedy that tonight.

A dim lamp burned in the hallway downstairs and the one in the parlor window sent a yellow slant of light across the otherwise-dark front porch. The house was quiet except for the intermittent creaking that seemed to come from first one place and then another. Only the ordinary noises of an old house settling for the night, Lily told herself. Strange she'd never noticed them before, but of course there were always others about, as well as the usual sounds—a radio show, kitchen clatter, water running in the bathtub, doors opening and closing.

After Phoebe left for the wedding, Lily'd made sure to lock the door behind her and had checked to see the one in the back of the house was secure, as well. She made herself a cup of hot chocolate and took it upstairs, along with a few of the molasses cookies Augusta had made before she left. The four women had been gone a little over a day now and Lily wondered if they had met Dora Westbrook's sister and if she had been able to help them.

It was lonely here without them, and Lily wished she hadn't lost the key to the room she shared with Velma as she closed the door behind her, but the chocolate was hot and sweet and the cookies had just the right amount of spice. What would we have done without Augusta in Odessa's absence? she wondered. Lily admired Augusta, although she wasn't quite sure what to make of her. Why, she had even changed the way she wore her hair because of something Augusta said.

"You have a lovely wave in your hair but no one can see it when you pull it straight back like that," she'd commented one morning at breakfast. "Why not let it frame your face, so everyone can see?"

Lily wondered why no one had suggested that before, as the soft waves around her face seemed to make her look much younger, and, well, almost pretty, or at least she felt that way. Even Mr. Taylor, the assistant principal, had complimented her on her new look.

Not that his opinion mattered. Certainly not! Still, it was nice to be noticed.

Later in pajamas and robe, Lily curled up in the small boudoir chair covered in a cheerful yellow-and-blue print in the same fabric as the bedspreads. The light was just right, and with a cozy pillow at her back, Lily picked up the book to begin her adventure.

She had read as far as page two when the sound of breaking glass came from the kitchen below.

Chapter Twenty-three

"Bobby Tinsley was to have let Dora's sister know we were on the way, so she should be expecting us," Velma said at breakfast the next morning. All had ordered scrambled eggs and biscuits, and no one seemed to be in a hurry to leave, as a steady rain had begun to fall and the restaurant was warm and comfortable.

"I wonder what she said—Dora's sister, I mean. She must wonder why all of us are coming." Annie poured syrup over a steaming biscuit and licked her fingers, looking first to see if Miss Dimple was watching.

But Dimple Kilpatrick's attention was on the rain pounding the awning over their window and collecting in puddles in the asphalt parking lot below. Or that's where she seemed to be looking. They had spent the night near Lynchburg, would pass through Shelbyville before noon, and then Lewisburg, where they hoped to meet Dora's sister, Elaine. Dimple's memories of that area were of daisy-dotted meadows and winding streams, of vast fields of corn and tobacco, and of a tree-shaded village still in its youth. As she had been.

"My goodness, Dimple, you've hardly touched a thing," Velma said. "I hope you're not coming down with something."

"I'm just saving my appetite for that picnic lunch," Dimple said, "but it would be a shame to waste these biscuits. I'll ask our waitress if they could spare us a little wax paper to wrap them. You never know when they might come in handy."

Annie made a face. "I don't mind leftover biscuits, but I believe I'll pass on cold ones."

"Then you've never been hungry." The other three spoke at once, and then, of course they all laughed.

Later, they would have cause to remember that conversation.

The restaurant cook had packed a picnic of fried chicken, deviled eggs, pickles, and pimento cheese sandwiches; and for dessert had added crisp red apples from a nearby farm. The chicken smelled so inviting, they all agreed it should travel in the trunk of the car and away from temptation.

"I hope this rain lets up before we get to Lewisburg, or we might have to picnic in the car," Velma said as they left the motor court with its welcoming café behind them.

Glancing at the sky, Dimple said they all should look for a patch of blue large enough to make a pair of Dutchman's britches, because that meant it was going to clear.

"Poor Dutchman! Looks like he's going to have to wear his old pants," Annie observed a while later, as there seemed to be no letup from the rain. A little after noon, they pulled off the road and lunched in the car in a spot overlooking a narrow stream of rushing brown water.

"It looks like this weather's going to follow us all the way to Lewisburg," Velma said. "I was hoping we could find a nice place to take a break and stretch our legs."

Augusta ate the last bite of her pickle and announced that as far as she was concerned, fried chicken tasted just as good no matter where you ate it.

Rain and muddy roads delayed their arrival in Lewisburg, and they decided to spend the night in a tourist home there and try to visit with Dora's sister the next morning.

"After we see Elaine tomorrow, I would think our next step should be to try to locate the person Dora visited in Macon," Augusta said. "Dora must have gone there for a purpose, and whoever she went to see would be the last person she confided in before getting off the bus in Elderberry. Maybe Elaine will be able to come up with a name and address."

"I'm afraid none of us has the time or the money —not to mention the gas coupons—to go all the way to Macon," Dimple said, a bit peeved that Augusta suggested what she herself had in mind.

Augusta twirled her colorful necklace around her fingers. "I believe I know someone there who can help."

Velma avoided a huge puddle in the road as she

spoke. "My goodness, Augusta, you certainly know a lot of people. How did you come to know somebody in Macon?"

"I've been fortunate to meet a lot of people in my line of work, and I think I know just the one. I'll try to get in touch with Grace as soon as I can, as I believe she'll just be bang up to the elephant."

Annie laughed. "She'll be *what?* 'Bang up to the elephant!' What in the world does that mean?"

Augusta smiled. "That's just an old expression I picked up in London years ago. It means perfect, and I think my friend Grace should be exactly what we need."

"This agency you work for certainly covers a large area," Dimple said. "When were you in London, Augusta?"

"Oh, it was many years ago. I once had the good fortune to see the queen on one of her hospital visits to the troops. Always wore black—not a good color for her, I'm afraid."

"The queen?" Velma gasped. "Why, Augusta, Victoria's been dead for years! You're much too young—"

"Oh, Augusta, you're so funny!" Annie said, laughing, "and we can use a little humor on a dreary day like this, but do you really know somebody who might help us in Macon?"

"I'll see what I can do," Augusta said. "Now, where is this tourist home they told us about at the gas station back there? I'm ready to kick off my shoes and relax."

"And after wading through all these puddles, they should be soaking wet," Velma said. Augusta was the only person she knew who wore sandals in October. "We should be there soon. I believe it's in a small place called Willow, a few miles on the other side of town. Maybe that's the sign now. . . . Dimple, can you read it?"

But Dimple Kilpatrick had already gone back to Willow, Tennessee. It was August 1898, and she was nineteen.

Chapter Twenty-four

Upstairs in her room, Lily curled in the chair, afraid to move, as if the chair itself could protect her from whatever was going on below. Had she left a glass too near the edge of the sink? But, no, she had washed the handful of dishes she'd used at supper, dried them, and put them away. There had been no glass on the sink, no cup, no plate, and whatever had been broken was larger than that, much larger. Like the glass from a window.

Still, she froze, clutching the arms of the chair. She could call for help, but the telephone was downstairs in the front hallway. If only she could lock the door to her room!

Putting the scandalous novel aside (in the first

two pages, she was yet to be shocked), Lily turned off the lamp by her chair, but another burned in the window. Surely the intruder would notice the light and realize he was not alone. Terrified that whoever was below could hear her every breath, every footstep, she crept across the room and switched off the other lamp. Now the room was in darkness.

What would she do if he came upstairs? She had no weapon or any other means of defense, and there was no telling what ghastly things he might do. She was certain it was a man. Why, whoever heard of a female burglar? Oh, why had she insisted that Phoebe go to that wedding? Whoever was down there probably thought the house was empty, and she would be at his mercy.

Feeling her way in the darkness, she stumbled over a basket of magazines beside Velma's bed but regained her balance before she fell. Did he hear? Was he on his way upstairs? Shedding her slippers, Lily felt the edge of the rug beneath her bare feet and felt her way around the wall until she came to the door—the unlocked door. There was nothing here heavy enough to block the way. Besides, he would hear her dragging furniture about. There had to be something she could do.

Her heart was beating so fast and so loudly, she was sure he would be able to hear it. Why, Emma Elrod next door could hear it! What was it Augusta had said to do in moments of frenzy when it was necessary for one to react in a calm manner? *Think blue, of course!*

Lily Moss took a deep breath, closed her eyes, and thought *blue,* but instead of becoming calm, she became angry—no, not angry, *incensed.* The very idea for this intruder, this criminal, to break into this house that had become a home to all who lived here, a home filled with respect, and, yes, even love for one another, and it was up to her to stop him.

And now he was clomping up the stairs, not even bothering to tiptoe, as if he thought the house was his to explore. Well, he had another think coming.

Moving quickly but quietly, Lily grabbed an empty soft-drink bottle—Orange Crush, if she remembered correctly—from the desk she and Velma shared, and snatching a coverlet from her bed, inched into the dark hallway and waited. The pale glow from the streetlamp gave just enough light through the fanlight over the front door for her to make out the shape of a shadowy figure halfway up the stairs. And statuelike, she waited. And waited until the intruder was almost opposite and a few inches below her, and then with a shriek, she landed a blow with the empty bottle to the person's head.

The burglar's howls blended with her own, until it became impossible to tell whose was whose, and dropping the bottle, Lily shook out the coverlet and threw it over his head.

Hollering, he half-rolled, half-stumbled until he reached the hall below and bounded out the door. And Lily, gripping the banisters, yelled a word she wasn't even aware she knew, and then she cried.

"Looks like whoever it was is long gone," Bobby Tinsley said after searching the house and surrounding area, "but if you hit him as hard as you say, all we have to do is look for somebody with a big knot on his head." He knew he shouldn't smile, but the very thought of timid Lily Moss lurking in the hallway to attack a burglar was as rewarding as a big piece of sweet potato pie. Warren Nelson had found Lily's coverlet draped over a leafless forsythia bush on the front lawn, and the two of them had checked for footprints under the kitchen window, but the ground was hard and covered in leaves. They did dust for fingerprints and took pictures of the broken window before boarding it up temporarily.

Lily had brought out the broom and dustpan, intending to dispose of the shattered glass, but Sergeant Nelson immediately took them from her.

"My goodness, I can help," she announced in a voice that still sounded frail, but he would have none of it.

"Heroes shouldn't have to sweep, and tonight, Miss Lily Moss, you are one brave hero." And she didn't even correct him to say that in her case she'd be a *heroine.*

"I wonder if this has anything to do with what happened to little Willie Elrod yesterday afternoon," Warren said as the three sat in the parlor, where Lily had insisted on serving tea.

Lily quickly set aside her cup. "My goodness! What happened to Willie?"

Bobby told her about the bicycle accident, except, he explained, it wasn't any accident. "And he got a pretty bad lump on his head, too. His mother called Doc Morrison just in case, and she's keeping an eye on him, but they think he'll be just fine."

"Why would anybody do such a thing?" she asked.

"Willie blames it on a boy in his class. Seems they recently had a difference of opinion," Warren said, "but of course the boy denies it, and we have no way to prove he's not telling the truth."

When Phoebe arrived a short time later, she was surprised to find two members of the local police department being entertained in her parlor by none other than Lily Moss, and she was even more surprised to hear how Lily had sent a would-be burglar running.

"We've checked to see if anything's missing, and Miss Lily here seems to think nothing was taken," Bobby told her, "but you might want to look around just to be sure."

"Silver's all here, and I can't think of anything else valuable enough to steal," Phoebe told them later. "I don't like this at all, Bobby. What do you suppose he was looking for? I've lived in this house more years than I care to admit, and this is the first time anything like this has happened. Thank goodness you weren't hurt, Lily! But what if this person decides to come back?"

"He'll be afraid to if he knows what's good for him," Bobby said, smiling, and then he grew serious. "I don't know what's going on, but we'll be checking around here on a regular basis, and if you have even the slightest sense that something's not right, promise you'll call me right away." Yawning, Lily agreed.

At the Methodist church on Sunday, just about everyone in her Sunday school class had heard of Lily's remarkable bravery, and although she put on a modest face, Lily had to admit to herself she enjoyed the rare attention.

"I suppose you've all heard what happened to Willie Elrod." Geneva Odom, who had taught Willie in the second grade, told them what had taken place. "Thank goodness the little rascal's going to be all right," she added, remembering how she had wanted to wring his neck one minute and hug it the next when Willie had been in her class.

"Well, that's just plain mean," someone else said. "Why would anybody do that? Willie wouldn't have any money or anything else to steal."

"Sounds like it was all because of a quarrel with another boy, but of course they aren't sure," Geneva said. "And his mother told me he was worried that he'd lost his library book. Emma couldn't find it when she went back to look for it, but Marjorie Mote discovered it the next morning underneath that big boxwood at the edge of her walk.

"Willie was really upset about it, Emma said. He had to get on a waiting list to read it."

The police had lifted fingerprints from the outside and immediate inside of the kitchen window where the intruder had entered, and had also taken prints from Lily and Phoebe. It would have been almost impossible, they said, to distinguish between the jumble of prints left by everyone who lived there, as well as the ones belonging to Odessa.

Halloween was only two days away and the two women spent the afternoon decorating the house with festive yellow candles and vases of chrysanthemums in autumn colors. The year before, someone had purchased from the dime store a papier-mâché jack-o'-lantern, which Phoebe centered on the parlor mantel, and on the porch a fat orange pumpkin waited for Augusta to carve.

Lily felt lonely without the others and wished they would hurry and return, but she didn't want to hurt Phoebe's feelings by mentioning it. Well, it wouldn't be long, she thought. If all went as planned, their friends were due to get home sometime that night, as they were expected at school the next day.

Earlier, Chief Tinsley had dropped by to tell them they hadn't found a match for the prints lifted from the window. "But that doesn't mean we won't," he added. "There's still a chance they might turn up somewhere down the road."

"Speaking of 'down the road,' " Phoebe said after he left, "I wonder where Dimple and the others are now. If they left there early this morning, they should be well into Georgia by this time, don't you think?"

And Lily agreed that they should.

An hour or so later, when the travelers had still not returned, the two wondered again. They had eaten a light supper, washed the dishes, and turned on the radio to listen to the *Jack Benny Show*. Both admitted they would miss Dennis Day, the sweet Irish tenor, who was joining the navy, but looked forward to the hilarious comments of Jack's butler, Rochester, and the "tightwad" jokes from Jack himself. The show, they noticed, was now being sponsored by Lucky Strike cigarettes, whose acronym, LSMFT meant "Lucky Strike means fine tobacco." Earlier in the war, the packaging had been changed to red instead of the original green, as an ingredient in the green coloring was needed in the war effort. The company took advantage of the change to advertise: "Lucky Strike has gone to war," and many Americans took exception to that.

"They really should be here by now," Lily said at the end of the show. "I hope they haven't had an accident or something."

"I suppose they stopped somewhere for supper," Phoebe said, and going to the window, searched for approaching headlights. She didn't want to alarm Lily, but she was worried, too. "I'm sure they'll be home by ten," she said in an effort to calm herself as well as Lily.

But the four did not return by ten, nor did they by eleven.

Chapter Twenty-five

"You'll be living with the Applewhites," they told her. A farm family, they said. Well, that was all right with Dimple Kilpatrick. She had been raised on a farm and lived there for most of her life, except for the time away at college to earn her teaching certificate.

As long as Dimple could remember, she had wanted to teach, and here she was at nineteen, certified at last to begin teaching in her first school. But *Tennessee?* Dimple had never lived that far from home and was yet to set foot in any state but the one she'd been raised in. And what about Henry? Her younger brother had been eight and she fourteen when their mother died, and he was still attending the same small school where Dimple had received her diploma a few years earlier. Her papa hired someone to cook and clean, but Dimple had been responsible for her brother for almost half his life. Who would see that he did his homework and went to bed on time? Who would make sure he had clean clothes to wear? She had always known Henry was bright, and hoped he would someday be able to fulfill his ambition to attend college at Georgia Tech, in Atlanta. Their papa loved them, of course, but he worked hard all day and was too tired at night to do more than eat supper and go to sleep in his chair.

Dimple had hoped to find a school closer to home, but teaching positions were scarce in their area, and because of a drought, her father's crops had been disappointing that year. He had assured them they weren't in danger of losing the farm, but Dimple was aware she needed the income to help out.

A few weeks before she graduated, one of her professors told her of a teaching position near her hometown in Tennessee, and with her recommendation and Dimple's outstanding record in college, she soon received a letter of acceptance from the school board there.

The Applewhites raised dairy cattle in the small community of Willow, she was told. And that was all she was told.

This is not the same as leaving for college, Dimple thought as she and her papa began the long buggy ride to Atlanta. *This is forever.* In Atlanta, she would board the Louisville and Nashville train to Lewisburg, Tennessee, and there would be met by her hosts for the coming year.

What if they didn't like her? What if she didn't like them? A portion of her small salary would go to the Applewhites for her room and board, and she couldn't help worrying about the "board" part. Dimple was accustomed to hard work and sacrifices, but she appreciated a well-cooked meal. What if her hostess was an indifferent cook, or, worse, a bad one?

For heaven's sake, what a silly thing to worry about, she told herself. Just eat what you're given and be glad of it, as she and her fellow students had been reminded in college where the fare was often less than desirable.

"Now, you take care of yourself, little girl," her papa said as she boarded the train, and she had held on to him until the conductor yelled "All aboard!"

Papa hadn't called her "little girl" since . . . well, since she was one, and she felt a terrible emptiness as she watched him disappear from sight.

Neighbors had packed her a box lunch of tiny

ham biscuits, deviled eggs, a small jar of fresh peach slices, and a generous wedge of chocolate cake. She thought of them fondly as she ate and wondered if Papa would reach home before dark, and if Henry would remember to write. Dimple watched the rolling hills of home turn into higher ones, and then to mountains as the train took her far from the people she loved best, and she allowed herself a few tears—but only a few—before settling down to begin a new book, *The Mystery of Mr. Bernard Brown*, a gift from her college roommate. Saving the cake for last, Dimple finished it as the train chugged its way into Tennessee, and wondered if it would be the last piece of cake she would have for a long time.

Dimple sat up with a jolt when the conductor called out the next station as Lewisburg. Why, it was almost dark outside! How could she have gone to sleep at a time like this? She smoothed the wrinkles from her gored skirt (navy, so it wouldn't show dirt), straightened the collar of her new white blouse with its tiny bit of lace at the throat, and checked to see if her hair was in place. Dimple had thick chestnut hair with a slight wave and wore it in a bun on top of her head, but strands were always coming loose and falling about her face. She wore her mother's watch pinned to the short piqué jacket that matched her skirt, and now saw that it was after seven o'clock.

Before stepping from the train, she set her small

straw hat in place with a hat pin and pinched her cheeks as her mother used to do, "just to give them a little color," she'd said; gathered her valise and a small purse and stepped down into Lewisburg, Tennessee.

The man who greeted her at the depot was the tallest man she had ever seen, and Dimple found herself looking up—up—up and wondering if she'd ever reach the top. He introduced himself as McKinney Applewhite but added that everyone called him Mac and he hoped she'd do the same. He had warm brown eyes, a mustache like her papa's shaving brush, and wore overalls that still smelled of wash day.

"Sadie's home keeping supper warm," he told her as he hoisted her luggage into the back of his buggy. "Thought you might be hungry after this long trip. Hope you like fried chicken and sweet potato pie."

And Dimple thanked him and smiled. Maybe she wouldn't go hungry here after all.

The Applewhites lived several miles out of town on a large farm they called Willowvale, Dimple was told, named after the nearby village and the graceful trees found along the wiggling water-ways that meandered through the land.

"I understand you raise dairy cattle," Dimple said as the two of them jounced along.

And that was just about the last thing she had a chance to say, as her host began praising the advantages of the Jersey cow and all its glorious attributes. "Best cow God ever made," he said. "Gentle, too, and wait till you taste that milk!

"Now, Glory, she'll follow you around just like a dog," he continued. "I reckon we've had her the longest." He laughed. "And Matilda—well, she likes her head scratched."

"Do you name all your cattle?" Dimple asked.

"Well now, don't reckon we'd be able to do that, but they're a good sort, every one of them."

For the better part of an hour, he talked of the land where he had been raised, as had his father before him. He told her of the big red oaks that shaded the yard, of the vegetable garden behind the house, and the black-and-white sheepdog, Ernie, who herded the cattle and slept near the kitchen stove on winter nights. He spoke of the delights of a watermelon keeping cold in the creek at the end of a hot summer day, and the sleepy sound July flies made at twilight. Dimple tried her best to see beyond the yellow glow of the carriage lamps, hoping to glimpse the welcoming light of the place she was soon to call home, but they were surrounded in darkness.

"Step it up, Polly!" Mac said at last, giving the reins a shake, and the horse slowly picked up her pace, until all at once she began to put on speed.

"Knows she's nearing home," Mac said. "Wouldn't be surprised if she could get here blindfolded."

Dimple thought she might as well be blind-folded for the little she could see ahead of them until, reaching the top of a hill, she saw a tiny light ahead, and it seemed to be moving back and forth.

"That's my nephew, Ned," Mac explained, "waving that lantern at the gate like, after all these years, Polly and I wouldn't know where to turn in!

"His papa, my brother Edward, farmed here with me until he died a couple of years ago, and now Ned's stepped into his shoes. He and Ellie—that's his mama—and his sister, Kathleen, live just over the hill there. I expect you'll be seeing them tomorrow."

Dimple covered a yawn and hoped she wouldn't be meeting anyone tonight, except for her hostess, Sadie, of course. It seemed like a hundred years since she'd left Papa and home, and all she wanted to do was crawl into a comfortable bed and close her eyes.

Sadie Applewhite greeted her on the wide front porch of the farmhouse and, ignoring Dimple's outstretched hand, pulled her into her arms in a warm embrace. She was what Dimple's papa would call "comfortably plump," and was probably a foot shorter than her husband. She wore a large white apron over a dress in a colorful patchwork print, and as soon as she had welcomed Dimple, kissed her husband *right on the mouth.* Dimple had never witnessed an older couple behaving in such a manner, and modestly looked away.

"I know you must be about ready to drop after all that long trip," Sadie said as she ushered Dimple into the house. "I'll show you to your room and give you a chance to freshen up, and afterward I've saved you a little bite to eat before you go to bed."

Upstairs, Dimple found a lovely cherry spool bed made up with plump pillows and a light bedspread. A delicate watercolor of a vase of roses hung over the mantel, and an oil lamp burned on a small table beside the bed. When left alone, Dimple would have liked nothing better than to fall on that bed, clothing and all, and sleep. But, removing her hat, she took time to wash her face and hands in the washbowl provided and tried her best to control her unruly hair.

The room was fairly large, with sheer white curtains at the windows and a faded rug in a floral design in the center of the floor. A small rocking chair waited beside the fireplace, empty now, and a table at the window might serve as a desk.

Dimple frowned as she looked at her wrinkled skirt, the blouse, no longer white, as she'd dribbled peach juice down the front. Well, it was too late to change or to search through her luggage for something else to wear. Maybe nobody would notice if she stayed in the shadows.

After all, her gracious hosts were the only ones here, and she hoped they were too polite to stare.

But who should be lingering in the wide front hall other than the Applewhites' nephew Ned. He was not as tall as his uncle, but looked to be a little over six feet. Clean-shaven, he wore his light brown hair parted in the middle, or Dimple supposed it should be that way, but it seemed to have a mind of its own, as if it couldn't decide where to go.

"As weary as I am, my heartless uncle insisted that I stay," he told her.

Mac Applewhite laughed. "Pay no attention to that rogue, Miss Dimple. He took one look at you and I couldn't pry him out of here with a crowbar."

But Dimple Kilpatrick hadn't heard a word they said. She could only see the easy way Ned stood as if he were ready for whatever life had in store. She saw the way his hair fell over his forehead. And there was something about the expression in his eyes that made her want to smile. Were they blue or gray? At the last minute, she remembered the peach stains on her blouse, but it was too late to do anything about it.

"Enough of this," Sadie announced, setting serving platters on the table. "This young lady is tired, and I imagine she's hungry. If I remember right, Ned Applewhite, you had your supper earlier, so go on home now and leave our guest in peace. You'll have a chance to visit with Miss Dimple in the morning."

And suddenly, Dimple wasn't tired anymore. She ate her "little bite" of supper, consisting of fried chicken, creamed potatoes, and sliced tomatoes, and even found room for sweet potato pie, and then, thanking her hostess, hurried off to bed.

She wondered what the morning would bring.

Chapter Twenty-six

"Dimple, wake up. We're almost there." Velma rolled down her window to signal a right turn and the icy air brought Dimple back to the present with a cruel awareness. "Here we are—Applewhite Road," Velma continued cheerfully. "House shouldn't be too far now. I believe she said it's the fourth one on the left."

Applewhite Road. Could it possibly be . . . Dimple unclenched her hands and began to breathe easier when they turned into the drive of a two-story brick house that sat a few yards from the road. In the dusk, she was able to make out a large cedar by the corner of the house and another on the other side of the drive. The meadows around Willowvale Farm had been dotted with cedars, and a lazy creek provided water for thirsty cattle. Often she and Ned, sometimes joined by his younger sister, Kathleen, had circled the property on horseback, taking their time on sweet autumn afternoons; picking wildflowers in the field; resting under the big sycamore by the bridge.

On warm fall days when they thought no one was looking, she and Kathleen held their skirts up high and waded in the creek, splashing water on each other until both were soaking wet. Cool nights when Ned was busy with outside farm-work, the two women popped corn and Kathleen taught her to make molasses taffy. After that, Dimple never saw a piece of the candy or smelled the syrup cooking that she didn't think of Kathleen.

Where was the bridge? Had they passed it? And who had divided this beautiful farmland into residential lots? The house was not new, she observed. It had probably been built sometime in the thirties, when the country was dealing with the Great Depression. Had Mac Applewhite, an old man by then, been forced to sell the land he loved so much? What about Kathleen, who at sixteen had spent her last year at the tiny school in Willow before going off to college? Sadie Applewhite had been like a second mother to Dimple—where would they go? What would they do?

The Applewhites had two daughters, Dimple remembered. Annette had been married to a physician and lived somewhere in Kentucky;

Aggie, the younger sister, was a talented artist who taught in a small college at the other end of the state. Her watercolors varied from landscapes and flowers to quaint vignettes of farm children and had been featured prominently in almost every room of the house. She must remember to ask about the family as soon as they were settled, Dimple decided.

It soon became obvious that their hostess, Fannie Templeton, had several sons in the military, as their photographs in uniform lined the mantel in the living room. At first, the women listened with interest while she described in great detail the fine qualities of each, until it seemed she planned to elaborate all the way back to their births. When she finally paused for a necessary breath, Dimple immediately jumped in to ask about the Applewhites.

"Well, I didn't know them, of course, but from all I've heard, they were well thought of in the community," Fannie told her. "In fact, we bought this lot from their daughter Annette. She still lives somewhere in Kentucky, I believe."

The younger daughter, Dimple learned, had been killed a few years before in an automobile accident.

Sadie had sent her a copy of the obituary when Ned's mother died, but she wondered what had happened to Kathleen, who had been so vivacious and full of fun in and out of the classroom and had insisted on calling her "Joy" because she claimed it suited her better than Dimple. From all reports, her brother's death had left her shattered. Dimple had felt deeply for the family and kept in touch for many years after she left, until the letters stopped coming.

"Annette's father died a good while ago," Fannie continued, speaking of Mac, "and I believe her mother was living with her in Kentucky when we bought the lot for this house." She smiled. "A few here still remember the Applewhites and speak well of them, and I believe Annette had an aunt who owned property on the other side of the creek. I suppose you were acquainted with the family?"

Aunt Mattie, Mac Applewhite's sister. Dimple remembered going with Ned to a barn dance with her daughter Amelia and her new husband. She'd heard later that several of Amelia's pregnancies had ended in miscarriages.

"Yes." Dimple gripped the handle of her small overnight bag until her fingers became numb. "Not only were they fine people; they were excellent guardians of the land." Long-suppressed emotions swelled inside her. *How long must she stand here and appear to be composed?*

Their hostess turned again to the display on her mantel. "Now, you won't believe what our David did when he was five," she began. And that's when Augusta started to cough.

"I wonder if I could [cough, cough] trouble you for [cough] a drink of water?" she sputtered. And when Fannie hurried to the kitchen to get her a glass, Dimple escaped to the room she was to share with Augusta.

"I don't know if I should thank you or mix you up some honey and lemon," Dimple said when Augusta joined her.

Augusta laughed. "Neither will be necessary," she said, and went about hanging her wraps in the closet. Dimple had done the same, and now sat by the window, looking out at the dark, rainy night, and for a while, neither spoke.

A lamp burned beside the bed and Augusta took needlework from her bag and pulled up a chair to the light. Her needle wove in and out as the colors took form, until a scattering of violets appeared on the cloth. "What was his name?" she asked, not looking up.

Dimple turned, startled. "What?"

Augusta set her stitching aside and looked at her. "What was his name, the one you loved? I can see this place holds meaning for you."

"Ned. His name was Ned." How long had it been since she had spoken his name aloud, and still she was caressed by the sweetness of the sound. Tears came slowly as she told Augusta of the time she spent on the Applewhites' farm during her first year of teaching at the tiny school in Willow.

She told her how she had lived in the comfortable rambling farmhouse, where Ned's aunt Sadie made her welcome, and how his kind uncle Mac named the cows in his herd. Ned had gone away to college for two years, and when his father died, she said, he had come home to help his uncle on the farm.

"He had planned to major in English and literature," Dimple said. "He loved books, loved to read."

She spoke softly. "I had him for too short a time."

Augusta picked up her stitching. "But you should have no regrets."

Dimple turned to her then, her face dark with sorrow. "Oh, but I do," she said. "I do. I should've married him when he asked. And then it was too late."

She remembered the day Ned asked her to marry him. It was April and the apple trees were in glorious bloom as they strolled beneath them hand in hand. A pale pink petal drifted onto her cheek and Ned brushed it away with a kiss. "You are the apple of my eye . . . my nose, my lips, my ears," he said, kissing each place in turn, and Dimple threw her arms around his neck and laughed. They laughed a lot when they were together. How could she possibly be this happy?

And then he proposed, getting down on one knee in the wet spring grass.

"Oh, Ned, do get up," she pleaded. "You're soiling your clean trousers."

"Not until you agree to marry me," he said. And of course she did.

Later, at twilight, they sat in the porch swing, both reluctant to go inside, although a chill wind had picked up, blowing leaves across the floor. Sadie stepped outside long enough to call to them. "Aren't you two freezing out here?" she asked.

But they only snuggled closer, lulled by the rhythmic squeaking of the swing, and quietly, Ned took Dimple's hand in his and slipped a ring on her finger, an amethyst set in white gold, with a tiny diamond on either side.

"It belonged to my grandmother," Ned told her, "and I hope it will do for now. Later we can look for a diamond."

"But I don't want a diamond. This is perfect, and I never want to replace it. Purple is my favorite color."

Ned laughed. "Really? I'd never guess." He touched the purple grosgrain ribbon at her neck and glanced significantly at the violet-colored skirt she wore. "It suits you, sweetheart. I'll love you in any color, but I'll always think of you in purple."

But their happiness was shadowed by the dark threat of war. Anger against Spain had simmered since the U.S. battleship *Maine* was blown up in

Havana harbor in February, and earlier in the month, when President McKinley asked Congress for authority to send troops to Cuba, most felt war was imminent. As a member of the National Guard, Ned would have to go, and his company had already begun to plan for their departure.

But for the next few days, Dimple allowed herself to bask in her newfound happiness. School would soon let out for the summer, and she busied herself by readying her students for exams and planning an end-of-school program with readings, essays, and songs. Life couldn't have been better if it had been presented to her gift-wrapped and tied with a ribbon—purple, of course.

According to the president, a state of war had existed since the blockade of Cuba began on April 21, but the situation became official four days later, on the twenty-fifth, and the United States went to war with Spain.

She wasn't going to cry. What would Ned think if his intended turned out to be a weak, weeping milksop? No! She would be positive and strong and they would plan a wedding in the fall. Meanwhile, she would continue to teach.

Dimple wrote to Papa and Henry and told them of her good news. She would travel home when Ned left in June and ask their neighbor's assistance in altering her mother's simple wedding gown. Meanwhile, dear Sadie offered to help with her trousseau and had taken what to

Dimple seemed at least a million measurements.

And then on a gentle evening in May, Ned suggested they alter their plans. "Is a big church wedding important to you?" he asked one night after supper. They sat on the back steps with the dog, Ernie, at their feet and Ned stroked him as he spoke.

"Of course not," she told him, "as long as we have our families there, I don't care where we're married."

"Then what about here? What about now?" Ned asked.

"Now?"

"I mean a few days from now, before I leave for Cuba. I'll need time to get the license, of course, and we'll have to be sure your family can get here in time."

Dimple wanted to say yes. She wanted to throw herself into his arms and shout "Yes! Yes! Yes!" But the practical Dimple whispered in her ear.

"But, Ned, I can't teach if we marry now."

He frowned. "Why not?"

"Married women aren't allowed to teach. Just think about it. How many of your teachers were married?"

Ned shook his head. "Well, that's a ridiculous rule, but, sweetheart, it has nothing to do with us. Everybody knows this war won't last long. Why, I shouldn't be away for more than a few months at the most, and you don't teach in the summer anyway. I'll be home by the time school begins."

"But, Ned, what if you aren't? What if the war lasts longer?" Dimple said. "I wouldn't know what to do with myself, and I can set aside what I earn for later, when we set up housekeeping."

Ned stood and pulled her into his arms. "Honey, I don't care about that. I want you now," he said, and kissed her deeply.

With his arms holding her close and his lips warm on her own, Dimple felt they had already become one person. "You know I will always be yours," she said.

But she had never been apart from her brother this long, and for years Henry had been her responsibility. He was fourteen now and had two more years of school ahead of him. If her papa and Henry were in agreement, she planned to ask Ned if her brother could complete his schooling here with her, but of course she would think about that later.

"Oh, Ned, wouldn't it be wonderful to have the wedding right here in the front parlor with all our families together? It's so beautiful here in the fall, and the war will surely be over by then."

The dog frolicked at their feet and Ned stooped to pet him. For a long while, he didn't speak. "Sweetheart," he said finally, "whatever you want will be all right with me, as long as I know I have you to come home to."

And she held him close and assured him that he did.

• • •

Weeks later, Dimple and the Applewhites, with Ned's mother and sister, took the long buggy ride to Lewisburg to see Ned off on the train with his National Guard unit. In a few days, the men would board a ship to assist the Fifth Army Corps in establishing an American base of operations in Cuba.

As Ned kissed her just before boarding the train, he took the purple ribbon from her hair and tucked it inside his jacket. "I'll always think of you in purple," he said as he climbed aboard.

What had she done? "Oh, Ned, I love you so!" Dimple called as he disappeared in a sea of khaki. And feeling a great, painful emptiness, she watched the long train round the bend and wished with all her heart she could run after it and bring him back.

She never saw him again.

Chapter Twenty-seven

Augusta continued to stitch as Dimple told her story, and when Dimple was finished, she tucked it away in her bag and went to sit beside her on a small chest at the foot of the bed. The sadness and regret in Dimple's heart, Augusta experienced in her own, and reaching out, she touched her hand.

"You've carried this burden for too many years. Oh, Dimple, I'm so sorry."

"I do feel lighter somehow for having shared this," Dimple said. "Thank you, Augusta, for listening."

"Well, you know I'm here to help," Augusta said, smiling. "I'm sure your friend Odessa would have done the same."

And Dimple agreed that she would, but she had never had the courage or the justification to share it.

"Why have I never seen you wear the ring?" Augusta asked.

"The ring was for a promise I didn't keep. It's in a box at the bottom of my dresser drawer."

Augusta fingered her necklace and the stones in rose and lavender, burning amber and twilight blue slipped slowly through her fingers. As Dimple watched, she began to sense a calmness akin to peace.

"Your Ned, how did he die?" Augusta asked softly.

"Yellow fever. The terrible virus took many of our young men—too many. He had only been there a little over a month when he came down with the illness. I read about it, Augusta. It was horrible! They began with severe headaches, fever, pain in the arms and legs, and then it progressed to something much worse. When I thought of my Ned suffering so in that place so far from home—his beautiful home—I could hardly bear it.

"They said he called for me in his delirium just before he died, and of course I wasn't there."

Augusta took Dimple's hand in hers and there was comfort in her touch. "And don't you think that during his rational hours, Ned would've been at peace to know you were safe and well hundreds of miles away?

"Too, if you had married him, Dimple, you might have been left with a child, and that would've concerned him, as well."

Dimple smiled. "Oh, I wish I had. Do you think I haven't felt that loss? I've often wondered about our might-have-been children. Would they have Ned's gray eyes and unruly mop of hair? Would they enjoy reading the classics and refuse to eat tomatoes?"

"Or perhaps they would prefer the peace of early-morning walks, the excitement of a good mystery book, and the knowledge that they have helped to form more young lives than they can possibly count," Augusta said. "You have hundreds of children, Dimple Kilpatrick, there is no way to measure your value to your town and your friends, and you have been loyal to your Ned for all these many years. Don't you think he knows that?"

Dimple nodded. "Yes, I believe he does."

"Then never forget you have loved and been

loved, and for heaven's sake, go home and put that lovely ring on your finger, where it belongs!"

And Dimple smiled and promised that she would. "But first," she added, "I think we need to try to find out who is responsible for Dora Westbrook's death."

We should get an early start in the morning, Dimple thought as she lay in bed that night. They hoped to visit Elaine before the long drive back to Elderberry, and they had to be at school on Monday. Augusta had fallen asleep immediately, and Dimple listened to her companion's peaceful deep-sleep breathing and wished she could do the same. Flipping her pillow to the cool side, she thought of all the events of the day and wondered if she would ever go to sleep. And then she closed her eyes.

"Wake up, you sleepyheads! We have to call on Dora's sister before we get on the road for home," Velma called, knocking on their bedroom door.

Dimple sat up and looked around. She couldn't believe she had slept the entire night without waking. "Coming," she said, fumbling for her robe. Augusta, already dressed, sat by the window, plaiting her long hair into one braid that trailed over her shoulder. "Good morning," she said.

"My goodness, Augusta, why did you let me sleep so late? We should've been on our way by now."

"It's not even eight o'clock," Augusta told her.

247

"It's too early to go calling just yet. Besides, you needed the rest."

"I think you're right about that," Dimple said. "I don't know when I've slept so well. I don't believe I moved all night."

"Sleep knits up the raveled sleeve of care, the poet says. I think you were long overdue."

Dimple touched her toes and stretched. "It's a brand-new day, Augusta. I wish I had time for a walk."

Augusta glanced out the window, where rain came down in a curtain of gray. "Then I hope you know how to swim," she said.

"Shouldn't we telephone before we show up at the door?" Annie asked as water sprayed from both sides as they looked for Elaine Arnold's address. Outside the small car, the world was awash with rain, making it difficult to see street signs and house numbers.

"You're right. That would be the proper thing to do," Velma said, frowning as she tried to see the road ahead, "but Chief Tinsley didn't think to give us the phone number."

"And we didn't think to ask," Dimple reminded her.

"Well then, we'll be a surprise," Augusta piped up from the backseat. "I should think Dora's sister would welcome a chance to find out more about the circumstances of her death."

Miss Dimple adjusted her bifocals in an effort to see through the rain. "I can't imagine why she wouldn't," she said, "and I've made a list of questions I want to ask her when we get there."

"But what will we do if she's not at home?" Annie asked.

"In that case, I suppose we'll wait," Velma told her, slowing as she came to an intersection. "I believe this might be the street. . . . Dimple, can you make out that sign?"

"Yes! Duncan's Ferry Road. Turn right here, Velma. It shouldn't be far now."

A sycamore tree, still holding on to a few brown leaves, stood in front of the small brick house. A bicycle waited on the porch, and a jack-o'-lantern grinned from the front steps.

"They must have children," Velma said as they pulled into the driveway. "This could be difficult. . . . I suppose I never thought . . ."

"We'll worry about that later." Dimple stepped in ankle-deep water and popped open her lavender umbrella as she got out of the car. "Right now, I suggest we make a dash for the porch."

Elaine Arnold must have been watching, because she met them at the door and immediately ushered them inside, where a wood fire burned on the hearth and a large calico cat slept on one end of a faded slipcovered sofa.

"You must be drenched. Slip out of those wet shoes and we'll put them by the fire, and I imagine you'd like something hot to drink. I've Russian tea keeping warm on the stove."

From what Dimple had learned, Dora and her sister were close in age, but there the similarity ended. Where Dora had been awkward and shy, with dull brown hair, her sister was warm and welcoming. Small and slightly plump, she wore her hair in a pompadour, with the sides rolled back and pinned in a style that had become popular during the war years.

Her friendly smile, however, didn't mask the sadness in her eyes. "Please sit down," she said, shooing the cat off the sofa.

"You have children?" Dimple spoke softly, and Elaine nodded, smiling. "Cindy spent the night with a friend, and Eddie's youth group's responsible for decorating the church fellowship hall for a Halloween party, so he won't be home for a while.

"Both are aware of my sister's death, but we haven't discussed the details with them. Frankly, I have a lot of questions about what happened and why."

"And so do we," Dimple told her, "and we're hoping that with your help, we might be able to come up with some answers."

Over tea and gingersnaps, Elaine told them of Carolyn Freeman, her sister's college friend from Macon. "It took some searching, but I finally found a snapshot of the two in an old Christmas card. Our parents died when my sister and I were young, and Dora and I were raised by our grandmother. We were still living with her then, and Carolyn had sent it to that address. Our grandmother even kept the envelope, as she probably wanted to save the address for the next Christmas, but she died a few months after that. I've always wondered if Dora would've married Leonard Westbrook if she had lived."

Miss Dimple examined the envelope. "Have you tried to get in touch?"

"I wrote, but it came back," Elaine told them. "For all I know, Carolyn married and moved away."

"So who do you think Dora went to see in Macon?" Velma asked.

Elaine shook her head. "I can't imagine. I believe Carolyn was her closest friend at Wesleyan, and I wouldn't be surprised if they kept in touch, but except for Carolyn, I don't know why she would make it a point to stop there."

Augusta ran fingers through damp hair that curled about her face. "In Macon, she bought a bus ticket for Elderberry, but no one there seems to know her or understand why she came," she said. "It would appear more likely for her to have come here to you. From what the police found out, she had enough money with her to have purchased a fare all the way to Lewisburg."

"If she was planning to come here, she didn't let me know," Elaine said. "She and Leonard were to come for Christmas—or at least Dora was. She wasn't sure if Leonard would go off and leave his mother."

Annie made a face. "I've heard about his mother."

"Lucille." Elaine groaned. "Frightening woman."

"Do you think she might've had something to do with what happened to Dora?" Velma asked.

"It wouldn't surprise me, but I can't imagine why, unless she just wanted her out of the house," Elaine said, "but that seems pretty drastic, even for her."

"Some friends of ours recently made a trip to Fieldcroft to talk with people who might have known Dora," Dimple told her, "and it has come to light that Dora had been in communication with someone from South Carolina—Columbia, I believe. Do you have any idea what that was about?"

"Columbia?" Elaine frowned. "She didn't mention it to me, and I can't imagine who it might be. Your friends," she added, "did they have a chance to speak with Leonard while they were there?"

"They didn't see Leonard," Annie told her, "but they did speak briefly with his mother, and she accused Dora of being a thief. Do you have any idea why she might've said that?"

"*A thief?* Why, my sister was as honest as the day is long! And what on earth would she steal? I can't imagine why Lucille would say such a thing." Elaine closed her eyes and shuddered. "That woman has done her best to make life miserable for my sister!

"This has all been a nightmare for me. Dora was my only sibling, and even though I didn't see her often, life won't ever be the same without her."

Dimple took her hand. "I'm so sorry, and we'll do our best to find out who's responsible." She couldn't imagine how she would feel if she lost Henry. She had received a brief note from him a day or so before and made up her mind to write him as soon as she had a chance.

It was obvious Elaine was making an effort to fight back tears. "Do the police in Elderberry have any idea who might've done this to Dora?" she asked.

As far as Dimple knew, they didn't, but she wasn't going to admit that to Dora's grieving sister. "They're doing their best to find out," she told her, "and I promise we'll keep you informed."

They were preparing to leave, when Dimple noticed the two photographs on the small end table beside the sofa, and for a few seconds she found it difficult to breathe. Others were talking, making polite conversation as they gathered shoes and wraps, but they might as well have been in another world as Dimple reached hesitantly for the black-and-white photo of a young man in his teens. *How could this be?* Her legs gave way beneath her, and clutching the arm of the sofa, Dimple fell back against the cushions, the framed picture still in one hand.

"Your shoes are almost dry, Dimple," Velma said, then, noticing her friend's demeanor, went to her side. "Dimple, what is it? Are you all right?"

Concerned, the others gathered around as Dimple's face seemed to crumple right in front of them, and Annie, thinking the older teacher might be suffering some kind of attack, dropped to her knees beside her. "Something's not right," she said with a sob in her throat. "I think we should call a doctor."

But Dimple held up a hand. "No. Please, no. I'm all right, just a bit shaken." She held the photograph in front of her and with one finger traced the image of the boy's face. "This young man . . . is this . . . is this your son?" she asked Elaine.

Puzzled, and a bit alarmed, Elaine sat beside her. "Why, yes. That's our Edward, but we call him Eddie. He's named for a great-uncle of mine, who, I understand, was our grandmother Mattie's only nephew."

Relinquishing the photograph at last, Dimple shook her head. "I didn't mean to give you such a turn, but your Edward is the image of someone I knew long ago. His name was Edward, too, but everyone called him Ned."

Ned! Could it possibly be the same? "When did you know him, Miss Dimple?" Elaine struggled to speak calmly.

Dimple sighed. "Years ago. He's been gone so many years now. Too many. Ned never lived to see the turn of the century. He died during the Spanish American War—died on foreign soil."

Crying silently now, Elaine took Dimple's hand. "Of yellow fever. I know. I never knew him, of course, but our grandmother spoke of Ned often, and our cousin Kathleen, as well. She showed me his picture once, and you're right, there's a strong resemblance to our Edward.

"And . . . oh, my goodness . . . you're *Joy*, the one he loved. The one he left behind."

Dimple fumbled for her handkerchief, and minutes passed before she was able to speak. "No one's called me that since I left here that last summer. Ned's sister, Kathleen, named me that—said I looked like a Joy to her, and she never called me anything else. I taught at the little school here, lived with your great-uncle and -aunt. It was the happiest year of my life—well, until Ned was taken from us, and I remember your grandmother Mattie. She always seemed to find pleasure in everyday living, as many of the Applewhites did."

Dimple frowned, remembering. "And you must be Amelia's daughter."

"That's right. Our mother was always frail, and she died much too soon. Our grandmother gave us a good home, though, and we never lacked for love." Elaine smiled. "I remember family gatherings at Willowvale with Uncle Mac and Aunt Sadie—and Kathleen, too, of course. She was teaching then, but always joined us in the summers."

Kathleen. Dimple remembered the pretty young girl who loved to have fun and took delight in helping in the classroom. "And Kathleen," she began, "is she—"

"Still teaching, and she'll be excited to hear about you. You're the reason she went into teaching, you know, but I never knew your real name. She always referred to you as Joy, and I don't suppose you knew this, but she named her daughter after you."

"Dimple?" Annie asked.

"Why, no, she named her Joy." She went on to explain that Kathleen and her husband also had a son and were the grandparents of three.

"Oh, how I would love to see her!" Dimple said, slipping at last into warm, dry shoes. She had kept in touch with the family for years but Kathleen moved several times during that period, and Dimple lost track of her address.

"I blame myself for not trying harder to locate Kathleen," Dimple admitted, "but I couldn't bear the thought of reopening old wounds. She was my closest link to Ned, you see, and I thought I could bury my grief. I was wrong."

"I believe Kathleen and her husband plan to come here for Thanksgiving," Elaine whispered to Dimple as she left. "How do you feel about surprises?"

Chapter Twenty-eight

As it was too late to stop in town for breakfast, Elaine had recommended a small restaurant between Shelbyville and Lynchburg that served excellent waffles and pancakes. "It's called Bertie's," she told them, "and it's on a side road only a few miles on the other side of Shelbyville. I promise it will be well worth the detour," she said, "and it's about the same distance to Lynchburg, so you shouldn't lose any time."

Everyone had agreed that they preferred to get on the road and put some miles behind them before stopping, and they would all be ready for Bertie's when it was time to stop.

The rain had slacked by the time they drove through the outskirts of Lewisburg. Dimple took charge of the map and felt encouraged when they reached Shelbyville sooner than expected. A short time later, they turned off on the detour route Elaine had told them about, which would take them to the restaurant and then on to connect with the main road to Lynchburg.

"Finally! I thought we'd never get here," Annie said as they pulled into Bertie's parking lot.

"The first thing I want is a cup of coffee," Augusta said.

"Make that two cups," Velma suggested, and once inside and seated, they found the food as good as they had expected.

It would have been pleasant to linger over a second cup of coffee, but no one wanted to be on the road after dark. The rain held off briefly as they got on their way, but the sky opened up a few miles down the road and Velma slowed to be able to see where she was going. "It can't be much farther to Lynchburg," she said. "Please, Dimple, tell me we're almost there."

Dimple frowned over the map. She had no idea how far they had come. "I'm sure we'll be there soon," she assured her, hoping she was right.

The old Ford sloshed along over water-filled potholes, and everyone sat on edge when a tire hit a large rock in the road.

"Uh-oh! All we need now is a flat tire," Annie said.

"Don't say that. We need to think positive," Augusta told her. "We aren't going to have a flat tire. We just aren't."

But they did.

Here they were in the pouring rain, out in the middle of nowhere. Velma began to wish she had never agreed to this trip, but it was too late for regrets. "It looks like I have no other choice but to change that tire in this rain," she said. "The old thing is held together with patches. Let's hope the spare's in better shape."

"I think I see a shed of some kind just up ahead." Augusta pointed it out. "At least we can get the car off the road and out of the rain." And after thinking about it for a minute, Velma decided the tire probably wouldn't suffer much more damage than it already had.

"I suppose it's worth a try," she said. "We have to do something soon."

Fortunately, the shed, which seemed to have once been used as a blacksmith shop, was close to the road and there was just enough room inside for the four of them to stand beside the car. Spiderwebs shrouded the few rusty farm implements on the walls, and water from a leak in the roof formed a puddle on the floor.

Annie watched Velma wrestle to jack up the car. "Let me change that tire, Miss Velma. You must be worn out from driving, and I used to watch my brother. I think I can remember how."

"Very well." Velma seemed relieved. "The spare is mounted on the rear. You'll need a hand to get it out."

"And that hand will be mine." Augusta stepped

up. "I don't know how to change a tire, but I can learn."

"First we have to get this one off," Annie said, welcoming the help. She knelt beside the deflated tire and took a deep breath. The old place smelled of earth and mildew and . . . something else—rats? But she wouldn't think of that.

"What will we do if this one's flat, too?" Annie asked as the two worked together to remove the tire.

"But it won't be," Augusta said. "Remember, think pos—"

"And if I remember correctly, that didn't work the last time," Velma reminded her. "Let's just hope we don't have to spend the night in this shed."

Finally, the two managed to get the spare tire in place, and although it wasn't completely flat, it definitely needed air. "We'll just have to hope we can make it to Lynchburg," Velma said as they were once more on the road. "I've a feeling we're not too far away."

"The sky seems to be clearing up again," Dimple said. "Surely nothing else can happen."

But of course it did.

Velma threw on the brakes as soon as she saw it. They had rounded a blind curve, only to be confronted with a large pool of water stretching all the way across the road. "Do we dare try to cross it?" Annie asked.

"No!" The others spoke in unison. "There's

probably a dip in the road there," Velma explained. "We have no idea how deep it is."

Annie frowned. "So what do we do now?"

"We back up and find a place to turn around, and hope we can get back to Shelbyville," Velma told her.

It was then that Augusta noticed Annie's hand was bleeding. "What happened to your hand, Annie? It seems to be bleeding quite a bit. Here, let's use my scarf and see if we can stop it."

"Better still, use this." Miss Dimple offered her ever-present handkerchief. "I always try to keep a clean one in reserve."

But even with applied pressure, the wound continued to bleed. "I must have cut it changing the tire," Annie said. "It doesn't seem to be deep."

By this time, Dimple's handkerchief was useless, and Augusta removed the scarf from her hair. "It's not white, but it's all I have. Maybe it will do." And she folded the scarf of silvery blue and gold and pressed it against Annie's cut. But blood still seeped through and soon the scarf had turned to red.

"I hate to ruin your pretty scarf, Augusta," Annie said. "I hope you can save it."

"I'm more concerned about your hand." Augusta frowned. "I've a gown in my overnight bag I can tear into strips."

"No, wait!" Dimple searched her handbag. "I'd almost forgotten about this." And she unwrapped the biscuit she'd saved from breakfast at the motor court. "I had a feeling this might come in handy."

"Dimple Kilpatrick!" Velma said as she turned the car once again toward Shelbyville. "How do you think eating a stale biscuit can stop the flow of blood?"

"You don't eat it," Dimple replied, breaking the biscuit apart. "You press it on the wound. It would be better if it were fresh, but it should help to absorb the blood." She passed it back to Augusta, who did as instructed and the piece of biscuit did exactly what it was supposed to do. "Why, for heaven's sake, it *is* slacking," Augusta said.

"Spiderwebs would probably do just as well, but this is what we have on hand," Dimple told her. "Now, take that one off and put the other half in its place. We'll need a clean sock or stocking to hold it there."

"Use one of mine." Annie, who was relieved they didn't have to rely on spiderwebs, gestured to her bag on the floor. "Hate to mess up another of somebody else's accessories."

By the time they returned to Shelbyville, the cut had finally ceased to bleed, and when they stopped on the outskirts of town to have one tire patched and the other inflated, Dimple poured antiseptic over Annie's wound and bound it with a strip torn from her extra petticoat. When Annie protested at her sacrifice, Augusta assured both that she could mend it as good as new. "Just give me a few minutes when we get back, and I promise you won't see the difference," she said.

And Dimple knew it was so.

"How did you find a dry place to change that tire way out in the middle of nowhere?" the filling station attendant asked before they left. "The few people who live out there are so far from the road, you'd never know they were there. If you ask me, it's a dad-blamed long way to go for pancakes, and if that Bertie didn't serve such good food, he wouldn't stay in business a minute."

Velma explained to him about the deserted blacksmith shop. "It was just off the road, and we would've all been soaking wet if we hadn't found it."

The man took off his cap and scratched his head. "Ma'am, I've driven down that road just about all my life. *There is no building like that between here and Lynchburg.*"

Chapter Twenty-nine

"I don't understand how that man at the service station could miss seeing that old blacksmith shop," Annie said as once again they left Shelbyville behind. "It's *right there* next to the road. He must need his eyes examined."

"It does seem peculiar," Velma agreed. "I

suppose we become so accustomed to things on a familiar route, we don't always take note of what we see."

Miss Dimple nodded and said that was probably the case.

Augusta only smiled.

The rain finally stopped and a hint of sunlight broke through after they passed Lynchburg, but darkness fell quickly as they crossed the state line into Georgia. Having bypassed lunch, they pulled into a drive-in in the small city of Dalton and ordered hamburgers all around.

Dimple examined the watch she wore pinned to her dress and saw that it was after eight. "It's going to be late when we get back home. I'm sure they must be worried. Do you think we should telephone?"

Everyone agreed that would be a good idea, but when Annie tried to use the pay phone, she found others in line ahead of her.

Velma blinked her lights for the carhop to collect the tray. "We don't have time to wait. If we get back on the road right now, we should be home before midnight."

But it was almost one o'clock when Velma finally parked her old reliable Ford V-8 in the garage behind Phoebe's house. "I expect everyone's asleep by now," she whispered as they made their way wearily across the lawn and crept in the front door, attempting to be quiet.

"Where in the world have you been?" Both Phoebe and Lily waited in their robes, faces shiny with cold cream. "We were just about ready to call the State Patrol," Phoebe said. "Did you have an accident? What happened?"

Velma yawned as she started for the stairs. "It's a long story. We'll tell you all about it in the morning."

But Lily stepped in front of her. "Oh no you don't! We've been pacing the floor for most of the night, and frankly, you've given me a headache."

"And that goes for me, as well," Phoebe added. "I think you owe us a few minutes at least. It won't take long to heat up the kettle, and there're still some of Augusta's molasses cookies."

"Cookies? Well, why didn't you say so?" Annie said, as she had been a little miffed since Velma wouldn't wait for her to order ice cream at the drive-in.

And so the six of them gathered around the kitchen table while the four tardy travelers took time about telling their story of rain and mud, flat tires, and a return trip filled with delays.

"But what about Dora's sister?" Phoebe asked. "What about Elaine?"

"You'd never guess the two were related," Annie told them, describing Elaine Arnold and her warm, welcoming home.

"And guess what? She turned out to be a relative of Miss Dimple's fiancé."

And of course everyone wanted to hear about that.

"She gave us the name and address of a college friend of Dora's," Dimple said after that subject was exhausted. "A Carolyn Freeman who lived there in Macon, but a letter to that address was returned. Elaine assumed she probably married or moved, or both."

"Then how do we go about finding her?" Lily asked.

"I can take care of that," Augusta assured her. "I've a friend in Macon and will get in touch with her tomorrow."

Yawning, Velma rose to put her cup in the sink. "I don't suppose anything exciting happened while we were gone," she said, and everyone looked bewildered when Lily and Phoebe laughed.

"What is it? What did we miss?" Annie, who had stood to follow Velma, sat abruptly.

"Yes, tell us, please," Augusta said. "Don't keep us in suspenders."

For a few seconds, everyone was quiet, and then Phoebe laughed and said, "I wouldn't dream of it, Augusta." And then Lily took a deep breath and told them about the break-in.

"You mean you were here all alone?" Annie gasped. "Weren't you afraid?"

"Of course I was, but I had to do something. Nobody was here to help me," Lily told them primly.

"Have the police found out who it was?" Velma asked, and Lily shook her head. "Not yet, but whoever broke in here should have a great big lump on his head," she told her.

Miss Dimple, who had been longing for her own bed, suddenly became wide awake. "I wonder what they were looking for. Did the authorities find any prints?"

"Looks like he was wearing gloves," Phoebe said. "They dusted all around the window over there, which is how he came in. Chief Tinsley had it boarded up for us, but we won't be able to replace the glass until tomorrow." She shrugged, glancing at the kitchen clock. "I mean today."

Augusta rose and studied the boarded-up window. "Has this kind of thing happened here before?"

Phoebe's eyes widened. "Oh, good gracious, no! Why, what would anyone want to steal? None of us has anything valuable that would make it worthwhile."

"Then the person must have been looking for something else," Augusta said.

"Like what?" Annie asked.

"It might be something that seems worthless to you but could actually be valuable."

Velma laughed. "I can't imagine anyone risking his life to steal my grandpa's pocket watch. It doesn't even run."

"Or my aunt Chloe's recipe book," Phoebe

added, "although it does have a really good recipe for apple brown Betty."

"What about postage stamps?" Dimple offered. "Some of the rare ones can be worth quite a lot of money."

No one remembered having anything like that but agreed to look through old letters just in case.

Augusta turned to Lily. "Could you tell where this intruder was searching?" she asked.

"It would be hard to say. I was afraid he would know I was there if I moved about too much, but I could hear him just below me in the parlor, and then he seemed to linger for a short time in the hall."

"What could he possibly have been looking for there?" Phoebe asked. "Although Odessa tells me she sometimes finds coins under the couch cushions." She smiled. "I tell her, finders keepers—"

She paused. "Do you think it was the same person who broke into the library last week?"

Miss Dimple spoke quietly. "That happened a week or so after Dora was in the library. Someone must have believed she left something there."

"Was she in there long enough to do that?" Phoebe asked.

"Yes, I think she was," Dimple told her. "And then she came here. She certainly had time to hide something in this house."

"Whatever it was had to have been in that paper bag she carried," Velma reminded them.

"They obviously didn't find what they were looking for in the library," Augusta pointed out.

"And I didn't give them a lot of time to look for it here." It was obvious to the others that Lily struggled to control her emotions. "Thank goodness the four of you are back safely from Tennessee!"

Rising, Phoebe wiped crumbs from the table into her palm and whisked them into the sink. "It's become obvious that Dora planned to meet someone here in Elderberry. How do we know it isn't a person we see every day, somebody we wouldn't suspect? I wonder if Bobby Tinsley has considered this. I'll phone him first thing in the morning. Now, I think it's time we all got some sleep."

Yawning, Annie reminded her that it was already morning as she stumbled off to bed.

The others followed. To Dimple Kilpatrick, the stairs seemed steeper somehow, and it took all her energy to wash her hands and face and brush her teeth before climbing into bed.

But first, she took the ring from its small box in her dresser drawer and slipped it onto her finger.

The next day was Monday and four weary teachers straggled in for dinner at noontime that day. Even Miss Dimple had forgone her usual sunrise walk that morning, and although the idea of a nap seemed appealing, the conversation of the night before weighed heavily on her mind.

"Did you have a chance to speak with Chief Tinsley?" she asked Phoebe over tuna croquettes and turnip greens fresh from the garden.

Phoebe paused as she spooned chow-chow over her greens and glanced up with a frown. "I don't know what's going on down there. I called and left a message with that woman who answers the phone—what's her name . . . Shirley . . . Shelby?"

"Shelly," Velma told her.

"Well, anyway, Shelly told me he wasn't in, so I asked to speak with Warren. Turned out, *he* wasn't in, either, and neither was anybody else! Shelly said she'd have somebody get in touch soon, but I haven't heard a mumbling word."

"Good thing an ax murderer wasn't chopping at the door," Lily said. "Will somebody please pass the catsup?"

"That seems most unusual," Miss Dimple said. "There must be a reason no one's returned your call, and I'm very much afraid it's not good."

Augusta was spooning up a dessert of boiled custard with a sprinkling of nutmeg when Warren Nelson telephoned to tell them there had been another break-in.

Chapter Thirty

"Seems Rose McGinnis took her aunt Trudy to visit her sister over in Eatonton yesterday, and when they got home last night, somebody had gotten in through that little room off the back porch. Looked like they'd jimmied open the door," Warren told them when he came by the house that afternoon.

Phoebe frowned. "What on earth could they be after? Gertrude doesn't have any money except what she takes in from her sewing."

"Told me she keeps that in a pillow—one of those fluffy things with a cat or something on it, just for looks, you know—that stays on her bed," he said.

"Chenille?" Velma offered, and Warren nodded. "I reckon. Anyway, the burglar didn't know to take that, but whoever it was did make off with a silver punch ladle that had belonged to Mrs. Hutchinson's grandmother. She's right upset about that."

"It's a good thing they weren't at home when that happened," Lily said, hugging herself. "I'd hate for anybody else to go through what I did. I'll swear, I think it took at least a year off my life!"

"And that's not all they took, either," he

continued. "Miss McGinnis says she's missing two china vases, an antique platter, and a brass candlestick from that little shop she has. I reckon the person would've gotten more, but she says she thinks they might've scared the thief away when they got home last night. Seems kinda funny to me, as it doesn't look like anything was stolen from here or the library."

"I believe we all need to put some thought into this," Miss Dimple said. Gray skies threatened rain, and they gathered in the parlor, where not even autumn leaves and paper jack-o'-lanterns seemed to lessen the gloom. The next day would be Halloween, and earlier Augusta had carved for the porch a large orange pumpkin that looked suspiciously like Adolf Hitler, complete with painted mustache.

"Do you think whoever broke in here might be the same person who caused that disturbance at the library the other day?" Dimple asked.

"They seemed to be looking for something," Phoebe added, "and we think it might have something to do with Dora Westbrook, as she spent some time at both places."

"But she never went to the Hutchinson place," Warren pointed out.

"It seems the intruder didn't know that," Miss Dimple reminded him.

Velma spoke up. "Well, if Rose hadn't bragged about that shop she runs, the thief probably would've left them alone. She's always talking about the nice things she buys from estate sales and places like that, and I'll be willing to bet those things came from the Cunningham estate near Athens. Old Mrs. Cunningham didn't have any heirs, and that sale was advertised in the Atlanta paper not long ago. Rose ought to keep her mouth shut or invest in stronger locks."

The policeman shifted in his chair and sighed. "What do you suppose *your* burglar was looking for?" he asked.

"Something that was valuable to Dora. Something she wanted to keep safe," Annie volunteered.

He frowned. "Didn't you just get back from seeing her sister? Did she know what it might've been?"

Velma nodded. "Yes, and Elaine couldn't imagine what it was. She said her sister didn't have anything valuable."

Annie idly adjusted the burgundy-colored sweet gum leaves on the mantel. "But don't forget what Lucille Westbrook said. Dora's mother-in-law accused her of being a thief when Charlie's mother and aunt were there last week."

"What did she think Dora took?" Warren asked.

Annie shrugged. "She didn't give them a chance to ask."

"Do you suppose that woman could be behind all this?" Phoebe asked.

"I can check with the police down there, see if

they can find out if she left town recently," the officer told them.

"From what we've heard, you'd better be careful if you plan to mess with her," Annie said.

Warren stood to go, tucking his notebook into a shirt pocket. "Maybe we can at least find out what she *thinks* Dora took.

"Now, be sure and lock your doors and fasten all the windows. We'll be in touch as soon as we know anything."

Annie laughed after the policeman left. "He talks like we're going to be invaded by spooks tomorrow."

"I think he has another kind of spook in mind," Miss Dimple said.

But Halloween passed peacefully enough, except for a multitude of small costumed callers.

"I hear the Methodist church is having a Halloween carnival for the children tonight," Phoebe said as it began to grow darker outside. "Maybe that will keep them out of devilment— for a while at least."

Velma nodded. "Remember last year? Most of our downstairs windows were soaped and the porch furniture ended up at the top of the schoolhouse steps."

"And somebody put the Olivers' lawn ornament —you know, the one that looks like a dwarf—in the lily pool down in the park," Lily added. "It never has looked the same."

Velma shook her head. "Pity," she said, trying not to smile. She considered that no great loss.

"I'll bet it was Junior Henderson." Annie laughed. She had taught that rascal the year before.

"Or his buddy Marshall Dodd," Lily said. "Of course they'd both deny it. At least with the paper shortage, they won't be decorating all the trees with toilet paper like they used to."

But this year, they would be prepared. When it was time for the carnival to be over, Annie, wrapped in one of Phoebe's worn-out sheets, greeted the children as they passed. Augusta had made popcorn balls with honey and molasses, and word spread quickly among them that this house was to be spared from their usual pranks.

"I didn't know we had that much popcorn on hand," Annie said as Augusta passed around a tray for the grown-ups after the young goblins had left.

But Augusta smiled, explaining that popcorn usually makes more than expected.

"It's still hard for me to believe there's someone in Elderberry who is bold enough to invade our homes," Velma said as they sipped hot spiced cider in front of the fire.

"Speak for yourself!" Lily snapped. "It doesn't seem hard for me." And everyone, including Lily herself, laughed at her retort.

Augusta stole a glance at herself in the hallway mirror and brushed back a lock of hair before joining them. "I've been in touch with my friend in Macon," she told them, "and asked her to inquire around the neighborhood where Dora's friend Carolyn lived. Perhaps one of them will be able to tell her how we can get in touch."

"If we can locate Dora's friend, she might be able to tell us what everyone seems to be looking for," Dimple said.

Velma stared into the amber flames. "Can you believe it has been just over two weeks since Dora Westbrook stumbled into our lives?"

"Seems to me she did a lot more than *stumble,*" Annie said.

"Annie Gardner!" Lily gasped. "Shame on you! The poor woman's dead."

"Don't I know it? If the silly thing had just stayed with the Nelsons like you planned, she'd probably still be alive, and we wouldn't be on this wild-goose chase." Annie quickly drained her cup and announced she was going upstairs to write to her fiancé.

Phoebe nodded wisely. "War nerves," she whispered after Annie left the room. "I don't think she's had a letter from Frazier in a while."

Lily groaned. "How long is this miserable war going to drag on?"

"If you think you're tired of it, remember the ones who are over there fighting," Miss Dimple reminded her, and then went to her room to write her brother.

"My goodness, Phoebe, where are you going with all those heavy books?" Augusta said the next morning as Phoebe slid several volumes into a canvas handbag, grabbed her purse, and started for the door.

Phoebe paused in front of the hall mirror to adjust her green knitted hat. "I promised Dimple I'd return her two books, and Velma just finished reading that funny *See Here, Private Hargrove.* . . . I plan to check that out for myself, and there's that book of house plans Annie's been poring over."

"Why not let me return those for you? I have to stop at Mr. Cooper's anyway. We're almost out of onions."

Relieved, Phoebe wasted no time shedding coat and hat. That would give her time to gather the few cabbages left in the garden before the first frost.

Arriving at the library, Augusta was a bit surprised to find Rose McGinnis at the piano, her arm finally free from the sling. "I see you're learning 'Let Me Call You Sweetheart,'" she said, wandering over. Rose looked up in chagrin. "Well, it's *supposed* to be 'My Darling Clementine.' Guess I need a little more practice."

"I understand you and your aunt suffered the same misfortune that we did," Augusta continued. "You must be relieved that it happened while you were away. Let's hope the police will soon find out who's behind all this."

Rose slid her fingers along the keyboard and frowned. "Oh, I think whoever took those things knew very well when we'd be gone. The vases I lost were fairly expensive, but that silver ladle has been in our family for years and Aunt Trudy is just sick about it."

"I'm so sorry. I hope they can recover it before it's too late. Officer Nelson explained to us that thieves usually don't wait long before finding a market for stolen goods." Augusta shook her head. "I just don't understand why someone would do a thing like that. It seems they don't care for anyone but themselves."

"That's one reason I'm here," Rose said. "Aunt Trudy's feeling so low, I thought I'd try to find a book to make her smile."

Augusta knew just the right one, but she didn't want to mention it before making a phone call.

"Well, of course, I can read that book later," Phoebe said in reply to her question. "I think Gertrude needs cheering up more than I do. At least the thief didn't take anything here—thanks to Lily."

"Tell Phoebe I'll put her at the top of the list," Virginia said when Augusta passed the book along to Rose. And then she frowned. "It seems to me some of this might be connected to Dora Westbrook. Just think of it—we had that break-in here and then the one at Phoebe's, the only two places Dora spent any time. Somebody seems to think she left something behind and it looks like they're determined to find it."

"What do they think she left?" Rose asked as Virginia stamped her books.

"I wish I knew," the librarian told her. "From what I've heard about Dora's mother-in-law— what's her name?"

"Lucille," Augusta said.

"I'd be willing to bet that woman knows more than she lets on." Virginia snatched wilted chrysanthemums from a vase on her desk, tossed them into a trash can, and dusted off her hands. "If anybody knows what Dora might've taken with her, it's bound to be Lucille. Why else would she accuse her of being a thief?" She frowned. "Do you think she might be behind this?"

"I believe Officer Nelson is looking into that," Augusta told her. "He was to find out from the police in Fieldcroft if there's a way they might learn if and when she left town."

"How are they planning to do that?" Rose asked. "She's free to come and go as she pleases, isn't she?"

"Of course, but there's the bus station, for one thing," Virginia told her, "and you know as well as I do people talk in a small town like that. I suppose when it comes right down to it, they could even ask her son."

On her way to the grocery store, Augusta saw Warren Nelson coming out of the barbershop and asked if he'd heard from his counterparts in Fieldcroft.

But the officer, cleanly shaven and smelling of Old Spice, said that as far as the authorities in Fieldcroft knew, Lucille Westbrook had been sticking close to home.

Later, leaving Cooper's, Augusta saw Jesse Dean taking groceries to the car for Charlie's mother, Jo, and stopped to say hello. She had spoken to him several times when shopping for groceries but never had had an opportunity for a conversation.

"I hope you know you have many supporters here who are sick at heart that someone would try to link you with what happened to Dora Westbrook," she told him. "Your friends at Phoebe Chadwick's—and I hope you'll count me among them—are determined to learn who's behind this and why."

Recognizing her, Jesse Dean smiled. "It sure came as a surprise to me," he said, shaking his head. "For the life of me, I can't figure out who would do a thing like that!" And then he shrugged. "I wondered why the Presbyterians ordered vanilla wafers when they usually want graham crackers."

"My daughter Charlie speaks highly of you," Jo said to Augusta, introducing herself when the young man returned to the store. "I'm perfectly capable of carrying out my own groceries," she added, smiling, "but Jesse Dean insists—and he refuses to accept any money." She sighed. "I hope we can get to the bottom of this thing soon. It all seems to hinge on the person Dora planned to meet here." Jo stepped closer to whisper, "I just hope it's not anyone we know!

"Believe me, when this finally comes out, the whole town will learn the truth." And Jo confided her intentions for a front-page story.

"Let's hope it's soon," Augusta said.

On her return, she put away the onions and tumbled apples into a wooden bowl, filling the parlor with the sweet scent of autumn. Then, passing the console table in the hall, saw a letter waiting from her friend Grace in Macon.

Chapter Thirty-one

"I can't remember when I've been this tired," Velma said after supper that night, kicking off her shoes in front of the fire. "Maybe I'm just getting too old to travel."

"I think it's taken a toll on all of us," Dimple admitted, "but I'm so glad you convinced me to go along."

"Just think what you would've missed," Phoebe reminded her, "meeting some of your Ned's family after all these years."

Dimple touched the amethyst ring on her finger and smiled. "And I have all of you to thank for that. Elaine has invited me there for Thanksgiving, and I believe I'm going to accept."

"What about Henry?" Phoebe asked, surprised.

"I believe he and Hazel—and Imogene—plan to have dinner at the Winecoff Hotel in Atlanta. It's lovely, of course, but I think I'll pass this time."

Phoebe hid her smile. Good for you, she thought. It will be a wake-up call for Henry Kilpatrick to realize his sister has a life of her own.

"We always spend Christmas together," Dimple added, "and naturally I look forward to that." Perhaps by Christmastime, she thought, Henry will have come to terms with the stressful demands that weigh so heavily on his mind.

"Surely by Christmas we'll know more about what really happened to Dora, poor thing," Annie said. She was in a more tolerant mood since receiving a letter from Frazier that day.

Augusta pulled up a chair beside her, the firelight reflecting off her dazzling necklace. "Maybe I can move things along," she began. "I heard today from my friend Grace in Macon."

"Did she learn anything about Dora's college friend?" Velma asked.

Phoebe leaned forward eagerly. "Did she find anyone who remembered her?"

"Oh, I hope she found out where we might locate her!" Lily said.

Augusta smiled. "To answer your questions, yes, yes, and yes! Grace spoke with a former neighbor of Carolyn's who has known her for most of her life. She told her Carolyn married soon after graduating from Wesleyan and still lives there in Macon."

Taking out her handkerchief, Miss Dimple polished her bifocals. "That's grand news, Augusta. Has your friend had an opportunity to speak with Carolyn yet?"

"I believe that's where I come in," Augusta said. "Unless there are objections, I prefer to speak personally with Dora's friend. Grace has been an angel to help, but sometimes she can be a bit flighty, and being here from the beginning— well, almost the beginning—I'm more familiar with the background."

Everyone agreed that would be the best solution, although they disliked the idea of having to cook for themselves.

"I've left marinated slaw in the refrigerator," Augusta reminded them, "along with a casserole of macaroni and cheese. All you have to do is pop it into the oven. I should be back in a couple of days."

"But, Augusta," Annie asked, frowning, "how are you planning to get there?"

"I happen to have a friend passing through town

in the morning who is going in that direction, and I'm sure I can arrange a way back." With long, slender fingers, Augusta smoothed her ocean blue skirt and adjusted the filmy scarf in her hair.

"I declare, Augusta, if you don't beat all!" Lily said. "How do you come up with all these convenient connections? What kind of agency do you work for anyway?"

"I suppose you might say my orders come from the top." Augusta smiled. "And now I think I should say good night, as I plan to leave early in the morning."

Phoebe was waiting when Miss Dimple returned from her morning walk the next day. "Did you happen to notice when Augusta left this morning?" she asked.

"I believe she had already left." Dimple smeared margarine on one of her Victory Muffins. It really didn't look appealing at all after Augusta's tempting fare, but she knew she must think of the nutritional value. Maybe it would go down easier with a glass of milk.

"It must've still been dark, and I didn't hear a thing." Phoebe shook her head. "It's uncanny, don't you think, how Augusta manages to do some of the things she does? But I'll have to say, she certainly has been a godsend."

Miss Dimple smiled in agreement.

●●●

A chill wind whipped around the corner of Oak Lane and Partridge Avenue when Augusta arrived in Macon, and she tugged her hat snugly about her ears and wished she'd thought to wear something warmer. Making note of the correct address, Augusta remembered that Grace had told her Carolyn had two school-age children who boarded the school bus on that corner. Soon a young woman emerged from the yellow-brick house in the middle of the block, herding two little girls in front of her. Thinking it best not to be seen, Augusta stayed out of sight until all the children boarded the bus and the handful of parents drifted away. Carolyn chatted briefly with a neighbor until, shivering, each went her own way.

Quietly walking behind her, Augusta hesitated. Well, there was no use in putting it off; it simply had to be done, and gritting her teeth, she cried out and fell smack in the middle of the sidewalk.

"Oh my goodness! Are you hurt?" Whirling, Carolyn stooped beside her.

Augusta moaned. It wasn't necessary to fake pain, as her elbow burned like fire and she was sure she had bruised her knee. "Must've turned my ankle. I think I'll be all right," she answered in as feeble a voice as she could manage.

Carolyn offered a hand. "Here, let me help you. Do you think you're able to walk?"

Augusta thanked her and nodded. "I think so," she gasped.

"Look, it's freezing out here. My house is just down the street. Why not come in and get warm until you're sure you're all right?"

Augusta nodded her thanks and hobbled along beside her.

"I'm Carolyn Lowe," her rescuer said once inside the house. "I don't believe we've met. You must be new in the neighborhood."

Augusta introduced herself and explained that she was looking for an address a few blocks away. "My mother lived there years ago and I promised her I would stroll by her old neighborhood when I was in town." She disliked telling a fib, but after all, it *was* for a good cause.

Her hostess brought a warm washcloth for her injuries and dabbed her elbow with antiseptic. Augusta tried not to wince. She'd had no time for breakfast before she left and would dearly love a cup of coffee.

"There. That ought to do it," Carolyn said, rising to her feet. "Do you think you'll be all right now?"

Augusta thanked her and said she was sure she would be fine.

"Good. Then how about a cup of coffee to warm you up before you go?"

Thank goodness! I thought she'd never ask. "That would be wonderful," she said.

"I would offer to drive you to your mother's

old neighborhood, but I don't have a car today." Carolyn brought cream and sugar and joined her.

"That's all right. I really don't have much time before I meet my friend for my ride back home." Augusta sipped and waited.

"And where do you live?"

"Fieldcroft, but I've only been there a short time." Augusta closed her eyes. *Sorry, but that was necessary.*

"Fieldcroft! Why, you must know my friend Dora Westbrook."

Oh dear! She didn't know. Augusta hesitated before telling Carolyn what had happened to her friend.

Carolyn's eyes filled with tears. "I don't understand. Why would anyone want to do that to Dora? Are you sure it wasn't an accident?"

Augusta told her what she'd learned of Dora's peculiar behavior when she arrived in Elderberry and how she had chosen to take shelter in a church rather than spend the night in a tourist home run by a local policeman and his wife. "Some of the people there believe she might still be alive today if she hadn't made that choice," she added.

Carolyn shook her head silently. "I'm sure it was because she didn't want her husband to find her. I wondered why I hadn't heard from Dora, but frankly, I thought she must've decided to join her sister in Tennessee. I suppose all that's been in the newspapers, but I give piano lessons several after-noons a week, and with my girls and their activities, I don't always have time to read them."

Augusta noticed the piano in the corner of the room and on it a framed photograph of a naval officer she assumed was Carolyn's husband.

"I guess it's all right to say this now, but Dora was unhappy in her marriage, and she planned to get away. Tell me, do they believe Leonard had anything to do with this?"

"The police checked, of course, but he never left home during that time."

"What about her mother-in-law? They never did get along."

"She was in Fieldcroft when it happened, but there have been recent reports about robberies or would-be robberies in the town where this took place. Someone seems to be looking for something Dora might have hidden, and they believe it's somewhere in Elderberry. I wouldn't be surprised if the authorities had their eye on Lucille Westbrook."

Carolyn sighed. "There must've been something I could have done! Did you know I was the last person Dora saw before she took that bus to Elderberry? She came here first to throw her husband off track so he wouldn't look for her there."

"I'm sure you did all you could," Augusta assured her, and when she touched her hand, Carolyn seemed to visibly relax. "Carolyn, do you know why Dora planned to go to Elderberry?" Augusta asked.

"She told me she was to meet someone there." Carolyn dropped her head, and Augusta could barely hear her when she spoke. "She took something," she whispered. "Something valuable she planned to sell so she could begin to live independently of Leonard—for a while at least."

"What? What did she take?" Augusta found she had forgotten all about her cuts and bruises.

"It was a book. Dora said it would be worth a lot of money."

Of course! What better place to hide a book than in a library?

"What kind of book?" Augusta asked. "What was the title?"

"Dora was afraid to tell me in case somebody came here looking for it," Carolyn said. Her eyes widened. "I wonder if they've found it."

"I don't believe so, at least not yet." Augusta gathered her cape, adjusted her hat, and started for the door. "After all, who would know the title but Leonard Westbrook and his mother?"

The wind had settled some when Augusta left Carolyn's snug bungalow, and the midmorning sun felt warm upon her face as she started down the street. Bare branches of hardwood trees arched overhead, and now and then, piles of newly raked leaves waited by the curb to be collected. Augusta resisted the temptation to jump in one, but this was neither the time nor the place, she reminded herself, however she relished the crisp, tingling smell of them just the same.

If Leonard Westbrook or his mother hadn't been the one who caused Dora's death, then who could it have been? And had Dora known the person who might purchase the book? Walking cleared her mind, and Augusta found herself wandering into the Cherokee Heights section of homes, and admiring the lovely Georgian, Tudor, and Craftsman houses. Along the way, she passed several women pushing baby carriages, and on the corner across the street, two ladies in hats and gloves talked as they waited for the bus. With the shortage of gasoline, most people now relied on public transportation. But young men were obviously absent from the picture, and it made life seem out of kilter. Augusta crossed over onto Napier Avenue, where an older gentleman walking his dog removed his hat and smiled as they met, and smiling in return, Augusta hoped with all her heart the world would soon be at peace.

Walking past Mercer University, in the center of town, she noticed young men in uniform who, she learned, were there to be trained as naval officers. Carolyn had said that the campus of Wesleyan, the college she and Dora had attended, was on the outskirts of town.

Finding a convenient drugstore, Augusta settled in a back booth and indulging in a chocolate soda, found it every bit as good as she'd remembered. Taking her time to sip the delightful concoction through a straw, she scooped up ice cream with a long-handled spoon, and saved the whipped cream and cherry for last. Augusta closed her eyes and decided it was *almost* heavenly.

As she ate, Augusta decided the most logical person to want to find Dora's rare book would be Lucille Westbrook, rather than her son, who, from all she had heard, seemed to appear indifferent to the whole affair.

As she left the drugstore, a sharp gust of wind brought November's brown crumpled leaves tumbling through the street. This would be a good time for a brief visit farther south, Augusta thought. Perhaps someone in Fieldcroft might know if Lucille had left town recently. However, her friend Celeste, she remembered, was on another assignment.

But hadn't Annie's friend Charlie told them her mother had mentioned that the woman who ran the grocery store there knew everything that went on in Fieldcroft? So why not pay her a visit, she reasoned. If anyone would know Lucille's whereabouts, she seemed the likely one to ask.

The main street of Fieldcroft was almost deserted when Augusta dropped in later that afternoon, but a few customers still lingered at the small grocery store in the center of town. Augusta took her time browsing among the root vegetables until she could approach the woman behind the counter and tactfully ask about Lucille.

But according to Edna of Edna's Groceries, as far as she knew, Lucille had been keeping close to home until earlier that day, when she'd bought a bus ticket to Elderberry.

Chapter Thirty-two

Although she was disappointed not to be able to visit awhile with Celeste, Augusta thought it best to get back as soon as possible after learning of Lucille's recent departure for Elderberry. While speaking with Edna, she had noticed a rather large woman with hair a more vibrant yellow than any dandelion shopping nearby.

"That's Linda Pearl, Lucille's niece," Edna whispered, drawing her aside. "Works part-time at the police station."

Augusta bought winter vegetables for a hearty casserole, thanked her, and left. Looking back as she reached the corner of the street, she saw the shopper with the yellow hair step outside the store, as if to follow her.

It was time to cut her travels short and return to Elderberry.

• • •

"Why, Augusta, we didn't expect you so soon!" Phoebe opened the door to find Augusta standing on the porch with her large bag in one hand and a sack of groceries in the other.

"We've just finished supper, but there's plenty left if you're hungry," she said.

Augusta said she thought she might be able to eat a bite or two, and joined the others, who were lingering over tea and cookies.

"How in the world did you get to Macon and back so quickly?" Velma asked.

Augusta helped herself to the macaroni. "I left very early this morning—way before anyone was up."

"Did you learn anything there?" Phoebe asked, passing her the slaw.

"Yes, I did, and I'll tell you all about it after supper." Augusta found she could eat a bit more than a bite or two.

"The meal you left was delicious," Lily said, and everyone agreed. "Thank you for looking after us."

Augusta smiled. "That's the very reason I'm here . . . but I didn't make the cookies," she said, noticing the platter on the table. "They look delicious."

"They are delicious," Miss Dimple said. "Annie made them this afternoon."

Annie smiled. "They're called crybabies. It's a recipe that I saw in the paper. They're made with molasses, brown sugar, and spices, and they're supposed to be especially good for shipping. I'm going to make more to send Frazier."

Augusta found the cookies to be moist and flavorful and took hers into the parlor with a cup of tea while she told everyone about her visit with Carolyn Lowe.

"I think I know now why someone broke into the library," she began. "They were looking for a book."

Lily frowned. "Why couldn't they just check it out like everyone else?"

Augusta laughed. "Because it was a particular book. Carolyn said it's probably worth a good bit of money, at least enough so Dora would have had the means to leave her husband and begin a life on her own."

Of course everyone wanted to know the title, but were disappointed to learn that Carolyn wasn't given that information. Dora was afraid someone at home might come there asking questions and didn't want to put her friend in that position, Augusta explained.

"So, what did she do with the book? Where is it now?" Annie asked.

"We'd all like the answer to that," Augusta told her. "Carolyn said Dora took it with her when she left."

"Then it has to be somewhere in Elderberry." Frowning, Phoebe set her mending aside.

"Well, it's not here," Velma insisted. "I've looked everywhere I know to look. Besides, Dora wasn't here very long."

"And it's certainly not at the library," Phoebe added. "Augusta, you helped put all those books back on the shelves. Don't you think we would've noticed it?"

"But we didn't know to look for something like that," Augusta reminded her.

"Evidently, whoever broke into the library didn't find it, either," Dimple said.

"What about the church?" Annie suggested. "When Dora left here, she went to the church—or at least she ended up there. Do you suppose she hid that book somewhere in the church?"

Lily sighed. "Well, if she did, they'll never find it. How would anyone know what to look for?"

Augusta nodded. "A thimble in a haystack," she said, and of course everyone looked at her oddly until Annie finally laughed and said that was close enough.

"I'll telephone Evan Mitchell tomorrow," Dimple said, referring to the minister there, "and ask them to be on the lookout for it. I just wish I could be more specific."

"What about Odessa's husband, Bob Robert?" Phoebe suggested. "After all, he works part-time as sexton there and was the one who found her. He might remember seeing it somewhere."

"It won't hurt to ask," Augusta said, "but if we only knew the title!

"By the way," she continued, "I heard from an acquaintance in Fieldcroft that Lucille Westbrook bought a bus ticket for Elderberry this morning, so it appears she's up to something."

"That's comforting," Velma said, frowning. "We should all sleep soundly tonight."

Going to the window, Dimple pulled aside the curtain and looked out on the street, now dark except for a dim light on the corner. "If she left this morning, she should be here by now. I wonder where she went."

"Didn't Jo Carr tell us the police officer there in Fieldcroft—what's his name? Reece something—anyway, he told her he'd let us know if Lucille left town. Do you suppose he forgot?" Phoebe said.

Dimple closed the curtains with a twitch and glanced at the clock on the mantel. "I think we should let Chief Tinsley know what's going on. Perhaps he can get in touch with the officer in Fieldcroft."

Dimple relayed the information to Warren Nelson, who assured her they would patrol the neighborhood that night and keep an eye out for Lucille's whereabouts. "Meanwhile," he told her, "be sure to keep your doors locked, and call us if you hear anything out of the ordinary."

"Huh! He won't have to worry about that!" Lily snorted. "I doubt if I'll close my eyes all night."

"I worried about that Lucille woman all night," Lily said at breakfast the next day. "I don't think I got a wink of sleep."

Velma laughed. "Then what was all that noise I heard coming from your side of the room? I thought we were being attacked by the enemy."

Fortunately, Augusta placed a dish of steaming waffles on the table, delaying Lily's response. Later, as the teachers were getting ready to leave for school, Phoebe telephoned Odessa, who said her aunt was improving, although not fast enough for her, and left a message for Bob Robert.

"Are you all all right over there?" Odessa asked, her voice dark with concern. "I hear there've been some funny goings-on."

Not wanting to worry her, Phoebe assured Odessa that they missed her but that everyone was fine.

"Humph!" Odessa responded. "So, who's taking care of all of you while I been gone?"

Phoebe told her a temporary worker from an agency was filling in to help out.

"She feedin' you all right?" Odessa wanted to know, and Phoebe whispered that the temp was doing fine *for now* and they were doing their best to get by without her, so please not to worry about them. How could she admit they looked forward to Augusta's meals as much as they had Odessa's?

"Humph!" Odessa said again.

• • •

Bobby Tinsley dropped by around noon, just in time for some of Augusta's apple cobbler with whipped cream on top. He had been in touch with the authorities in Fieldcroft and was told that Reece Cagle hadn't been aware that Lucille had left; he found out later that Edna Watson had dropped by the day before while he was out and left a message on his desk, but it had somehow disappeared.

"I wonder what happened to it?" Annie asked.

"I think I know." Augusta passed a cup of coffee to Chief Tinsley. "My friend there tells me his receptionist is Lucille's niece."

The chief finished the cobbler and leaned back in his chair. "Sounds like he might want to keep an eye on that one."

Phoebe told them she had spoken with Evan Mitchell at the church and that he promised to remind Bob Robert to keep an eye out for the mysterious book. "If Dora meant to sell that book, she must've had a buyer in mind," she added, frowning. "I wonder who it might've been."

"Probably the person who killed her." Annie's words were stark.

"I'll be willing to bet that's what Lucille Westbrook is after," Bobby said. "Unless she got off the bus somewhere between Fieldcroft and here, she should've been here already," he said, "but so far, nobody's seen hide nor hair of anyone new in town."

"Wait a minute," Miss Dimple began. "Didn't Jo or Lou mention something about a fellow in Fieldcroft who ran a small library? I believe they said he was a friend of Dora's, and there may be a chance he knows something about the book she planned to sell."

"It's worth looking into," Bobby said. "I'll try to check with one of the ladies this afternoon."

"You'll have to wait until the bus gets back from Milledgeville," Annie warned him. "They work three days a week at the munitions plant over there, and so does Bob Robert.

"I don't have anything special to do after school this afternoon," she added, "and if the minister doesn't object, I'll be glad to look around the church and see if anything interesting turns up. I'm sure Charlie will want to help, too."

Evan Mitchell said that was fine with him as long as they left his office alone, and he didn't see how Dora could've had access to that, as he kept it locked when he wasn't there.

"Why don't you search the balcony and I'll look in the choir loft, then we can go over the rest of the sanctuary together?" Annie suggested when they stepped inside the narthex that afternoon.

The day had been drizzly and gray and the stained-glass windows made the small church seem even darker. The minister had left for the day, planning to visit sick parishioners, so the church had an empty, eerie feeling, and Annie hurried to turn on a light. The old stone building, constructed soon after the turn of the century, consisted of the church proper, an office, and the belfry. A tiny kitchen, bathrooms, and a few Sunday school rooms made up the basement area. The sanctuary always remained open for worshipers, but on weekdays the floor below was locked.

"All I can find are hymnals and a few forgotten Sunday school papers," Charlie reported after searching the balcony, "and it looks like somebody has been here before us. Everything's in a mess."

Annie had no more success in the choir loft, where sheet music seemed to be strewn about. "If only we knew what to look for. These hymn books are far from new, but there's nothing rare about them."

Charlie stood in the middle of the sanctuary and shrugged. "Beats me. Hey, you don't suppose we're looking for a Gutenberg Bible, do you?"

Annie laughed. "I don't think we'd have trouble recognizing that. It's huge—two volumes, I think—and written in Latin. I can't see Dora lugging that around in a paper bag!"

"Bob Robert will have a fit when he sees this mess, so let's try to straighten things as we go. Why don't I take this side of the aisle and you take that one," Charlie suggested. "And hurry! I know it's a church, but this place is giving me the creeps."

"Oh dear, looks like somebody forgot their gloves." They had been searching silently when Annie held up a pair of tan leather gloves she'd found on the end of a pew. "Nice ones, too. I'll turn them in at the church office tomorrow, as I'm sure someone will be missing them."

"Look and see if they have a name inside," Charlie advised. "I'm always losing mine, so I try to put at least my initials in there."

Annie sat down to examine the gloves, straining to see in the poor light. "*Charlie* . . . These gloves belong to Lucille Westbrook. Come and look. Just inside, it's clearly marked *L. Westbrook.*"

Joining her, Charlie gripped the back of the pew for support. "Looks like she got here before we did. Annie, what if Lucille's *here?* In this church. Right now?"

"But why would she bother us? That book— whatever it is—probably belongs to her or her son. We're not trying to claim it."

Charlie sighed. "No, but from what I've heard about Lucille, I doubt if she'd believe us. Look, I'm beginning to feel uneasy in here. Let's get out of this place."

"I'm with you, but I left my coat down front."

"Yeah, my hat and gloves are down there, too, but let's hurry!" Charlie urged.

They had almost reached the front of the sanctuary when Charlie froze in place. "Somebody's here!" she whispered, crouching behind a pew.

"Oh, you're just trying to scare me."

"No, I'm not. Get down and be quiet. *Somebody's in the narthex.*"

Annie was just about to tell her it was probably a worshiper who had come in to pray, when the lights went out overhead.

Chapter Thirty-three

Charlie crept close beside Annie. "We're sitting ducks," she whispered.

"No, we're not. Whoever that is can't see any better than we can," Annie reminded her. "I think I know of a place we can hide, but we'll have to stay down. Just follow me." Earlier, while searching the choir loft, she had noticed a small closet partially concealed by a dark curtain off to the side, and it was the only place she could think of to hide—if only Lucille, or whoever was out there, hadn't noticed it, too.

On their hands, knees, and stomachs, the two of them more or less shimmied under the pews to the open area in front of the pulpit, where Annie whispered directions. "Let's make a dash to the choir loft and see if she follows. If not, we can slip into the closet." Charlie was jammed beside her so tightly, she could feel the imprint of her friend's jacket zipper on her shoulder, and she had encountered several hardened wads of chewing gum—at least she *hoped* it was gum—underneath the pews along the way.

How many steps up to the choir loft? One or two? Annie wished she could remember. Thank goodness the carpet softened their movements as they crawled quickly behind the first row of seats in the loft, hardly daring to breathe.

Where was she? Crouching, they listened as their eyes became adjusted to the dim interior of the church. *Just as Lucille's were doing!* Annie felt as if the world stood still, and all she could hear was the drumroll beating of her heart—plus, she was getting a cramp in her leg. Finally, after squatting statuelike for long, painful minutes, the two made their way to the covered doorway and slipped inside.

Feeling her way in the dark, Charlie bumped into a cardboard box, which threatened to tip over until she managed to get a firm grasp. The small closet-like room smelled musty and stale and she tried to calm her breathing and hoped she didn't run across a mouse—or vice versa. "Quick, lock the door!" she said in what she thought was Annie's direction. *Where was Annie anyway?*

"I can't. There isn't a key." Her words seemed to hover in the darkness.

Well, this is another fine mess you've gotten us into. Why now, of all times, to remember the famous words attributed to comedians Laurel and Hardy? Annie thought.

"Then we'll just have to block it somehow." Charlie's bleak words seemed hopeless.

"How?" Annie pressed an ear to the door. Nothing.

"Our bodies. We can block it with our bodies. After all, there're two of us and only one of her."

"Charlie . . ."

"What?"

"I hate to have to tell you this, but . . ."

"But *what?*" Charlie hissed.

"We can't block the door," Annie explained. "It opens *out.*"

"Oh . . . Annie, I'm scared."

"So am I, but get off my foot."

Shuddering, Charlie clawed at a spiderweb. The place must be covered in spiders, and there were probably mice in here, as well. "Can you hear anything out there?" she asked.

Annie shook her head and then realized Charlie couldn't see her. "Nothing. Maybe she's gone."

"How long do we have to stay in here? I'm getting claustrophobia. What if that was just Bob Robert or somebody cutting off the lights to save electricity?"

That sounded like a lifeline to Annie, but, she reasoned, surely whoever did it would have heard them in the sanctuary, even if they didn't see them. "Let's wait awhile, okay? I'll think about Frazier, and you think about Will."

"I *am* thinking about Will. I'm thinking I want to live to a ripe old age with him and have our children and grandchildren over on Sundays." Charlie swallowed a sob. "And I think I'm about to sneeze."

"Don't you dare! Hold a finger under your nose."

Charlie clamped a hand over her mouth, smothering the sneeze just in time. "I hear somebody moving about out there. Listen!"

Annie groaned. "It's pitch-black dark in here. I can't see a thing. Feel around and see if there's anything we can use as a weapon."

Charlie blindly groped the wall behind her, inching along until she came to what felt like a flagpole, but when she attempted to lift it out of its stand, the staff slipped from her hand and rolled to the floor with an enormous clatter.

"Well, that does it! Now everybody will know where we are," she said, retrieving the pole at her feet. "Quick! Get back as far away from the door as you can and we can try to fight her off with this flagpole."

Silence prevailed during the seconds that followed, and Charlie was beginning to wonder if they were truly alone, when her foot nudged something soft and bulky. "Annie? Where are you? What are you doing down here on the floor?"

"What? I'm over here!" Annie replied from the other side of the room.

Charlie knelt, and reaching out a trembling hand, drew in her breath when it met with another hand in the darkness, but this one was cold and still. "I think I've just found Lucille," she said, and dropping the flagpole, ran screaming from the stifling room right into someone's outstretched arms.

"Charlie! Charlie!" Someone clasped her in a firm grip. "Honey, it's all right. It's me!"

Dazed, Charlie looked up into her mother's face and threw her arms around her. "There's a dead woman in there and I think it's Lucille Westbrook. We have to get out of here *now*.

"Annie? Where's Annie?"

"She's over here with me," her aunt Lou said. The two huddled nearby in the choir loft, where Annie seemed to have a death grip on the older woman's arm. "Miss Dimple phoned your mother to ask if you had returned, as they were concerned you and Annie were taking so long over here."

"So here we are," Jo chimed in, "and thank goodness you're all right. Hurry now. We'll call the police from Phoebe's."

Annie snatched up her coat and threw it around her shoulders. "How long have you been here?"

"Were you the ones who turned off the lights?" Charlie asked.

"Why no. It was so dark in here, we couldn't see, so we turned them on," Jo told her. "We'd only been here a few minutes when there was a loud racket somewhere near the choir loft, and then we heard you scream."

Minutes later, Charlie telephoned Chief Tinsley from Phoebe's to tell him what had happened, and was relieved to hear that he and Warren Nelson would immediately head to the church, along with Doc Morrison, who acted as coroner in addition to his other duties. As eager as they were to find out what had happened, not one of the women complained when advised to stay away.

Augusta brewed several pots of tea, for which everyone was grateful, but no one seemed hungry for the shortbread cookies she offered.

"Could you tell how she died?" Annie asked Charlie after her second cup of tea. But Charlie shook her head. "Are you kidding? You know how dark it was in there. I couldn't get away fast enough."

"Miss Dimple, I can't tell you how grateful I am that you called attention to Charlie's absence," Jo said. "I just assumed that she was here with Annie."

"Yes, thank you," echoed Charlie and Annie at once. "I've never been as glad to see anybody in my life," Charlie added. As a rule, she would've been annoyed her mother and aunt had felt the need to check on her, and was certain Annie felt the same. After all, they were grown women and respected teachers in the community, but in this case, all that didn't matter one whit.

"I wonder if the one who killed Lucille followed us into the church," Annie said. "Whoever it was must've been looking for something in there and turned off the lights to scare us away."

"Do you think they came to get the gloves?" Charlie said, remembering she'd left them behind.

Annie frowned. "But why worry about her gloves when the killer must have known somebody would eventually find Lucille herself?"

Charlie shuddered. "Can we please talk about something else?"

Eager to oblige, Phoebe called attention to the war overseas. "I was just reading about our forces landing on Leyte, where General MacArthur was finally able to say 'I have returned.'" She shook her head. "I'll have to admit that earlier in the war, I had my doubts."

"It does seem like things are looking up," Velma added. "I heard a few days ago that U.S. forces captured Aachen, their first major German city."

"Aachen! That sounds like a sneeze." Charlie tried without success to suppress a laugh, and soon everyone else joined in.

"I feel thankful every day we're so far removed from what's going on over there," Lily said. "Those people live in fear for their lives every time a plane flies over, and many are even starving. I heard on the news that British forces have been delivering food because of a famine in Athens."

The others nodded in agreement, and Annie, who was just about to reach for a cookie, decided she really wasn't hungry. For a while, they sat in silence around a low-burning fire in the parlor, until Lou could keep quiet no longer. "I'm sure everybody else is wondering the same thing I am," she began in her loud, take-charge voice. "Is the person who killed Dora also responsible for what happened to Lucille, or do we have more than one murderer in town?"

"Wait a minute," Charlie said. "We're not sure yet if that *was* Lucille. I didn't actually look at her."

"I believe we'll soon find out," Miss Dimple said from her position at the window. "I see Chief Tinsley headed this way."

"The woman's body has been taken to Harvey Thompson's," the chief told them upon entering, "but we'll need to find someone who can identify her."

This was greeted by silence, until Jo spoke up. "Lou and I spoke to her only briefly, but if it's Lucille Westbrook, I think I would know her if I saw her." She glanced at her sister, who nodded in agreement.

"How was she—Could you determine how she died?" Annie asked, hoping against hope the woman had died a natural death. A heart attack maybe, or a sudden stroke.

"Looks like she was strangled from behind. The scarf was still around her neck, but Doc will be able to tell us more later." Hat in hand, the chief sat in the nearest chair and took a minute to choose his words. "Does anyone know what this woman was doing here? And why the church—that particular church?"

"We believe she was looking for a book," Miss Dimple told him. "It seems Dora took this book with her when she left home, and from what we've learned, it's supposed to have some value, but no one knows what or where it is."

"When Dora left here, we assume she went straight to the church," Velma said, "and it would be reasonable to believe she might have hidden the book there."

"If she did, we couldn't find it," Annie said, "but then, we had no idea what we were looking for."

Bobby Tinsley got to his feet and sighed. "Well, if you ladies don't mind, let's get this over with. If this is Lucille Westbrook, we'll have to get in touch with her next of kin."

"That would be Dora's husband, Leonard," Lou explained. "Lucille is—or was—his mother."

"If you do speak with him," Charlie said, "ask him the name of that blasted book."

Chapter Thirty-four

"Well?" everyone asked when Lou and her sister returned a short time later. "Were you able to tell if it was Lucille?"

Jo made a face and nodded. "I hope I never have to do anything like that again! Poor thing, you should've seen her face."

"Her son will be here tomorrow," Lou added. "He must think we're the murder capital of the world."

A solemn group gathered around the supper table that night after Charlie left with her mother and aunt. Augusta served a platter of sliced ham and homemade bread with cups of winter-squash soup and the conversation was subdued until Miss Dimple again raised the question of the puzzling murders.

"This is not going away," she reminded them, "and we're going to have to deal with it one way or another."

Velma glanced up over her cup of soup. "Any suggestions?"

Augusta frowned. "First of all, what brought Lucille here to Elderberry after all this time? If she was looking for the book, it seems she would've been here earlier."

"I suppose we'll know more after the authorities

speak with her son tomorrow," Velma said. "I hope he'll be able to give us some answers."

Phoebe suddenly put down her fork. "I believe someone invited her here," she said.

"Who?" Lily asked.

"And why?" Annie echoed.

"I think Phoebe has a point," Augusta said. "After all, by this time most of us know Dora at one time had on her person a valuable book, but who, other than Dora, and possibly her husband and his mother, knew the title?"

"As cold-blooded as it seems, I think that's something to keep in mind," Miss Dimple said. "It's beginning to look as if someone may have asked her here and pretended to help her look for the book, then killed her as soon as they learned the title."

Annie covered her face with her hands. " 'That it should come to this!' " she said, quoting a line from *Hamlet*. "Who would *do* such a thing?"

"Someone who obviously doesn't know or care about the difference between right and wrong," Miss Dimple said. "Someone who's extremely dangerous."

Lily shuddered. "Well, I certainly hope he doesn't come here again!"

"I don't believe he will." Augusta helped herself to one of Odessa's green tomato pickles and passed them along. "I think whoever it is will try once more at the library."

"Virginia!" Miss Dimple tossed aside her napkin and stood. "She's weeding out a lot of those books that are either out of date or way beyond repair and might be working late. I have to warn her."

But no one answered the telephone at the library, and Dimple was relieved when she finally reached her friend at home.

Virginia and a few volunteers had accomplished a lot that day, she was told, and planned to continue tomorrow.

"Since tomorrow is Saturday, you can count on me to help," Dimple promised, and Augusta volunteered, as well. "Meanwhile, I plan to ask the police to put a special guard at the library tonight. With luck, we might be able to put a stop to this before this person kills again."

"Woodrow Malone." Jo Carr stood on the threshold of the library the next morning and tossed her beret on a chair. Lou would have joined them as well, she told them, but she had talked her husband into taking her shopping in Atlanta.

Virginia frowned. "Woodrow who?"

"Woodrow Malone, Dora's friend in Fieldcroft. I've just remembered his name. I have a feeling he might be able to help connect the dots on Dora's mysterious letters from Columbia."

"Then let's not waste any more time." Virginia reached for the telephone. "Florence, can you please ring Bobby Tinsley for me?" She knew the operator would stay on the line, but in this case, what did it matter?

"Well, when do you expect them back?" she asked. "Oh my goodness! Really? Whenever he gets in touch, please ask him to call me at the library . . . no . . . we're all right, but I really think he should know about this."

Hanging up the receiver, she couldn't resist a chuckle. "That oughta keep Florence guessing for a while!"

"What is it?" Miss Dimple hurried from the back room, where she had been working, followed by Augusta.

"I was just speaking with Shirley—Shelly at the police department," Virginia said, "and she told me Chief Tinsley had been called to Harris Cooper's store. Seems Jesse Dean was looking for cleaning supplies this morning in that little storeroom in the back and ran across those things taken from Rose McGinnis and her aunt."

"I know Gertrude will be glad to have her silver ladle back," Dimple said, "but who in the world would put them there?"

"I suppose anybody could," Jo said. "I don't think they ever keep it locked."

"But why hide them there?" Dimple frowned. "Unless they meant to throw suspicion on Jesse Dean."

"From all I've heard about your friend Jesse

Dean, that would be the last thing on his mind," Augusta said. "Besides, if he really meant to take them, why turn them in now?"

"It seems to me whoever put those things there meant not so much to throw suspicion on Jesse Dean as to direct it away from himself," Dimple said. "And I still can't see what it has to do with Dora Westbrook's death."

"Nor can I," Virginia added. "At least we should learn the title of that book when Leonard Westbrook gets here this afternoon."

It seemed like forever before Chief Tinsley finally returned Virginia's call, but actually it was less than an hour, and when she told him about Woodrow Malone, he decided it would be best to ask the police in Fieldcroft to take care of it. After the turmoil of finding Lucille Westbrook's body, the matter of Woodrow Malone had taken a backseat, he admitted.

"Jo said he spends most of his time at his fix-it shop," Virginia told him, "so he'll probably find him there. You will let us know when you hear from him, won't you?"

And the police chief promised that he would.

Expecting an unwelcome visitor, they took time about going home for the noonday meal, and upon returning to the library, Dimple brought along Annie. "With all of us helping, we should soon be through," she said.

By midafternoon, they were close to finishing when Virginia, becoming impatient, shelved the last of a stack of books and started for the telephone. "It doesn't look like Bobby's going to call to tell us what he's discovered, and I'm tired of waiting. Maybe he's forgotten."

"No, wait just a minute," Dimple cautioned her. "I believe I see him coming now."

But it was Warren Nelson, not the police chief, who crossed the porch and stepped inside. "The chief has gone to meet Leonard Westbrook at the funeral home," he told them, "and I can't stay, but he wanted you to know what he found out from that fellow in Fieldcroft."

Jo nodded. "You mean Woodrow Malone?"

"According to this Mr. Malone," Nelson began, taking a piece of folded paper from his pocket, "Dora Westfield had asked his advice about finding someone who might help her sell a book she considered valuable."

"Did she tell him what it was?" Jo asked. But the officer shook his head. "No, just that it had been a wedding gift from a relative and she wanted to know what it might be worth."

Warren smoothed out the paper on Virginia's desk. "Here's a short list of names and addresses he gave her. Now, whether she contacted any of them or not, he didn't know."

Miss Dimple studied the list silently. "Oh, yes. I believe she did," she said, passing the paper to Augusta. "There's an address in Columbia, right at the top, and it seems that would be the nearest person to contact. I think we should find out if she got in touch."

"Tell you what," Warren offered. "I've got to get back with the chief, but it shouldn't take long after that to put in a call to this fellow and find out if he heard from the Westbrook woman."

"Then you'll give us a call?" Virginia asked.

"I'll do better than that. I'll drop by as soon as I know anything. We want to keep an eye on this place anyway, and I might just be able to find out the title of that book that's responsible for all this."

"So, what do we do now?" Annie asked after he left.

"I suggest we sit tight," Miss Dimple said.

"And keep the door locked," Virginia added.

"Do you really think they'll come back?" Annie asked.

"I believe whoever it is is only waiting for us to leave," Augusta said.

"Well, they'll be wasting their time. We've looked through every book in this library and I haven't seen one that looks remotely valuable," Virginia said.

Annie went to the piano and ran her fingers up and down the keys. "Anybody want to play 'Chopsticks'?"

"It's been a while, but I'll try," Augusta said, joining her.

"Don't you all know anything else?" Jo asked after several fractured attempts.

"Let's see what we can find in here," Annie said, and lifting the seat of the piano bench, she brought out a thick copy of *Songs for the Hearth and Home.*

But it wasn't a songbook underneath the tattered cover, but a very old edition of *Adventures of Huckleberry Finn.*

"I think we've just found what everyone's been searching for," Annie said, hugging the book to her chest. Tenderly, she turned the pages. "And it's signed by Samuel Clemens with 'Mark Twain' in parentheses beneath it."

"There seems to be an envelope glued to the inside, as well," Augusta said. "It's addressed to a Mrs. Richard Mayfield and there's a note enclosed."

The note, they discovered, consisted of only a brief paragraph to "Dear Miss Millie," thanking her for "a pleasant weekend among delightful company." It was signed "Truly yrs, Samuel Clemens."

"And it's been sitting in there all this time!" Jo sighed. "What do we do now?"

"I think we should put it back where we found it for now and telephone the police," Miss Dimple advised.

"What is it, Virginia?" she added. "You don't look well."

Virginia waved that away. "It's that book, *Huckleberry Finn*. Remember how Willie Elrod was shoved from his bike on his way home with a copy of this same book?"

"Yes, but that one wasn't worth anything," Annie said.

Virginia nodded. "True, but whoever shoved him didn't know that yet. The next day, Marjorie Mote found the copy he borrowed under some bushes near the sidewalk. I think the person who made Willie fall returned the book sometime during the night."

"Do you remember who was here when the boy checked out the book?" Augusta asked.

Virginia thought for a minute. "Why, yes. It was just Phoebe and myself. And Rose McGinnis."

Going to the telephone, Miss Dimple picked up the receiver.

"Who are you calling?" Jo asked.

Miss Dimple held up a hand for silence. "Florence," she said, "connect me with Gertrude Hutchinson, please."

After a brief conversation, during which she discovered the older woman was alone, Miss Dimple invited her to join them for a cup of tea at the library. "We've been having such dismal weather, we thought it would cheer everyone up to spend some time together this afternoon," she told her.

"Gertrude said she'd be happy to join us," she said, hanging up the receiver.

"Then I'll run over to Cooper's and pick up some cookies," Jo offered.

"And I'll collect our guest." Pocketbook under her arm, Virginia prepared to leave. "Somebody call Bobby Tinsley *right now*," she directed. "And lock this door behind us."

Virginia was relieved to find Gertrude waiting on the doorstep when she arrived.

"I was glad to hear they found your missing punch ladle," she said as they got under way. "I know it must be special to you."

"Oh, yes. Yes, I was happy to get it back. . . . It's just that . . ."

Virginia glanced at her passenger as she waited for a light to change. Gertrude seemed ill at ease. "Is something wrong?" she asked.

"Well, I suppose it is. Virginia, how did those things end up in a storeroom in Cooper's store? It doesn't make any sense."

Virginia agreed that it didn't. "Trudy, is everything all right at home? What did Rose have to say about those things turning up?"

For a minute, Gertrude didn't answer. "Actually, it's been a while since I've spoken with Rose. She's been behaving a bit strangely lately, and frankly, I'm concerned."

"How do you mean?"

"Well, for one thing, she finally admitted her

fiancé broke off the engagement during her visit at Camp Gordon. Naturally, she's upset about that."

"Oh, Trudy, I'm so sorry! It does seem she's had more than her share of troubles after losing her job, and now this robbery at her shop." Virginia glanced at her passenger. "I can only imagine how she must feel."

"And there's something else, too," Gertrude continued. "We had been to Harris Cooper's for groceries weeks ago and I happened to mention that Jesse Dean's daddy, Sanford, worked for my husband's brother, Tate, years ago, before he just up and disappeared. Sanford came from that little town in south Georgia—Fieldcroft—and I remem-bered how his folks used to send pecans from there."

"Was this before or after Dora Westbrook was killed?" Virginia asked.

"Oh, before. Weeks before. Then Rose went to visit her fiancé at Camp Gordon and was in that awful bus accident on the way back. That was when she started asking questions about Jesse Dean's daddy being from Fieldcroft. I never understood why she wanted to know all that."

Virginia thought she understood but believed it best to keep quiet.

"I think losing her job at the defense plant and then a broken romance on top of it have probably been more than Rose could take," Trudy said.

"And I'm afraid her little shop has been a disappointment, as well."

Both Chief Tinsley and Warren Nelson were waiting when they returned to the library for the impromptu tea party, but cookies and tea took a backseat to the discussion that followed, and with a solemn face, Bobby Tinsley told them of his meeting with Leonard Westbrook.

The rare copy of *Huckleberry Finn* had been given to them as a wedding gift from his favorite aunt, Leonard told them. She loved reading, as Dora did, and was particularly fond of her. The book had been a gift to her mother by Samuel Clemens, who had been a guest in their home, and she especially wanted Dora to have it.

Although it belonged to both of them, Leonard admitted he had forgotten all about it. Apparently, his mother hadn't. He had no idea Lucille planned to come here until he found a note from her saying she had received a letter from someone here who promised to help her find the missing Twain book.

"Did he say who sent it?" Miss Dimple asked. But Bobby shook his head. "It appears the note wasn't signed, or if it was, Lucille didn't say."

He frowned. "I can't be sure, but I believe Lucille was told to meet this person at the church where Dora died. . . . Poor woman, she must have felt she'd be safe in a church."

"Dora certainly wasn't," Jo said. "But I don't understand how anyone here could possibly know about Dora or that she had with her a rare edition of Twain's work."

"I think I can answer that," Warren said. "I followed up on that address from Columbia and found that the person Dora had been corresponding with was killed in a bus accident while en route to meet her here in Elderberry. His wife told me he had been looking forward to seeing what seemed like a genuine first edition and hoped to help Dora find a buyer. They had agreed to meet in Elderberry, as it was an equal distance between them."

The room grew suddenly silent as everyone did their best not to look at Gertrude until she spoke up at last. "I knew something was wrong. Bad wrong, but not this. Nothing like this."

Augusta went to her and put her arms around her while Chief Tinsley drew a packet from inside his jacket. "And by the way, Leonard Westbrook tells me the scarf used to strangle his mother didn't belong to Lucille."

Gertrude grasped Augusta's hand. "I think we all know whose scarf that is. I gave it to Rose on her birthday."

"So that's why Rose came back to the church," Annie said. "She was after her scarf."

"Miss Trudy," Bobby said gently, "I think you should make arrangements to visit your sister for a while until all this has been worked out." While Virginia telephoned Trudy's sister and made arrangements for her to stay, Warren agreed to take her home to pack a few things before driving her to her sister's.

"What now?" Annie asked as the two drove away. "Surely Rose won't show up after all this."

"A rational person wouldn't, but Rose isn't thinking rationally," Miss Dimple pointed out. "She must have been that fellow's seatmate before the bus accident, and I imagine he shared his excitement over the possibility of finding such a rare edition."

"Just imagine all the times she sat at that piano, and all the time that book was in the very bench she was sitting on," Virginia said. "And by the way, Bobby, if Leonard hasn't already left, you might want to take the book to him. After all, it belongs to him, and I don't want to be responsible for it."

The police chief shook his head. "He says he doesn't want it. Says it's caused enough heartbreak. He wants Dora's sister to have it. Frankly, I think he regrets the lack of warmth in his marriage. He can't bring Dora back, but at least the book can go to someone who can appreciate its value."

"Then I'll take it when I go there for Thanksgiving," Miss Dimple said. "My goodness, it will be here before we know it."

"And what does Henry think about that?" Virginia asked, and Dimple smiled. "I received a call from my brother yesterday and he's treating me to dinner in Atlanta next weekend—just the two of us. It's been a long time since we've done that!"

Annie looked out the window. "Where do you suppose Rose is now?"

"I don't know, but I don't want any of you around if she does come back," Bobby said. "The woman's completely off balance. She had no reason to kill either of those women. Dora's death might have been an accident, but of course we'll never know for sure. I believe she became frightened when Rose approached her that night at the church and fell while attempting to get away."

Annie frowned. "Why do you think she killed Lucille?"

"I think she knew the book she was looking for was a rare edition by Mark Twain, but she wasn't sure of the title. As soon as Lucille told her what to look for, she signed her death warrant."

"Is it really worth that much?" Jo asked.

"I'd guess several thousand, maybe more. Leonard says it's one of a limited number printed with a sheepskin binding. Of course Rose has blown that all out of proportion in her desperate search to find it," he said.

"It seems odd when you think of it," Virginia said, "but like Dora, Rose must've been desperate to have enough money to start all over again somewhere else. I wonder if she was the one we saw under the magnolia that day. Remember, Dimple? Someone seemed to be stalking the library but ran when the police came. Why didn't she just show herself?"

"Probably because that was exactly what she was doing—stalking. I imagine she was trying to decide the best way to get inside and didn't want to be seen."

Annie put the untouched cookies back into the box. "So, what now?" she asked.

The chief looked at his watch. "Now, I believe it's time for all of you to go home. I'll park my car out of sight and keep an eye on the front while another officer watches the rear. I've noticed a window unlatched off the porch, so I imagine she'll try to come in that way. Probably unlatched it herself the last time she was here."

"You will let us know what happens, won't you?" Jo asked, and was assured that he would.

Carrying the book, carefully shrouded in brown paper, Dimple walked home flanked on either side by Annie and Augusta, with Jo bringing up the rear, as Virginia had come in her car.

"I feel like a pallbearer," Annie joked as they paraded down Katherine Street and paused to cross at the corner.

"I'll take that!" Suddenly, she was upon them, and if it hadn't been for Annie and Augusta blocking her way, Rose would probably have been able to wrestle the book from Dimple's grasp.

"I don't think so!" Augusta said, and Rose felt herself falling facedown on the pavement, just as if she had slipped on a banana peel.

Meanwhile, Dimple regained her grip and sent Annie to call the police from the nearest house, which happened to be the Motes. Every time Rose regained her balance, she slipped again. And again, until finally she lay prone on the sidewalk, at which point Bobby Tinsley arrived.

"Well, if that doesn't beat all!" he said, pausing for breath. "How'd you manage this? Is this some kind of voodoo or something?"

Augusta smiled. "Oh, just something I learned years ago. It comes in handy now and then."

The chief cuffed Rose and put her in the back of his police car. "Looks like you won't have to worry about this one anymore."

"How *did* you do that, Augusta?" Annie asked after Jo parted from the three of them. But Augusta only smiled.

"I'm not sure why you're here, Augusta," Dimple said as they neared home, "but I'm awfully glad you came."

Augusta smiled. "And so am I, but I believe your friend Odessa will be able to join you as soon as her aunt is up and about."

"But can't you stay, as well?" Annie asked.

"You know what they say about too many

cooks spoiling the broth," Augusta reminded her, "but I do plan to be here through Christmas, and I'm so looking forward to the music."

The others agreed that they were, too.

"I understand the Methodists are planning a cantata this year," Augusta said, humming a sort of tune under her breath. "I wonder if they need another soprano."

Center Point Large Print
600 Brooks Road / PO Box 1
Thorndike, ME 04986-0001 USA

(207) 568-3717

US & Canada:
1 800 929-9108
www.centerpointlargeprint.com